The Plentiful Harvest

Also by John A. Torres
On Higher Ground

The Plentiful Harvest

John A. Torres

NEPPERHAN PRESS, LLC
YONKERS, NY

Published by Nepperhan Press, LLC
P.O. Box 1448, Yonkers, NY 10702
nepperhan@optonline.net
nepperhan.com

PUBLISHER'S NOTE
This is a work of fiction. Names, characters, places, and incidents
are the product of the author's imagination or are used fictitiously,
and any resemblance to actual persons, living or dead, events, or
locales is entirely coincidental.

Printed in the United States of America

Library of Congress Control Number: 2012932996

ISBN 978-0-9839412-0-0

Cover art was provided by Craig Rubadoux

For Jen

This is a fictional story set in a fictional town in southern Sudan. Sadly, it is based on actual events that occurred in 1983.

Then he said to his disciples, "The harvest is plentiful but the workers are few."
—Matthew 9:37

ONE

JACK HOPKINS WAS awakened on what would be the hottest day of the year by the warm moisture of Felicia's nose rubbing against his lips.

Outside his window, Bruckner Expressway had been awake for hours and now seemed already tired of the 18-wheelers carelessly cutting in and out of traffic as if trying to find which rutted lane held the secret magical way to reach Hunts Point Market first. The choking exhaust mixed with the rising heat from the road itself and formed an unforgiving haze that covered everything in its path with scorched dust.

To look down the road, down toward the horizon, down towards New York City, reminded Jack of what the heat rising from the desert floor must look like. He'd squint his eyes and create mirages out of the rising heat. Not that he'd ever been to a desert or knew what a mirage would look like. He'd never been out of the tri-state area.

Jack never minded the racket, how the barreling trucks sounded like cannons going off, firing through the city like they couldn't wait to get out. Beyond his view were pockets of gorgeous purple loosestrife that seemed oblivious to the thundering around them as well, though they'd sway and dance caught in the gushes of breeze caused by the trucks.

The noise and the heat radiated the studio apartment that was so close to the busy Bronx highway that Jack could sit out on his fire escape and give a play-by-play account of the truckers jockeying for position. He could tell by the rattle and clangs which trucks were hauling full loads and which were heading to a final stop. Sometimes he'd impress friends by telling them what the trucks contained—laughing when he'd predict how many broken eggs there were, though of course there was no way to really be sure if he was correct. He did the same things with planes, always hollering out above the roar of an incoming jet or prop-job whether it was a 707 TWA approaching LaGuardia or a Cessna 337 putt-puttering its way toward Long Island or making its way north toward White Plains.

The fire escape also gave him a view of the basketball courts in the schoolyard if he leaned way over to the left and then squinted his right eye tightly. The stifling heat wave made it almost too hot to shoot hoops down in the schoolyard the last couple of days.

It was so hot that the flies took the morning off from their usual routine of helping Felicia wake Jack up.

The boiling weather started about three days earlier and was showing no sign of letting up. A few elderly people, living without air conditioning, had already succumbed to the temperatures and Con Edison was starting to make noise about raising rates to keep up with the increased electrical demands and the possibility of rolling brownouts.

Jack's aunt, living in nearby Co-op City to the north and east on the border with Westchester County, had called three days straight to tell Jack that it was hotter in the Bronx that day than in Miami Beach. He made it a point to find an even hotter more northern city on the *Daily News* weather map page to counter.

"Yes, Nelly, that's true, but it's 98 today in Boston."

Felicia jumped out onto the fire escape to lap up some of the dripping water from the window air conditioner in the Hernandez' apartment above them. She jumped back onto the bed via the open drawer in the ratty old dresser and her tongue flicked Jack's lips quickly and evenly, picking off the droplets of sweat beading instantaneously on his upper lip and for a moment his waking dream transported him to the boardwalk in Wildwood, NJ where he lovingly and carefully bit into an oozing caramel apple. They had just finished riding the tilt-a-whirl when Jack spotted the apple stand and they had his favorite: the caramel apples sprinkled with nuts. His dad bought one too and in the dream he could feel the humidity of that night and how the ocean air deposited pockets of salt onto his skin mixing with the sweat of the night.

Jack purposely did not wipe his lips clean of the sticky caramel so he could lick them clean once he was done eating. It was the only proper way to eat such a delicacy and his father had expertly taught him to savor such tasty treats. The philosophy was simple: eat most now, save the best on your lips for later. To this day Jack applied the same technique, without his dad's direct approval, to soups, ice creams, frosted cup cakes, buttery corn on the cob, hot wings, barbecue ribs and the coquito ices he bought from Papo whenever he wheeled his cart into the neighborhood.

"Jack, if I had a prize I would give it you," Papo would inevitably say with each 50-cent sale. "You have devoured, licked, inhaled, and eaten the most coquitos of any non-Puerto Rican, of any gringo, in the entire Bronx. My children thank you and the nuns at Mt. St. Ursula Catholic school thank you as well."

"I am more than happy to help further the education of those two girls of yours," Jack would say before buying three or four more for the children playing basketball in the school yard. "And you provide me with this ethnic delicacy that is most refreshing."

He'd pat his belly with both hands as if to measure how many more coquitos would be enough, then sigh, before going back for more of the creamy coconut flavored icees.

"You know," the conversation would always turn, "school is not such a bad thing. You're an intelligent guy, Jack. Why not do a few years at Lehman or Bronx Community College? You could probably get somewhere. Don't wait too long, you're just about pushing 30, right? Maybe you could get a scholarship to a four-year school. Fordham is close by."

"What makes you think I want anything more than this, Papo? Look around me. Everything is here."

Then, prompted by nothing, Jack would rattle off the reasons, like Socorro's Bodega, the library, the basketball courts, affordable rent, the front stoop, easy access to mass transportation, Agrapina's *cuchifrito* joint where the workers didn't mind that he ordered *alcapurias* by asking for Puerto Rican burritos, Joe Tuckman's Army-Navy surplus store that stocked double extra large T-shirts, coquito ices, and Marci. What else could there possibly be?

No, he long ago stopped looking for some hidden meaning to life, that elusive secret that self-help books claimed to have. There was nothing better than spending his seconds, minutes, hours, days, weeks, months, and years right here. This was home.

Papo, always ready with an arsenal of answers that ranged from the philosophical expanding of horizons to the obvious economical reasons for wanting to improve one's lot in life, knew Jack well enough never to reply. He came close to mentioning the No Nukes concert in Central Park a few weeks earlier that starred Jackson Browne and Bruce Springsteen, but decided against it. And, deep down, Papo thought Jack might be right somehow. He was, after all, the happiest guy Papo had ever met.

Jack rarely dreamt of his mother but understood that there were so few memories of her. Every once in a while he dreamt that they were at his uncle's house in Throgs Neck, splashing around in his above-ground swimming pool and dropping down underwater to avoid the bees or the biting flies that sometimes came in with the breezes from Long Island.

Every time his mother made an appearance in the backyard to serve some sliced watermelon or to make sure Jack was wearing enough sunscreen, his father would sing out.

"There she is, Miss America!"

She would laugh, always covering her mouth with her freckled hands, and then pose in her Navy blue one-piece swimsuit as if acknowledging the cheering crowds.

It was his mother who loved airplanes. The daughter of a mechanic at Kennedy International Airport, she grew up learning the different planes, what the difference was between personnel carriers and transport planes and how to tell by the rumble of the engines the type of plane it was. She likely would have made an amazing mechanic, sometimes pointing out problems to her father when she tagged along. But she was born during the time when women were expected to be housewives, nurses, or secretaries.

Sometimes, with sunscreen in hand by the pool, she'd point to the sky and let everyone know what kind of plane was making that noise. It never amazed Jack, until she was gone.

He never got the chance to ask her if she had ever flown or if she had ever wanted to become a pilot. There were many things he never got around to asking her.

There were always flowers there at his uncle's red brick house, loads of them, roses mainly planted in wooden planters that always seemed to ready to burst apart and it was difficult to picture her without them.

Most of the time, Jack couldn't remember whether that was a memory or just a dream.

Tired of waiting, Felicia placed her left front paw on Jack's face and mewed loudly.

"I don't want to go to school today," Jack muttered as he tried to sit and open his eyes before flopping straight back onto his bed and nearly pancaking Felicia, causing her to shrill defiantly. "I'm sorry my girl," he said while yawning loudly and creaking his eyes open ever so slightly, while moving his hair back out of his eyes. He slept in a moth-eaten black Pink Floyd T-shirt that was now too snug to wear outdoors.

He yawned again before panning the apartment deliberately, squinting his eyes for better focus and clarity. It was on the third pass through, peering beyond the three weeks of newspapers, the stack of New York Mets yearbooks, the laundry pile that was now entering its second week sitting by the door, the crusty discarded cartons of Moo Shoo Pork and empty fortune cookie wrappers from Dragon's Gate Chinese Restaurant, the framed American service flag that he had yet to hang up in honor of his father, a TV Guide from 1977 and the growing pile of past due bills that he spotted her bag of Pathmark Supermarket brand cat food.

"I know, I know." He moved slowly rubbing his tummy with both hands as he maneuvered over the various obstacles littering the floor, careful not to land on anything too sharp. "It's breakfast time, rather past it, and we can both do with a little grub," he addressed the cat in his mock English accent that was a melding of Peter Cushing and Peter O'Toole.

Jack, pleased that he found the bag of food so quickly, lifted it up proudly hoping to hear the rattle of dry food but to his dismay the bag was silent.

Felicia mewed angrily, wondering why Jack didn't remember that he had performed the same exact routine yesterday with the same exact results.

"Never fear, Felicia my love," he continued with the English accent but added a fake monocle this time. "This only means that we must resort to 'plan b,' a smorgasbord of tastes, a carnival for the senses, a, a symphony of exquisiteness that begs the question why is it relegated to 'plan b' instead of being the initial, primary plan?"

He once again performed his custom ballet to avoid stepping on something painful while making his way to the small kitchen area. He shot a glance at the clock hanging on the yellowing wall—a baseball diamond with the words "Pelham Bay Little League 1965" across the outfield. The green paint had long ago faded and chipped but his photo was still remarkably sharp.

He reached up and touched it softly. He was the easiest to spot. His ball cap was pulled down tight and low and the brim was perfectly curved. It was a trick his dad had taught him, carefully folding a new cap into a coffee mug for the weeks leading up to the season. It would drive his mother crazy. He pulled his hand away slowly—the clock had stopped working years ago—and he smiled.

1965. That was his best year as a player. That was the year he made the all-star team, the same year his mother got sick.

Jack slid two of his three coffee mugs away from the front of his bread box and was thrilled that there were still several slices of Wonder bread left, including the ends.

He rotated his caps into two of his mugs, unless Marci was over for breakfast and then he'd have to have to work on curving only one ball cap. Currently in the mugs were his 1976 Bicentennial New York Mets cap and a Pittsburgh Pirates cap in honor of his favorite player of all time, Roberto Clemente.

Somehow, through the noise of the highway and Felicia's persistence, Jack was sure he heard some of the neighborhood kids laughing and the indistinguishable sound of a Rawlings rubber basketball hitting the blacktop of the courts at P.S. 152. Ignoring Felicia and the five slices of Wonder bread, Jack leapt out onto the fire escape, which bounced significantly under his girth, and peered around the corner to see if it was true.

"Alright!" he exclaimed, dropping the English accent and looking upward after being dripped on by the air conditioner. "Joselito, little Tony, Chumbley and Nelson are already out there. I need to get moving."

The park was filled with the neighborhood children and he could almost make out the clanging of Papo's *coquito* wagon nearby and the intoxicating smell of *pastelitos, alcapurias* and *rellenos de papa* starting to fry in yesterday's oil at Agrapina's for the pre-lunch crowd.

At that, Felicia mewed again and Jack quickly resumed the task at hand: making peanut butter and jelly sandwiches for the duo to share for breakfast. As he ripped little pieces off for his cat, Jack rummaged through the drawers, tossing all types of objects aside, looking for a roll of black electrical tape.

When he finally found the dying remnants of a roll, he hopped to the couch with a sock in one hand, his worn Converse All-stars in the other and half a sandwich stuck in his mouth. Dust flew up as he landed on what used to be his parents' couch.

"I promise, I promise, Felicia. If that unemployment check comes today you will feast tonight on the tenderest vittles you've ever had."

She cocked her head and looked at him quizzically.

"I'm serious," he said and swallowed down the last of the sandwich. "And maybe, just maybe, I'll treat myself to some of those Ballpark franks that plump when you cook them. But right now it's time to give these kids some pointers on the fine art of the fade-away jump shot. It's a dying art you know. Anyone can dunk the ball but the fade-away? Now that takes talent. I consider it my duty to pass along some of my knowledge on to them."

He fell backwards onto the couch and lifting his legs in the air, proceeded to pull his sneakers on. The right sneaker was far worse off than the left, though they both should have been retired a few years ago. The three big toes of his right foot pierced through his sock and out the very top of the sneaker. That's where the black electrical tape came in.

After sealing his toes safely inside his kicks, Jack filled an old milk carton with tap water, grabbed his keys and never noticed the circled date on the Liquor Store calendar reminding him that today was the two-year anniversary of his and Marci's first date, before heading out to the courts to shoot some hoops.

This time it was the phone that woke Jack at 9:17 p.m. and not a hungry cat.

Knees achy from basketball and a badly scraped elbow, he had fallen asleep in front of the television while Bob Murphy and Ralph Kiner gushed over this kid in the Mets' minor league system by the name of Strawberry.

Felicia, full from a dinner of Tender Vittles, had dozed early as well. The heat let up slightly though there was no breeze at all. Even Bruckner Expressway seemed to be taking the night off.

The minute, no, the second, Jack heard the phone ring, he was startled into remembering that tonight was a milestone of sorts, one he probably shouldn't have spent watching the Mets and Giants bore half of New York to sleep. Panic set in and he jumped up and down in front of the telephone knowing full well it would explode if he answered. He belly jiggled violently.

"Marci, I was kidnapped by the PLO.," he stammered still jumping and listening to the terrible ringing. "Marci, my building collapsed and I've been trapped all afternoon. Marci, remember seeing those headlines all these years at the supermarket about alien abductions? Well, guess what?"

For a moment he considered answering and feigning amnesia.

"Marci? I'm sorry, it doesn't ring a bell," he might try. "But this has been happening to me all day since banging my head against the cabinet door this morning. In fact, what's a cabinet?"

The phone kept ringing and that's when Jack realized that Marci was calling from the payphone in front of Socorro's Bodega. He snuck out onto the fire escape to look and the ring seemed to grow louder. He could hear Dexys Midnight Runners' "Come on Eileen" playing from a nearby radio.

Finally, he gulped and picked up the phone.

TWO

I_{T WAS A} tongue-lashing to remember, but Jack knew he was to blame and so he stood and took it like man, though the crowd that had gathered to watch probably didn't see it that way.

It started with Marci's broken-record ultimatum that he find a job and lose 50 pounds or else she would be on her way. It certainly was a browbeating and part of him wished he had not run down the stairs to catch her leaving the payphone at the bodega.

Maybe catching up to her the next day would have been better, though she wasn't the type to let her anger subside with time.

"You were let go from a very good-paying job at LaGuardia airport fueling planes," she said with disdain, "all because you wasted too much time gushing over the planes as they landed and insisting on sharing this incredibly vast amount of knowledge with your co-workers, keeping them from doing their jobs as well! Who cares what kinds of planes are landing or taking off or where they were going or where they had come from? Why couldn't you just do your job?"

Jack looked down, knowing full well that she was right. The small crowd grew in numbers and delighted in being witness to such a dressing-down.

"It's bad enough having a boyfriend who can't even afford to take you to a movie or buy you dinner but now I have a boyfriend who would rather play basketball with the neighborhood kids or watch the Mets on television than spend time with me. The Mets? They haven't won in decades. They stink, face it, Jack, they will always stink. And don't even get me started about your weight, I mean would it hurt you to walk around the block a couple of times a week for some exercise? And I don't think I will ever get over how you totally ignored our anniversary tonight."

"No, no, no, mister," she continued, not affording him a moment to break in or even a second to breathe, "things had better change and in a hurry or it is over."

The night was a total loss. Almost.

After being read the riot act, Jack was too depressed or too simple not to realize that he should have been depressed, so he decided to pound down a cold one or two at the Excalibur Pub, two blocks away from his apartment, away from the expressway. It was one of those bars that had been there for 50 years with very little changing. The dartboard was an antique and Jack couldn't remember ever seeing anyone play. There was no jukebox—only a small radio behind the bar, and the black and white television looked as if it might have broadcast Abraham Lincoln's inauguration. But Jack wasn't big on atmosphere or kitsch, he loved the 40-cent drafts and the captive audience of rummies and alkies that hung on his every word. In fact, they may have even cheered when Jack wandered in. At least it felt like they did.

"Jackie my boy," said Old Man Dukes, a 68-year-old black maintenance worker who could barely see two feet in front of him but who was always the first to recognize Jack. He was a big burly man who looked as if he could stop a bus with his bare hands. "What do you say? What do you know?"

Mike Morgan was there too, a union carpenter who would vanish for days at a time if the Jets lost a football game. His weakness was blended scotch, and the benders usually ended with him waking up on a subway car. It cost him two marriages and several good union jobs that could have led to full-time permanent work.

The Sullivan twins were there as well, signaling payday at United Parcel Service where they both worked loading trucks and taking heat for putting packages with the wrong zip code onto a truck bound somewhere else.

They had a few beers and pretty soon, as always, Jack was the center of attention as he regaled them with his self-deprecating stories and tales of growing up with a widowed father. They weren't sure how much of what he said was true but it never mattered.

"So there we were," he'd always start. "My dad and I having a terrific day at the Bronx zoo in the middle of what had to be the coldest winter in New York history. For most of the day we didn't see a soul. It was one of those gray days that just wanted to let loose a bucket of snow on you but held it all in keeping the sky one color throughout. We'd warm up in the reptile house and as usual my dad ignored the signs warning against tapping on the glass of the boa constrictors. This always caused me to back up, afraid the giant snakes would smash right through the glass and choke us to death.

"Just about all of the food concessions were closed but my dad had prepared for that, packing egg and pepper sandwiches we had purchased the night before from Busco's. We found a warm, quiet spot, ate our sandwiches and drank hot chocolate from the thermos we packed. My dad refused to make hot chocolate with water, always using milk instead. 'Why would anyone mix water and chocolate?' he'd ask. 'After all isn't chocolate made from milk?'

"Anyway, our great day was winding down and we found ourselves by the polar bear exhibit close to closing time. The sun was starting to set and the chill in the air became even more bitter. It was so cold that the air actually seemed to hurt your lungs as you sucked it down. And when we got there, to the polar bear, my dad threw his arms in the air in disgust. He couldn't believe that the polar bear was laying there sleeping by his swimming hole. 'For the love of Pete,' he said. 'This is the one animal in this whole entire zoo that should be up and at 'em. This is his type of weather.' So my dad reaches down and grabs a few small rocks."

"Oh my goodness," Old Man Dukes said, taking a long sip of his warm beer. "Oh my goodness. I know where this is going.

Your dad was one crazy guy. Shoot man, he was a crazy cat."

It wasn't an insult. Dukes meant it as a compliment and so Jack smiled and continued with his story.

"So my dad starts pelting the sleeping polar bear with rocks and the beast finally wakes up." Jack kneeled up on his bar stool to get taller, simulating the giant bear. "The bear starts pacing back and forth with foam dripping from his mouth. His head, which was the biggest bear head I had ever seen, was swaying back and forth in a scary, steady rhythm, going faster and faster and faster. His head was so gigantic that I couldn't figure out how his neck muscles could even support the weight of the darned thing. It was scary big. All the while my dad keeps chucking rocks and giggling.

"Part of me wanted to run away and tell my dad to stop but another part of me wanted to see what was going to happen next. One rock after another kept flying over the bars, over the moat that prevented the bear from reaching the bars, over the water and landing squarely on the bear's back. 'Now, that's more like it,' my dad laughed as the bear became more and more agitated.

"And as the words were coming out of his mouth, I mean so fast that it happened in between letters of a word being annunciated, the bear did the unthinkable, the simply unimaginable. This tremendously huge polar bear, the one with the incredibly large bulbous head, somehow hurled his 2,000-pound body in the air, clear across the swimming hole and onto the one foot of cement landing across the moat and by the bars. It had to be a 12-foot jump!

"My dad and I both fell backwards to the ground in horror as the bear pushed his massive paws through the openings trying to reach us. He snarled at us, drool oozing from his sharp teeth that looked more like butcher knives than anything. I could feel his hot breath cut right across the winter air right across my face. He was more than menacing and for a moment I absolutely knew that I was done for. He stood on his hind legs and roared at us, looking up at the top of the fence he was about to scale and almost smiling. But thankfully the landing was too narrow and suddenly the bear lost his footing and starting skidding backwards down into the moat.

"We were still sitting with our bottoms on the freezing ground when we could hear him groaning and growling in anger and despair at not being able to rip us to shreds. We backed up, scampering several feet, not yet daring to stand, before turning around and walking away from the enclosure without uttering a sound. We walked to our car in silence, drove home in silence and never spoke of the incident again. I don't think I saw my dad pester an animal again for as long as he lived."

Jack's friends at the bar were in silent awe.

"Good gravy, Jackie boy," Old Man Dukes finally blurted out. "You tell the most whopping stories of anyone I know. Get the boy a beer on me, will ya. I never met your dad but I gotta tell ya, I love the man."

Jack didn't buy a beer for the rest of the night and was happy until he started walking home alone and remembered Marci's ultimatum, his own stupidity at missing their anniversary, and the appointment he had with Mrs. Elysa Durchin at the unemployment office the following morning.

His apartment was a hot, sticky mess and Jack had a hard time getting to sleep. Finally, with the help of the midnight movie, Dana Andrews in *The Best Years of Our Lives*, Jack was able to forget everything and get some rest.

It was amazing to Jack that the black electrical tape held as he scurried wheezily up the platform stairs, through the turnstile, slithered past the hordes like a salmon looking to spawn upstream, and lunged for the collapsing double doors of the 6 uptown train.

Equally as impressive was the fact that his Mister Softee soft-serve vanilla ice cream cone with chocolate sprinkles had fared just as well. He sat in the near empty train car and stared in amazement at the dripping cone in his hand. Suddenly the train lurched forward causing Jack to misfire his first lick and winding up with a right cheek full of ice cream.

A little Puerto Rican boy who was on his mother's lap, erupted in high-pitched giggles. The boy's mother, a stern-looking woman with a kind face whose hair was pulled back tightly into a bun that looked painful, admonished her son in Spanish. The boy looked down in embarrassment.

"No, no, it's OK," Jack said to the boy and his mother. "It is funny. Look, I've got a face full of ice cream."

With that, Jack flashed the biggest, widest, silliest, grin he could muster and purposely smushed the ice cream cone on his face a second time. The boy laughed again.

The woman smiled politely and Jack did not feel it was necessary to continue the conversation, to mention that he was eating ice cream a day after his girlfriend ordered him to lose 50 pounds.

The little Puerto Rican boy kept looking up and smiling at Jack until he got off the train with his family at the Soundview Avenue stop. Jack's ice cream was long gone by then, though there was plenty of flavor left on his sticky lips. Jack waved goodbye and the boy smiled as the train pulled out of view. His mother, with the tightly-pulled bun, pulled him along sternly.

With a sudden lurch forward after the train had slowed, Jack lost his balance again and fell onto an empty seat, occupied only by a copy of *The Economist* magazine. He had never heard of it but started thumbing through the pages, while playing back every word that Mrs. Durchin had for him and his lack of initiative in trying to find a job.

"Mr. Hopkins," she said.

"Oh, please call me Jack."

"Mr. Hopkins," she continued, in her perpetually nasal and exasperated tone, "here is the bottom line because I know we both want to be bottom line types of people. You know there are really only two types of people in this world: bottom line people and people who say they are bottom line people but who really want nothing to do with knowing truly what the bottom line is. Do you follow?"

Jack nodded and gave a half smile.

"You strike me as a bottom line fellow. So here we go. The bottom line, the only line, is that unless you make an effort, a real effort in applying for several jobs in the next week or so, then your unemployment benefits will come to an end as of the 20th of this month. As it is, I cannot guarantee they will continue anyway. I've already extended you once and there has been a real crackdown on weeding out the deadbeats taking advantage of the system. The government helps tide you over, but the initiative, Mr. Hopkins, must come from you. You have been out of work for too long and you have not heeded any of my past warnings, Mr. Hopkins. I've even sent you on job assignments that come my way but something always seems to happen, doesn't it?"

"I won't let you down, Mrs. Durchin," a smiling Jack responded.

"Somehow I doubt that, Mr. Hopkins, but good luck and remember, you have until the 20th to show me you are serious about getting back to work. Send out some resumes, apply for some jobs. And remember, even that is no guarantee that we can continue to help."

Disturbed by the second ultimatum in as many days, Jack bought an ice cream cone from the Mr. Softee truck by the train station and ran up the platform stairs to catch his train heading home to the Bronx.

Jack thumbed quickly through *The Economist* and found it stuffy. It was filled with articles about the Soviet Union's banking system, the latest sexual scandal involving a British parliament member and his traveling secretary, and yet another speculating on what the coming year would bring to the bevy of Latin American countries which seemed to usher in new eras of ruthless dictatorships every couple of months only to rebel against them a few years later. No sports. There was not one article on Major League Baseball or even Magic Johnson and the Los Angeles Lakers basketball team or whether Joe Gibbs could get the Washington Redskins back to the Super Bowl.

Jack tossed the magazine down on the seat next to him, but it slid off the seat and fell to the floor.

Content to leave it there, Jack glanced down and saw that it was open to a most interesting page: Help wanted, colleges and situations wanted. Maybe this was a sign, an omen.

He picked up the magazine eagerly and scoured the jobs with a huge grin on his face. These jobs were not for gas attendants at the local Shell station or for peanut vendors at Madison Square Garden. No, these jobs were special. There was one that advertised for a Chief Advisor position for the New Zealand Commerce Commission, another to head up the Adriatic Sea and Southeast Europe Division bank's legal department, another to oversee a fairly new section of oil fields in Saudi Arabia, and then one that caught Jack's eye almost immediately.

He ripped the page from the magazine, shoved it into his ever shrinking dungaree pocket, and sat back in his seat and smiled widely.

THREE

JACK WAS ON his hands and knees scurrying through the dozens of ripped shoes, sneakers, boxes of baseball cards, crates of Marvel Silver Surfer comic books and too-tight sweaters that had long ago fallen from their hangers to the quiet, undisturbed oblivion of the closet floor.

Every once in a while he would stop and stare in amazement at something found that was once lost like the magic pen that showed the transformation of an old woman to a girl in a bikini when flipped or the cutout baseball cards that were on the backs of Hostess coffee cakes that he had clipped as a child. He also paused at the ticket stubs of Mets games—many from the improbable pennant run of 1973—and tried to remember each one as he found them. He paused and placed his hand atop a shoe box that was marked "pictures of mom," but did not open it. He moved it gently aside and continued his mission until he pulled the light blue Smith-Corona typewriter from the far recesses of his closet.

"Now to find some paper," he exclaimed to a very bored-looking cat before setting off on a similar search and rescue mission that yielded the typewriter.

Before long, and using nearly a half a sheet of Correcto Type, Jack pulled the one-page resume from the typewriter and proudly stared at it. He read the paper over and over again making sure it was what he wanted.

"Now this," he said aloud, "is too perfect. There is no way Mrs. Durchin can deny me benefits after learning that I've applied to this job. Yes, yes, it is far away, and chances are probably a hundred zillion to one that they would ever consider me, but it involves my background, my interests and she never said the jobs I applied for had to be local. It shows that I can dream and they can't really stop my benefits as long as I'm dreaming, isn't that right Felicia?"

Quite content with himself, Jack bounced to the kitchen where he placed four Ball Park franks into a pot of boiling water before quickly taking one out before the water got too hot and placing it back in the refrigerator. He tapped his tummy and for the first time in days was very happy.

Jack put all three hot dogs onto one hot dog bun, drowned them in ketchup then stuffed the resume into an envelope, taking care to correctly write down the complicated address. He only got one small ketchup smudge onto the resume. Stuffing the dogs into his mouth, he grabbed the envelope and ran out of the house as quickly as he could. The post office would be closing in 15 minutes and that was the only place he knew of to buy air mail stamps.

Posted on the refrigerator and held in place by a lighthouse magnet that said "Wildwood Crest, New Jersey," was the help wanted ad that Jack had ripped from the magazine on the train earlier in the day.

He ran past Papo without stopping to buy a coquito and whizzed by Agrapina's without even pausing to smell the frying *empanadas* or the *plátanos*. But most shocking was Jack's refusal to stop at the basketball courts where Lenny, Chumbley, Joselito, Teddy, and little Stevie Casanova were shooting hoops.

"Hey Jack we need a sixth," they called out but Jack waved the envelope at them as he continued running and blurted out something about the post office or unemployment.

"Don't look up," he told himself. "Just keep going, don't stop. If you don't look up you'll be alright."

Later that night, after dialing Marci 17 times with no answer, Jack went down to the Excalibur. He had some new stories he remembered and wanted to share but found instead that the regular crew spent the night trying to console Old Man Dukes, who had lost "Little Dukie" earlier that day.

It definitely was not a good time for another of his animal stories, the one about the pony ride at the Adventures Inn amusement park in Queens. Jack was only seven but as large round as he was tall. He finally mustered up enough courage to trust his life and limb to the wild beast. He got on the pony and the poor beast's legs buckled and the animal seemed to cry.

"Sorry, pops," the carnival worker told his father. "The boy's too big. Try the elephant rides."

No, that story would have to wait. Tonight was about Old Dukes.

"Good gravy," Dukes said, working hard to choke back the tears. "There couldn't have been a better dog in the history of pets than Little Dukie. That little white ball of fur had a little bit of everything in him: poodle, bichon, terrier, I don't know what else. But that dog was better than any purebred in the world.

"Sure he liked snooping in the trash more than the food I got him, but that was only because his instincts for survival were so great," Dukes continued. "That dog survived on the streets before I took him in and he knew how to get along. There wasn't a free meal anywhere that Little Dukes couldn't sniff out."

The mood wasn't completely black all night but things were definitely more somber than usual. There were no Jack stories, no off-color jokes from the Sullivan brothers and Jack walked home alone feeling that things were changing. He didn't like the feeling and stayed up late watching reruns of "The Rockford Files" and "McMillan and Wife" until his eyelids were just too heavy and trudged over to bed.

He didn't even open the bag of plantain chips he bought at Socorro's on his way home from the pub.

The stickiness of the night was gone and a slight breeze was kicking around from Long Island Sound. Surely tomorrow would be much cooler than it had been in days.

Despite his exhaustion and the sudden break in the temperature, Jack tossed and turned, flipped his pillow over several times and just could not fall asleep. His thoughts raced from topic to topic, starting with Marci then going to poor old

Dukes, his own weight and the need to start eating healthier food. But most of all Jack kept thinking about the amount of energy he wasted that day applying for a job he knew he would never get in order to try and keep collecting unemployment insurance.

"Imagine if I gave finding a job, a real job, that same effort," he said out loud.

Then, realizing he would never be able to fall asleep, Jack got up, stretched, and started cleaning his apartment.

He was done by dawn. He looked over his work and it was impressive. He had filled twelve large black plastic bags with trash—mainly old newspapers, fast food wrappers, Chinese food containers, empty boxes of cereal, empty rolls of electrical tape, and several discarded bags of cat food.

Then he went to work on his closet, tossing shoes with holes too big to be repaired, hanging up shirts that had not fit him in four years, and arranging boxes of collectibles and baseball memorabilia. He made sure to leave the typewriter out on the small metal kitchen table. He continued working straight through until the afternoon, stopping only to brew a pot of coffee and to sit on the floor drinking it while going through the shoe box filled with photographs of his mother.

She was beautiful.

Later that day, after showering and getting dressed, Jack went down to Socorro's bodega for copies of the *Daily News* and the *New York Post* to scour the classifieds. He even stopped to ask Papo if he was serious the other day when he said Jack should go back to college.

"Jack, are you kidding?" Papo responded. "You are one of the brightest guys in this neighborhood yet you waste your time with that collection of misfits at that run-down pub you hang around in. You should definitely get your butt in school and make something of yourself."

When he returned home Jack called information for the phone numbers of Lehman College, Pace University, Mercy College and others. He posted the list on the refrigerator, replacing the silly help-wanted advertisement he had found in the magazine on the train. He crumpled the ad and tossed it in the trash.

Not in the mood for the company of his friends at the Excalibur, that night Jack fixed himself a plate of instant mashed potatoes to go with a piece of "Shake and Bake" chicken and watched the ballgame with Felicia before conking out for the night.

The next morning Jack worked up the nerve to get on the scale that had been hidden away beneath his bed for several years. He gasped at the number and examined his profile in the bathroom mirror for several minutes, trying hard to hold his tummy in.

"OK, buster," he addressed himself in the same mirror after coming out of the shower and wiping the condensation away with his hand. "This is the day we start to win Marci back. It's time to get serious."

And he was serious for the first time in years. Jack called every college on his list and requested applications and course booklets. Then he started circling jobs in the newspaper and numbered them starting with the most desirable positions first like assistant boys basketball coach at Truman High School, head usher at Radio City Music Hall, and sports statistician for the Elias Sports Bureau. But he didn't stop with the jobs he'd love but he went all the way down to the jobs he'd accept like house painter and carpenter's helper.

Some ads requested a call and so he called while others requested something in writing and so he fired up the old Smith-Corona typewriter and typed out resumes, cover letters or anything else they asked for.

By the end of the day Jack was pleased with how his typing skills had improved so quickly.

It was this way for the next ten days as Jack worked hard to find a job and lose weight. But the 20th was looming and the dark day took on an even more dire hue when Jack received a certified letter from the landlord, or rather the management company that oversaw the maintenance and rent collection duties, serving him with an official eviction notice effective on the 20th.

"D-day minus five," Jack said out loud, smiling so as not to alarm Felicia or cause the cat any undue stress. "Well, my dear, something is bound to give. Let's see, I've inquired about 73 jobs, the odds are in our favor. And even if no one calls with an offer, Mrs. Durchin is bound to extend the benefits. She will fight for me. She will see how serious I am."

Exactly 6,334 miles away, as the crow flies, Clive Manchester Kennerly III frantically emptied the drawers of the small oak desk in his crowded office. Most of the papers were flying straight out of the desk and into the dusty air. Every once in a while he would snatch one he needed and grunt excitedly, stashing it into the already overflowing attaché case on the ground next to him.

He'd stop, wide-eyed and perspiring profusely whenever he heard footsteps outside his office in the hallway. One time the footsteps seemed to come to a rest directly outside his office door and he cowered beneath the desk holding his breath. When a set of keys dropped right outside his door Kennerly nearly screamed out loud.

He was able to accomplish the most, scouring the bulk of papers, whenever a plane roared to a landing just outside his window. First he'd crawl to the venetian blinds frantically and peek through to see if the plane was for him.

While peering through at a plane landing from nearby Uganda, Kennerly's bifocals slid from his greasy face off of his pointed nose and onto the floor where he proceeded to crush them with his left knee.

"Jiminy Cricket!" he squeezed out through clenched teeth trying to remain quiet while pulling small shards of fine glass from his knee. "That's just fantastic. That is just brilliant. What am I going to do now?"

His white hair was dusty from the red clay and his once impeccable dress consisting of the finest English suits and smoking jackets had now been reduced to wrinkly sweat-stained messes. His shoes were undone and there were dirty clothes sticking out from the lone suitcase waiting desperately by the office door.

The past month had certainly taken its toll on the 54-year-old.

Kennerly's ruddy cheeks were no longer sun burnt but still bright red from nervousness, exhaustion, and the fear of spending the rest of his days in a Sudanese prison.

Without his glasses the frantic paperwork search was more difficult but not much slower as he squinted tightly and glanced at every paper that came flying out of his desk. Despite the harried nature of the moment, the top of his desk was perfectly kept with pens, pencils, ledgers, and graph paper all in their proper places. There was a bin for outgoing mail, one for incoming mail and a third that was recently marked "Replacement Director: hire in this order" with a stack of resumes from qualified men from all over the world wishing to experience a bit of Africa while bumping up their own credentials of having run an international airport, albeit a small one.

It had been a month since Kennerly turned in his resignation but now the noose was beginning to tighten and it most certainly was time to get out of Dodge, or in this case the town of Jabra, a growing enclave directly between Juba and Rumbek. The local newspaper editor started making noise a few days ago and now there it was on the front page of the regional edition of the Al-Rayaam newspaper for all of Sudan to see. The headline—in English and Arabic—was larger than life: "Brit Kennerly Embezzler?"

The photo was just as bad. It was a shot of Kennerly counting several hundred pounds at the local bank. Was he guilty? Of course, but the photo was an innocent one of the ex-pat simply cashing his paycheck. Now it was time to get back home to Europe.

In three years Kennerly had managed to skim hundreds of thousands of dollars from the airport's revenues including kickbacks from pilots who didn't want their cargo searched or from passengers not having the right visas. But now the jig was up and in about 15 minutes he'd be on a chartered plane to Kenya where he'd hop a military transport back to Europe. He would avoid the United Kingdom and possibly settle in France. There was a chance he would still be extradited back to Britain where he would still have to answer to the airport's board of directors, all English. But the prospects of an English prison would be better than a Sudanese lynch mob.

When he finally had his paperwork in order, a relieved Kennerly took a deep breath and waited for his plane to land. Scurrying to the window one last time like a water bug, Kennerly slipped on a pile of discarded papers, sending several straight up into the air as he landed square on his chin, cutting and bruising it.

"Jiminy Cricket!" he exclaimed. "If I make it out of here alive it will be a miracle."

He never noticed, nor would he probably have cared if he had, that one of the papers sent flying during his spill seemed suspended in midair. It floated down slowly as if buoyed by the stifling hot air of the office—the way vultures use the thermals to soar for hours—and finally came neatly to rest atop one of the three bins on his desk.

As he grabbed the suitcase and attaché case and went scrambling from his office window out onto the tarmac to meet his plane, Kennerly never turned around. Squinting tightly, hoping he was not rushing out to the wrong airplane and holding his badly cut chin, he tripped and fell several times on his way out onto the tarmac. Remarkably, he lost none of the papers clutched in his hands and hanging precariously from his attaché case.

Had he turned around, it is likely he never would have noticed that sitting atop the "Replacement director: hire in this order" bin was an almost illegible resume filled with errors from a man with no experience and no education living on Bruckner Boulevard in the Bronx, New York.

FOUR

JACK SAT ON the dusty torn-up couch that used to belong to his parents stroking Felicia's back and trying not to look glum. The cat purred contently, apparently not taking notice that all the furniture in the apartment had already been donated to Goodwill, thrown in the trash, or rescued by some of the Excalibur crew.

The apartment seemed much bigger now with the clutter removed and Jack wished he had enjoyed the wide open spaces more than he had. The sunlight streaming in from the window danced off of the tiny particles of dust forever floating throughout the plaster-coated tenement. He wished for a lot of things now. Most of all he wished he hadn't waited so long to start looking for a job.

At Jack's feet were a half dozen boxes, the only things he cared to keep. In them were his baseball cards, coffee mugs, catcher's mitt, comic books, typewriter, and some of the clothes that still fit his expanding girth. On the couch next to him was the shoebox of memories, his mother's photographs.

He smiled at the cat, which looked away, and tried to put on a brave face. His aunt Nelly's one bedroom apartment was too small for a guest and she was much too old so Jack's next move, he figured, was to see if Old Man Dukes could take in a boarder for a few weeks until he landed a job or found a decent homeless shelter where he wouldn't have to fear for his life every time he closed his eyes.

It would be several months before the cold weather arrived and things would be alright. Shucks, he could probably even camp out under the City Island Bridge and catch enough flounder and striped bass to get by.

He tried remaining positive that one of the dozens of jobs he applied for would come through but it was difficult, especially now that he played this waiting game. Without a home telephone and a home address it would be even tougher. But Jack made sure to write down the telephone numbers of all the places that he sent resumes out to and would simply have to spend his time—and his dimes—at the public telephone booths checking in to see if he had been hired.

He never thought his life would change so much over the course of a few weeks.

But here he was now, $17 in his wallet from the very last unemployment check he would receive and sitting in an empty pathetic apartment five days past the eviction notice. His days were spent now waiting for the knock on the door telling him to leave. It never dawned on him to just get up and go. No, he felt obliged to wait and officially turn the apartment over to whoever came to enforce the notice.

He would have it no other way.

It seemed only proper and Jack did not hold any resentment or bitterness in his heart, knowing all too well that he would have been allowed to stay had he been able to pay his rent.

"Not one call, Felicia," he said desperately trying to sound upbeat and positive but doing a poor job of masking his disappointment. Even his mock English accent seemed forced now. "All those jobs and not one call. Looks like everybody would rather hire anybody than me."

Then he stood and walked over to the bathroom mirror where he leaned against the sink and smiled at himself.

"No use feeling sorry for yourself now," he chided. "That ship has long sailed. Nope. It's better to look at this as an adventure, a new challenge in our road to win Marci back. Isn't that how it always goes in the movies? Don't things always get blackest before getting better? The whole darkest hour before the dawn thing?

"Yes. That's right. We've got to keep a positive outlook, Felicia my girl."

The words made Jack feel better and he smiled, but the cat, distracted by a pigeon that landed on the fire escape, leapt from the couch to the window.

With that came a loud knock on the door and Jack's heart immediately sank and started racing simultaneously.

"I guess this is it," he smiled one last time at his reflection.

He walked to the door in slow motion, taking in every last second, every last chip of peeling paint or splintered plaster that he called home for years. He ran his fingers gently over the walls, patted the old couch, and stood frozen at the door.

The knocking continued.

"Mr. Hopkins, are you in there? I have very important papers for you." The voice was accented and deep and not what Jack expected.

Jack gulped and tried to answer "I know" but his throat was so dry that no sound came out.

Finally he clicked the swollen bolt and pulled the door open.

To his surprise, standing in the doorway was a well-dressed black man with perfectly shiny skin, who must have been about 6-foot 5-inches tall, wearing small round glasses that seemed tiny on his shaven head where sweat beads had formed a perspiration crown around his dome.

The man was pleasant-looking enough and started smiling, which Jack thought was a little inappropriate for someone about to send a tenant out to the streets.

"Mr. Hopkins?" he asked and this time Jack could hear what sounded like a British accent of some sort.

Jack nodded, fighting back the urge to answer in his own mock accent, perfected from studying Peter Cushing's accent in the Hammer horror films of his youth. He loved how Cushing could make you feel sorry for him even when he was clearly insane and pathological, especially during his numerous roles playing Dr. Frankenstein.

"Ah, perfect then. May, may I come in?"

Jack moved aside and motioned for the man to come in. The visitor lifted his glasses for a moment to take in the odd surroundings he suddenly found himself in. He thought it odd or genius that Mr. Hopkins had already packed his things and was ready for the move even before receiving the news. He looked at the couch and Jack nodded for him to sit down.

The man had a large manila envelope and started opening it.

"Mr. Hopkins, we are prepared to offer you three years at this rate right here," he said pointing to a number on a contract that had so many zeroes it made Jack's eyes water. "But you must be willing to start immediately. I can see you've already anticipated the hire and have succinctly packed your things. That is simply a brilliant maneuver on your part."

The man stood up and looked around the apartment. The quizzical look turned into one of admiration.

"I hope you don't mind terribly that we have taken the liberty of doing an extensive security background check, obtained a passport and necessary visas for you, and have a $5,000 allowance here for you to buy the appropriate clothing. It can actually get chilly there this time of year. People don't realize that we have winters. We don't get snow but it can get quite cold. We can fly out tonight and you can start your new position on Wednesday if that pleases you, sir. We have a charter at our disposal."

Jack kept his head very still but darted around the room with his eyes looking for some hidden camera. He grinned slightly, demurely. Finally he shook his head slowly and rubbed his eyes. It was a long time before he was able to remember how to speak. When he did, it felt as if there was an old dried out sweat sock in his mouth.

"I'm sorry. Who are you exactly and what on earth are you talking about?"

"I am so sorry," the man stood up again, looking even taller than he had before. "Please forgive my lack of manners and etiquette, my apologies. Allow me to introduce myself. My name is Jean Richard Baptiste and I represent the White Nile International Airport in Jabra, in the Sudan. I know what you are thinking. You probably have never really heard of Jabra but it is a growing little city, the next Juba maybe. It is very close to the

Nile River and though it is a southern city many feel it is close enough to the north to one day become a viable cosmopolitan city. Your name topped all other candidates for the job and we would like very much for you to come and, and be the airport's new director. Unfortunately there is quite a mess there for you to clean up but we are confident you will be up to the challenge."

Jack started laughing, quietly at first, like when you are holding back the giggles during church services or in class at school. But before long it was a full-out belly laugh complete with watering eyes and dripping nose. Jack stood up and grabbed a tissue for his nose.

"Oh my," he finally got out through the laughing. "Oh my, that is hilarious. You got me sir, you sure did. This was just priceless."

Jack wondered who was behind the prank but couldn't remember telling anyone that he had even sent his resume for this job.

"I'm sorry Mr. Hopkins. I'm not sure I understand."

"OK, where are the cameras, sir?

"Excuse me?"

"The hidden cameras, this is a gag, right? You got me good, look, my nose is dripping from laughing so hard."

"I'm not sure what you're getting at."

Jack sat down and started looking through the papers.

"Mr. Hopkins, I assure you this is legitimate. Now, will you sign the contract? As I said the previous director left quite a mess behind and someone needs to come clean it up."

Jack started giggling again when a short chubby balding man in terrible need of a shave knocked on the front door, which was still slightly open and pushed his head in.

"Mr. Hopkins? Jack Hopkins? I think you've been expecting this. It's time to go, mister," the man's voice was gruff and heavy like he had just smoked a pack of cigarettes on his way up the stairs. He was out of breath and seemed surprised to see the other man in the apartment as well.

"Oh, I see you've got company," he said slowly, clenching his fists. "Well, you'd better not be trying any funny stuff. There is no need for you to have anyone here, except of course if he's here to help you move. There's no need to make this harder than it has to be."

The man coughed and backed up slowly into a defensive position.

Jack rubbed his eyes again.

"OK, wait one second. Let me get this straight. You," he said pointing to the short balding man, "are here to evict me. Is that right?"

The man nodded.

"And you," he motioned to Jean Richard Baptiste, "are here to offer me the job of a lifetime and take me on a shopping spree. Is that pretty close to it?"

"Yes, sir, Mr. Hopkins. That is, if you sign the contract."

"Hold on one second," the landlord chimed in. "I've got papers for you to sign as well. And then I'm sorry, buddy, but you've got to go."

"Well," Jack laughed again. "Who's got a pen?"

That afternoon, whisked downtown in a limousine, while movers loaded a small truck with his belongings and carted them to JFK International Airport, Jack was full of questions for Jean Richard Baptiste.

He asked about lions, giraffes, tribes, spears, and malaria. He asked about hot dogs, hamburgers, and fried chicken. He asked about being able to get American newspapers in order to keep track of his beloved Mets and the rest of the baseball world.

Baptiste answered as best as he knew how and was bewildered at how this man, who had never stepped foot outside of New York could be the answer to problems at the airport. But having been trained and educated at the finest British boarding schools and the University of South Cairo, he knew better than to question—even privately to himself—his superiors. They must have a plan and they must know what they are doing, he thought as he kept a frozen half-smile on his face while answering Jack's queries, even the one about telling the difference between a hyena's laugh and growl.

Jack marveled at his first limousine ride and felt obligated to stick his head through the sun roof and wave at non-interested Manhattanites darting in and out of office buildings like bees heading back to the hive. At Jack's request the car pulled up to the Banana Republic store on 86th Street and 3rd Avenue. Jean Richard wanted to wait in the car with a sleeping Felicia and the amused driver but Jack insisted he come in to help him pick out the proper clothing.

Of course, Jack had his mind set up when he saw the "Safari" collection that included white vests with numerous pockets to keep matches, compasses, pocket knives, and extra rounds of ammunition safe and dry. He threw one into his cart, then decided better of it and put in three more. Similar safari-styled pants that zippered down into shorts, boots, waterproof socks, and even a pith helmet. All these purchases were made over Jean Richard's mild protestations who politely and delicately tried explaining that Jack would be in charge of running an airport not a safari-based comedy troupe. He also tried guiding him to more sensible purchases and pointed out that traditional western shirt and ties were appropriate for high-level business meetings and such.

After purchasing the goodies, Jack insisted on taking Jean Richard for a couple of hot dogs at Papaya King right across the street. Again Jean Richard protested to little avail and was forced to munch down two hot dogs with spicy brown mustard and diced raw onions and drink a cold papaya juice beverage. Despite his worldliness, he had never tasted anything quite like the hot dogs that were cooked to the perfect point where they snapped as you bit into them, squirting hot grease down the side of your mouth. It was only after this meal did Jean Richard start to understand the questions about hot dogs in the Sudan.

With shopping complete and lunch out of the way there were really only a few housecleaning items that Jack needed to take care of before they could head to the airport.

Not wanting his friends to worry, Jack had the limousine drive back to the neighborhood where he could say his goodbyes. The first stop was the schoolyard where Chumbley, Lenny, and little Stevie Casanova were playing basketball along with Jorge Blanco and Bobby Molettiere. They dropped the ball and stared in disbelief as Jack emerged from the limousine. He gave them all hugs, told them he would be back soon, and reminded them to keep their elbows tucked when shooting jump shots.

"Jean Richard," Jack said he got back into the car. "We didn't spend my entire allowance, correct?"

"That's right," Jean Richard responded as he observed Jack wipe a tear from his eye. "It is really yours to spend as you see fit."

"Good."

Jack pulled a few hundred dollar bills from the envelope and instructed the driver to go in and around some of the neighborhood streets.

Just as Jean Richard was going to complain about this seemingly endless joyride down through memory lane, Jack pointed.

"Ah, there he is, over there."

Papo had taken a break and was reading the sports pages of the *New York Post* on the stoop of the building where his mother—88-year-old "Mamita" Isabelle—had lived for the past 67 years.

Like the boys in the basketball court, Papo looked dumbfounded, mouth agape, as Jack jumped out of the fancy car.

"Jack, I know you're not stupid enough to be selling drugs. What's going on?"

"Long story, but the bottom line is I just landed a terrific job and have to leave pretty quickly. I'll try and send a letter explaining everything. But in the meantime, I want to buy ices for the boys."

"OK, how many?" he started to rise from the stoop.

"As many as these will buy," and he flashed several hundred dollars in Papo's direction.

"What?" Papo was flustered.

"This should cover them for a while," Jack smiled. "I don't want you charging those kids one cent for ices whenever they want one. Ices will be on me for as long as that money holds out."

Papo took the money and was still stunned. He shook Jack's hand without saying a word and watched as his most loyal customer started getting back into his car.

"Jack," he called out, finally able to speak.

Jack looked back over his shoulder.

"I don't know what this is about but I do know one thing. You're a good man. Take care of yourself."

Jack smiled and Jean Richard tapped the driver on the shoulder to start driving.

There was one stop left.

The neon gas filling the "x" in Excalibur was flickering sporadically as the sign became more visible with the setting sun. The limousine pulled in front of the pathetic looking bar and Jack bounced out, Felicia in arms and Jean Richard worriedly behind. His expression oscillated between fear and disgust. He tried not to let his clothes or skin come in contact with anything inside the wretched bar, sidestepping to make sure his clothes did not brush up against the wall or any of the patrons.

The Sullivan boys, Mike Morgan, and Old Man Dukes turned in bewilderment at the spectacle ambling toward them.

"Well, hot gravy on a griddle," Dukes exclaimed. "What are you up to, Jackie boy? You're wearing a grin on your face that tells me either you hit the lottery, robbed a bank or you've been signed by the New York Mets to play centerfield. But since most Major League teams are not in the habit of awarding multi-million dollar deals to chubby over-the-hill non-athletic ballplayers then I'm leaning toward the former rather than the latter."

"First things first," Jack said waving to the bartender. "Beers on me for the rest of the night."

"Huh?"

"Here you go, Rico." Jack smiled and handed him $200. Then he turned to Dukes. "No, the Mets have not called looking for my services, but someone else has." He looked over his shoulder and motioned to Jean Richard, who didn't know whether to laugh or speak so he simply waved and immediately felt foolish for having done so.

"I've got a job."

Everyone cheered and for the next two hours they regaled in Jack's stories and celebrated his good fortune. It was the best goodbye party anyone could ever have, he thought to himself, even if Jean Richard looked at his watch every fifteen minutes and sighed.

Finally when Jack had run out of stories and when everyone had had their fill of beer, he made his rounds saying goodbye to them all. Dukes was last and Jack motioned for him to follow outside.

"Well, what have you got up your sleeve there, Jackie boy?" the old man said in his high-pitched sing-song voice.

Jack looked up at his friend, who was still tall, strong and broad-shouldered from his days doing construction decades ago. His eyes were small and had large black rings around them. He was one of those people who looked strong and vulnerable at the same time.

Jack reached into the limousine and pulled Felicia out.

"Now Dukes, I know Felicia can never replace Little Dukie but I'm gonna need someone to look after her while I'm gone." He stopped when he sensed his voice was about to crack. "She's a good cat and won't be any trouble at all."

"But Jack—"

"Understand now that I'm not giving her to you to keep permanently but I know that you'll be kind to her."

With that Jack shook the old man's hand before placing Felicia into it.

"She'll be waiting, we'll both be waiting for you son," Dukes said, his eyes misting over. "Now you take care of yourself."

Jack smiled a sad smile, stroked the fur on Felicia's back all the way up to her head, and the little cat looked up and sneezed.

"I think that means 'I love you' in cat talk, Dukes," Jack whispered. "I love you too."

Then he turned to get in the car, which pulled away slowly and out of sight.

"JACK, EXCUSE ME, Mr. Hopkins wake up, sir. We should be landing in Jabra momentarily," Jean Richard said tenderly. "Perhaps you'd like to go wash up before we land, sir."

Jack yawned loudly and rubbed the sleep from his face. The soothingly loud engines of the 707 aircraft had put him to sleep shortly after leaving New York and he continued his lullaby even after they got on a much smaller aircraft in Cairo for the short jaunt to Jabra in the Sudan. There was something soothing about flying that Jack just found hypnotic. Despite all the sleep, Jack could have kept sleeping for several hours more. He wasn't quite ready to face his new life but there was little choice now.

He stood up, yawned and stretched and opened his bag to change his clothes. Jack had done a lot of reading during the 15-hour flight that stopped for fuel in Saudi Arabia then to switch planes in Egypt. He read over and over again how important it was for him to make a good first impression. This job would be the only way to win Marci back. He already pictured her face and her running toward him at JFK upon his triumphant return. If he played his cards right, he thought, there would be enough money for an engagement ring, wedding caterer, and a co-op apartment somewhere in Riverdale or Yonkers.

Yep, she would certainly be impressed. Jack was happy now that he had not spoken to Marci or left word concerning his plans before leaving. No, the plan now was to send a post card with whatever information he wanted her to have. Nothing, of course, was more important than letting her know he had a real job and was finally taking his life seriously.

He stretched again and carefully pulled his outfit from the bag so as not to wrinkle it. He also took his shaving kit and walked to the restroom. The aircraft, a modified Cessna 414A Chancellor, belonged to the pilot, George White, but he was contracted by the Jabra Airport and would basically be made available for Jack whenever he wanted. Maybe he could take a trip to see the pyramids or sphinx one of these weekends. Or maybe he'd fly back to Cairo then take a commercial jet if the miserable Mets somehow made it to the World Series again. He could propose to Marci right before the game at home plate, or maybe during the seventh-inning-stretch.

Jack shaved and bathed as best he could in the tiny sink in an even tinier lavatory area.

"Got to lose some weight," he muttered under his breath while squeezing into his new clothes. "Got to lose some weight."

The plane was descending rapidly now and Jack's ears were popping. The propellers seemed louder than ever. He held his nose closed and tried to blow it at the same time to alleviate some of the pressure.

The sleepiness was gone completely and Jack was nervously focusing on what he needed to do. Jean Richard had filled him in along the way and his words echoed in his head.

"Mr. Hopkins," Jean Richard had started, "this airport, well, the fellow that preceded you was playing fast and loose with things or so it seems. We'll let the courts have their final say. Do you follow?"

"Yes," Jack lied, nodding his head and trying to look thoughtful.

"However, we did not let his accounting snafus deter us from hiring someone he clearly thought so highly of. Despite the sticky fingers, the man knew how to surround himself with capable people. You'll find that you have a very good staff awaiting you."

Again Jack nodded and this time rubbed his chin in deep contemplation, suddenly realizing that he had no idea what he was doing.

"What I'm trying to say is that, well, he left this airport in an awful mess and everyone is counting on you to clean the mess up."

"Clean it up? You betcha. That's the first thing I will do."

Jean Richard had also given Jack a book of North African history, culture, etiquette, and traditions that might come in handy while he adjusted to the "different culture." Jack thumbed through it excitedly at first then a little less enthusiastically. His eyes widened at certain things, like how you should not touch someone with your left hand since that is the hand used for wiping, a passage that made him wish he had packed some toilet paper. He became dizzy when reading about the 200 ethnic groups and 900 languages. But that same dizzying thought later gave him comfort when he realized it was a melting pot of sorts, like the Big Apple, and that the people were obviously an accepting, welcoming bunch.

Jack looked in the mirror of the tiny restroom and then checked his smile carefully to make sure there was nothing embarrassing stuck in his teeth. One of the worst moments of his life had been on that first date with Marci. They went to the arcade at Nathan's on Central Avenue in Yonkers where he could bedazzle her with his skills playing Dragon's Lair. A crowd had gathered around as he was only a few moves from defeating the game but she would not look at him. He told jokes as he played, sang with the Clash as they poured out of the juke box and even had one of the bystanders cover his eyes during one sequence. Still nothing. She would not look at him. Finally, as he was entering his name into the high scorer's hall of fame he caught a glimpse of his smile in the reflection of the glass screen and was mortified. Seven, no less than seven kernels of corn had wedged themselves between his upper row of teeth as if he just rubbed the corn on the cob onto his closed mouth. It was hideous. He excused himself before entering his full name and ran to the men's room.

Now he always knew what was in his teeth.

He rubbed them vigorously with his finger then breathed into his hand to make sure his breath was not too offensive after sleeping. He wished he had a mint.

Jean Richard's eyes widened when he saw Jack emerge from the lavatory as the plane continued to descend.

There he was in full safari clothing including a pith helmet!

He had witnessed Jack make the purchase at Banana Republic and yet it was still nothing short of shocking to see the ridiculous get-up on this roly-poly person. He smiled politely and told Jack that he was sure to make an impression. Privately he fought the growing suspicion that a terrible mistake had been made during the hiring process.

"OK, gentlemen, let's sit down and fasten those seatbelts," the pilot George White called out. "I'm bringing Ti Burik in for a landing." He was a burly man originally from the Tennessee mountains where he learned to play the banjo and cultivate bonsai trees all by himself. The air force taught him to fly.

"Ti Burik?"

"It's what he's named this plane. It means 'little donkey' in Creole he once told me. I think it goes back to some rescue flights he made to Haiti in the 1970s. It all sounded a little mysterious and I never pressed him on it."

Jack jumped into the window seat and eagerly looked out the window. There were green mountains and large flat fields between. The colors were striking and Jack smiled widely.

"There is the Nile River," Jean Richard pointed.

Jack felt silly that he couldn't even respond because of the lump in his throat.

He mouthed the word "wow" but no sound escaped his lips. He looked back over his shoulder and smiled fondly at Jean Richard.

George White circled the plane slowly two full times so Jack could see the several dozen people jumping up and down and waving before he set the old bird down. Several children were running around with their arms spread wide pretending to be airplanes as well. The airport was little more than a landing strip with a building and small tower but Jack instantly felt proud. This is mine to take care of, he thought, at least until I make enough money to show Marci.

Jack walked slowly down the stairs from the plane to the tarmac. He was met instantly with cheers and a burst of hot breeze that blew red dust from the clay road onto his new pristine white clothing and all over his face, sticking to his sweaty cheeks and forehead.

There was a hush from his greeters as Jack paused to wipe his eyes and mouth. Even Jean Richard seemed anxious, moving slowly away from Jack.

But the newly appointed airport director burst out laughing, putting everyone at ease and immediately ingratiating himself to the Sudanese people, at least these. He shook hands with as many people as he could and they all seemed genuinely pleased to see him. The women wore tunics and scarves that looked like saris and the men wore traditional ankle-length garments that Jack soon learned were called *jalabiyas*. There were many children squeezing through the crowd to get a look at Jack, who immediately noticed that many were not wearing shoes or socks and some were wearing dark blue school uniforms.

As if reading his mind, Jean Richard leaned in and whispered to Jack that the teachers had given the children a holiday today for his anticipated arrival.

"Why are they still wearing their school uniforms? Won't they get dirty?"

"I'm afraid for many that is the only clothing they have."

Immediately Jack thought of Lenny and Chumbley and Little Stevie Casanova back in the schoolyard. He already missed them.

"Mr. Hopkins, come, let me show you the grounds and your office so you may get settled in."

But Jack had already stopped, plopped onto the ground and opened his brown leather-like suitcase. He dug furiously for a few moments looking as if the bag would swallow him up before a wide smile came to his lips. His left arm emerged holding a bag of Charms blow pops, with grape-flavored gum at the center. He ripped open the bag and started handing them out to the children. They came eagerly with shining faces and bright smiles and some, little Franco and Jo-Jo, dropped right down on Jack's lap and chewed on their lollies.

One little girl, the tiniest thing Jack had ever seen, moved close enough to see but would not take a treat nor would she smile or speak.

Jack tried everything to get a reaction from her. He made funny faces, quacked like a duck, and snorted like a pig but there was still no response. He held out his hand but she shrank back, somehow making herself even smaller. She had large brown eyes like baseballs and her hair was pulled into a dozen braids held together with brightly-colored berets. She reminded him of Dr. Seuss's Cindy-Lou-Who, who was no more than two.

"You are a tough cookie," Jack said kindly, reaching into his bag for something else.

"If you had the kind of life she's had, you would be a tough cookie too, Mr. Hopkins."

Jack looked up but the sun forced him to squint tightly to make out the face of the woman speaking. She was tall and wore western-style clothing, not unlike the school uniforms some of the children had one.

"I don't mean to sound ungrateful, Mr. Hopkins," she continued. "Obviously you have made quite an impression with the others with your sugary delights but I'm afraid it will take more than a lollipop to make inroads with her. She has not spoken for as long as I have known her."

"Do you know her well?" a puzzled Jack responded.

"Well, I am her teacher after all."

Jack continued digging in his bag and pulled out a plastic bottle of soapy bubbles.

"OK, OK, I understand," he said. "She won't go for just a lollipop. But I have yet to meet a kid who didn't love to chase, pop, or catch bubbles." With that Jack started blowing long streams of bubbles causing the children to go into a frenzy. When the crowd of children thinned momentarily to chase down the bubbles, Jack blew a slow fat bubble right at the young girl. It moved slowly at her, bobbing up and down before popping on her nose.

She barely blinked an eye.

"Like I have said Mr. Hopkins, it will take much more. Hopefully a breakthrough to this child will be made sooner or later."

"Can I ask what happened?"

"You can ask, Mr. Hopkins, but perhaps that is a conversation for another time and place. In any event, thank you for trying."

The teacher took the young girl's hand and started leading her away.

"Wait," Jack called out. "What is your name and where do you teach?"

"It's Miss Jenelle." She smiled and for the first time Jack could see how beautiful she was. "I teach at the Christian mission in town. It's a Catholic school. You can't miss it. It's right on the way to the market, Mr. Hopkins."

He instantly tried pulling in his gut.

"OK, so I will see you around," he answered. "And bye-bye to you too, little Cindy Lou." He squinted his eyes tight and tried making his face as small as possible, holding his hand up to his cheek and waving.

Jenelle gave a funny look and started to respond, to correct, but just turned and continued walking. By now the eager children were back for more treats and bubbles.

It would be a full forty minutes before the crowd dispersed and Jean Richard could finally show Jack around the grounds, the leaking underground fuel tanks, the pot-holed riveted runway, the littered grounds, and the not-so-skilled staff eager to impress their new supervisor.

Jack looked tired and a bit bored.

"Is there a place to get a *piña colada* around here?" Jack yawned as he spoke.

"I don't know what that is."

"Well, it's a cocktail made up of pineapples, coconut and, oh forget it," he said as if remembering something very suddenly. "I need to get started. There's something I need to do."

"Started, sir? But you must be exhausted. I merely wanted to show you around and you can get to work tomorrow."

Most of the employees stood around smiling, not understanding a word of what was going on.

"No, no," Jack replied. "I know what a mess this place is in."

"But I haven't formally introduced you to the staff, sir."

"That's OK. This, Jean Richard, is much too important to wait. I'm sure I'll have plenty of time to meet staff."

Everyone watched as Jack scurried around the airport to find some large black plastic bags. He was unsuccessful in finding a pointer or some object with a sharp end. Then, using the remaining 45 minutes of sunlight, he set out around the perimeter fence of the airport, red dust swirling up all around the heat choking him. The employees followed him, along with a curious Jean Richard.

Jack started at the far end of the fence, where a small mountain range could be seen far off and a great long flat plain directly in front. He stooped down and started picking up every single piece of trash he could find. He chuckled every time he picked up a Coca-Cola bottle. Wow, even in Africa, he thought to himself.

He grabbed plastic and paper and old newspapers and even things he did not recognize. Beyond the fence were little plumes of smoke rising where families were cooking their dinners. Goats bleated and scurried around but there was little sound otherwise. It was the first time that Jack truly realized he was in another country.

The workers watched and scratched their heads wondering what to make of it all. Then the youngest and tallest of the bunch, Matthew, who worked loading and unloading the planes, walked over to Jack and held his hand out for a bag.

He smiled and though his English was extremely limited Matthew wanted to impress the man in the safari suit.

"USA number one," he said in a heavy accent and a kind smile.

Jack smiled and patted the man on his shoulder. Before it had gotten too dark to continue, Jack taught Matthew his favorite chant.

"Let's go Mets, Let's go Mets," they called out together as the other wide-eyed workers continued staring at them. Jack had already proven himself different than anyone who had ever worked at the airport.

SIX

JACK'S ACCOMMODATIONS consisted of a single, though large
room, furnished with bed, armoire, and television set that barely
broadcast one channel that seemed to show the same man on it
all the time speaking quickly in an African or Arabic dialect.

There was a small kitchen area with a single burner stove,
coffee pot, frying pan, and small pot for boiling. To the left was a
small but rugged writing desk. The walls were bare and Jack did
not feel all that unfamiliar with his surroundings.

The room was upstairs from a small shop owned by a shoe
cobbler. They shared the same small entrance to the grimy
building that smelled of shoe leather, polish, and stinky shoes.

The best part of Jack's flat was the window—or rather, the
opening where a window would have gone in—where Jack could
look down and see the children playing soccer.

The first night was the most restful for Jack. He did not stir
when the neighborhood dogs got into a scrape shortly after
midnight, and he barely moved a muscle when the roosters
started heralding the dawn four hours before the sun would
actually start to rise. No, he was so tired from the flight, the
welcoming and the cleanup around the airport that he even
skipped dinner.

Needless to say, Jack was famished when he finally stirred
from his bed. For a moment he had no idea where he was but he
knew it was different. There was no Felicia to wake him, no
tractor-trailers barreling down Bruckner Boulevard, and no sound
of a basketball pounding on the blacktop. There were plenty of
sounds, just not ones you'd hear in the Bronx.

He stuck his head out through the window opening and
breathed in deeply. There was food cooking everywhere, it

seemed, and Jack's stomach growled. He instantly craved pancakes, butter, maple syrup, and a few sausage patties. He looked around his room for the first time really and noticed one very important element was missing—the bathroom.

Of course, realizing there was nowhere to go ignited his need to suddenly go and he started jumping up and down and squirming. He opened his door and peered down the long dark hallway. Nothing. He began jumping again and for a split second thought about using the window when he heard shouting from the shoe repair shop downstairs.

No one of Jack's ample girth had ever tested the structural integrity of the old wooden beams keeping the second floor from crashing down onto the first. He slithered quickly down the stairs and the need grew worse by the second. In a strange land, hoping to make a good first impression, the last thing Jack wanted was to meet someone for the first time clutching himself and writhing like a school child.

Ahmed, the similarly rotund shopkeeper downstairs who called out when it seemed as if the world was coming to an end—or at least the old, creaky building above him—jumped up and down himself at the awkward quasi-introduction. Holding his belly with one hand while laughing, he pointed across a dusty, grassless field behind the shop to a set of three outhouses.

"Over there, hurry before you let loose the river," he yelled in Arabic.

Jack's eyes widened with panic, causing Ahmed to laugh even harder. Again he pointed toward the rear and made an urgent wave for Jack to go.

"Over there? Outside? Really?" the words came out of his mouth in short bursts like a machine gun.

The portly cobbler waved again and continued to laugh.

Finally Jack took off running. He darted in and out of several goats who decided to compete for the one blade of grass popping up from the dry ground. As the handle to the door grew larger, everything slowed. Jack was now immersed in some classic football highlight reel running toward glory in agonizingly slow motion, shaking defenders and hurdling blockers. There were no words to describe the utter elation that surged through his body when his sweaty hand gripped the door handle and pulled the swollen wooden door open.

He didn't even bother to notice that the outhouse was nothing more than a hole in the ground, literally.

Walking back toward the building, his new home, Jack could feel everyone staring at him. Some smiled but most just looked on with curiosity. He smiled back at everyone, though most of it stemmed from the relief of having finally gone to the bathroom. Just before he reached the rear entrance of the shop, Jack felt a small, warm hand slip into his.

It was one of the children from the airport the day before.

"Hello," the little boy said.

"Well, hello yourself." Jack smiled and knelt down beside the child. "How are you this morning?"

"I am fine, sir, and you?"

Jack laughed good naturedly at the boy's impressive manners.

"I am doing well," he smiled. "I just found my bathroom. Now I need to find some breakfast."

The boy looked confused and did not answer.

Jack motioned his hand to his mouth, the universal sign for needing food.

"Where can I buy breakfast?" he asked slowly. "Maybe something along the lines of an Egg McMuffin?"

"Ah." The boy smiled and started leading Jack around the rear of the building to the front, where a busy street was bustling with shopkeepers putting their wares out on blue tarps set out on the ground. The bright colors of fabrics, spices, and flowers contrasted with the bluest sky Jack had ever seen.

Jack could barely keep up as the young boy pulled him eagerly through the growing crowds and down narrow alleyways that might impede a larger man. The boy kept looking back at Jack, nodding his head and smiling. His teeth were the whitest Jack had ever seen.

The boy wore no shoes. His T-shirt said "Hawaii '73" and was pocked full of small holes.

Finally the pair wove their way through a last maze of street vendors mainly showcasing baskets brimming with multi-colored beans. A white cloud was starting to break up and streams of sunlight danced from bean to bean. Jack stopped for a moment and admired the sight.

A woman quickly approached him, her hands clutching several types of soft scarves. She begged him to make a purchase.

Jack turned to another vendor and picked up two smooth flat stones and held them up in place of his eyes making the boy laugh. Later he grabbed two large dried peppers and held them to his face like tusks making an elephant sound. The boy nearly burst he was laughing so hard. Jack ignored the yelling vendors who he imagined were saying something like "If you touch it then you bought it."

The boy tugged on Jack's sweaty hand and they were off yet again until they reached a row of shabby lean-tos with corrugated metal roofs and walls made of what appeared to be stiff cardboard. There was a woman squatting outside each unit stirring with one hand and swatting at flies with another. Several young children, wearing not a stitch of clothing, chased a small goat through the dusty courtyard. A baby was crying in the distance.

The scene gave Jack pause and suddenly this game of finding breakfast and being led through the city by a little boy had lost its luster. Never before had Jack seen anything like this, poverty like this. There were no televisions, no radios, no beds, no nothing but a place for families to crowd together at night to fall asleep out of the weather.

He stopped walking and lost his breath.

When the people saw him they all stood up and gathered around him. Then at the same time they all seemed to start talking and tried pulling him toward their own little spaces. But the boy held tight and managed to get Jack through the crowd to his home, the next to last lean-to on the strip.

The boy's mother, a tired-looking woman with large eyes that had never seen the inside of a shopping mall, movie theater, nail salon, or beauty parlor, smiled widely and motioned for Jack to sit down on one of the mats. She kept her eyes on him while yelling orders at the children, including the little boy who had led Jack there. Before long, the little boy and two others, even younger, sat on mats as well. The villagers congregated and watched curiously.

The woman took a small bowl and poured out a large scoop of *ful*—a creamy spread made from fava beans. She yelled something and one of the children ripped a piece of pita bread and gave it to Jack. Then she gave bowls of food to her children who did not wait before digging in with their small pieces of pita or their fingers to scoop out every last bit of the mush.

The woman pointed to Jack to eat. But he looked and saw that the pot was empty. There was none left for the woman, the mother. Jack started rising and tried to give the bowl back but the woman would hear none of it. She insisted that he try her food and that he have breakfast.

He dipped the pita and felt incredibly guilty eating this woman's food but not because of anything she did. The smile on her face never wavered and seemed to grow with every mouthful Jack ate. When he had finished she clapped loudly, as did the other villagers who were still watching intently.

When the crowd dispersed, Jack tried to give the woman a few bills, not knowing whether he was offering ten cents or ten dollars for the meal. She refused.

Jean Richard smiled with relief when he finally saw Jack coming back through the crowd to his room holding the little boy's hand.

"Ah, here you are. Thank goodness."

"Oh hey, Jean Richard, meet my little buddy. He brought me back to his place for breakfast."

"Really? What did you have?" Jean Richard asked with a growing smile curling his lips.

"Hmm, not sure really."

Then Jean Richard asked the boy something in another language and the boy replied.

"Ah, you had what amounts to a spread made out of bean stew. Let's hope there is enough toilet paper for you at the airport today." Then he laughed heartily.

"Can't be much worse than the *cuchifrito* stuff I'm used to getting back home."

Jack stopped on the word. Home. It really held little meaning to him now. Then he smiled sadly at how his life had changed in the last two days.

"Let's get you cleaned up for work, Mr. Hopkins."

"OK, but can you ask my little friend why he's not getting ready for school?"

"Mr. Hopkins, not everyone here can afford to go to school. There are uniforms, books, fees. By the looks of things I doubt he has ever stepped foot in a classroom."

Jack turned to the little boy who was still holding his hand. He knelt down and kissed the top of the child's head and put a few of the wadded up bills into his hand.

SEVEN

THE CITY OF Jabra was alive.

Cars and old trucks maneuvered around each other honking their horns incessantly, more as a warning to other cars, pedestrians, goats, roosters, or whatever else was sharing the road with them. The diesel fumes were visible in the heat, rising along with the dust from the dry red clay roads.

There were smells everywhere too, from fresh produce to questionable fish and the occasional vendor frying meat on a stick or stirring some version of bean stew.

Meat on a stick is something you can probably find in every city in the world, Jack thought, his mouth watering at the thought of trying the Sudanese version of Satay Steak or a corn dog.

Two rows of immaculately dressed children in their sharpest blues—boys wearing white button-down shirts and girls wearing white blouses—walked hand in hand across the main thoroughfare as their teacher held up traffic with her arms. Jack recognized her immediately and called out.

"Jenelle!" He thought of hollering out and asking how on earth her school children keep their white shirts so white with all the swirling dust. It was as if the dust just swirled around them, never touching them. He jumped up and down waving, as if she would have trouble spotting the only white man in the city.

She gave an embarrassed wave and continued on with "Cindy Lou" clutching her hand tightly. The child turned to look at Jack with a blank look on her face and continued staring as she walked on.

"Where is the school?" Jack strained his neck to continue looking.

"Just up around that bend," Jean Richard answered. "St. Jude's Catholic school has been there only a few years and it appears as if they will need all of the power St. Jude can muster, Mr. Hopkins."

"Why is that?"

"This area, well let's say there are not many Christians in this part of Africa. The majority of the people are Muslim and there have been rumors that the government up north is looking to impose Sharia law, or basically a very strict form of Islam. I don't think a school like that can make it here long-term. There is a lot of pressure to make the entire country Muslim. I don't think they will do that but still it is a cloud that hangs over here in the south."

"So," Jack looked even more confused not knowing anything about Islam and never having heard of Sharia Law, "what can St. Jude do to help?"

"Well, the Catholics say he is the Saint of impossible tasks."

"Is, um, do you know if Jenelle is married or a nun or something? I have a girlfriend, I think. I'm just curious."

"St. Jude, help us all."

Jack was thoroughly impressed with his office even though there was an orange shag carpet and a very low acoustic tile ceiling. It was first-class all the way from the oak desk to the metal filing cabinets and huge electric typewriter in the corner. He had his own personal water dispenser and a boom-box type radio and a little Norelco coffee maker next to his very own Styrofoam cups. The chair, which felt like leather, reclined to a near vertical position and Jack felt right away that this might even be a better place to sleep than his apartment. He might even take a nap there this afternoon, he thought.

A ceiling fan rotated slowly above, and the room wasn't nearly as warm and uncomfortable as his Bruckner Boulevard apartment during the recent heat wave. There was a standing oscillating fan in the far corner of the office that was not plugged in. This would do very nicely.

Jean Richard went over the workings of the airport, the daily flights from Uganda and the weekly or monthly flights from Ethiopia or Egypt. He wasn't sure if Jack was paying attention or not but did observe him taking copious notes, or at least he was scribbling something.

Jack was completely disappointed—but worked hard not to let it show—when he went on the "tour" of the airport. There was no duty-free shop, no food court, no Waldenbooks selling the hottest paperbacks or latest sports magazines. The worst thing of all was that there wasn't even a place to have a cold one with your buddies. Nope, this was a far cry from Kennedy or even LaGuardia in Queens. This even made the White Plains airport look exquisite.

Making up for the lack of amenities however was the gregarious nature and overall goodwill of the small crew of workers who lined up on the runway ready to make a good impression on the new "boss." They were all eager to smile and talk with Jack, to practice their English.

They smiled widely and Jack went through and learned their names and what they did at the airport. He also wanted to learn about their families, how many brothers, sisters, aunts, uncles, children they had. He wanted to know what they did in their spare time, what their favorite foods were and hobbies. But he didn't stop there. When they were done excitedly telling him their stories, Jack insisted they escort him to their workstations so he could see firsthand what kind of work they did. Then he asked them to let him try as well. He especially enjoyed putting the thread on bolts in the small machine shop that was set off by a cage. He also loved taking a tour of the hangars with his new best friend, Matthew, who joyfully chanted "Let's Go Mets" every time Jack looked at him.

He liked Matthew and his easy-going nature. The tall, gangly 20-year-old said he supported his mother, father, three brothers and four sisters. He was the only one in the family with a steady job. That was an awful lot of pressure for someone so young and Jack admired how he went about everything with a smile on his face. He also liked that the young man could speak the best English of the bunch.

"I'd like to meet your family some time," Jack said, speaking slow enough for Matthew to follow.

"Yes, yes. Very good," he answered. "You come have falafel with us."

The hangars, housing about a dozen Cessna single and twin-engine aircraft, were where Jack felt most comfortable. He proudly rattled off facts and information about each model and whether they were designed primarily as personnel carriers or for transporting cargo. For some models he was even able to dictate what the flying radius of the plane was, that is, if the fuel capacity had not been modified. No one really understood what he was saying, except for Jean Richard, who felt slightly relieved that this American actually did know a thing or two about planes. He would be leaving in the next few days to Khartoum, Cairo, and then to England for other business. He wanted to be able to tell investors that the airport in Jabra was in good hands. He thought it funny that the English still held on to the belief that Jabra was an important transportation hub and that it could one day become important in the grand scheme if Southern Sudan ever became independent and aligned itself with British interests still operating in Cairo.

"Not going to happen," he thought. "At least not in this lifetime."

That night Jack felt a twinge of sadness and an enormous amount of loneliness when Matthew and Pubudu—another young man who worked as a handyman at the airport—said goodnight and headed home for the night. There were no landings or departures at night due mainly to there being no lights on the runway.

Jack fumbled with some papers that were left on his desk, not able to make heads or tails of any of the numbers written down before putting them back down. There was still a staffing meeting he needed to put together, a sort of first official act of his new regime. But he already felt overwhelmed and could probably put it off for another day or two.

He walked around the office three times, running his fingers over the coffee maker and radio. Finally, while there was still just a glint of sunlight left in the sky, he closed his office and headed home to his apartment.

He stopped at a street-side food vendor and bought a plate of fried meat with cheese in a spicy type of sauce. The vendor, a burly man with very few teeth left in his mouth, convinced Jack to also buy dessert. He had a dishonest smile and Jack knew he was likely being overcharged for the two pieces of a coconut cake called *baseema*, but he was tired and lonely and just wanted to get back to his flat and eat his dinner. He had never shied away from haggling with the street vendors back on Fordham Road.

Ahmed the shoe cobbler was sitting on a crate outside his shop smoking a cigarette. There was black polish on his cheeks, his fingertips, and spattered on his smock. His face was deeply wrinkled and his left eye sagged much lower than his right. An empty plate of fish and rice lay off to the side, attracting plenty of flies to feast on the remnants, though there was not much to choose from.

He smiled broadly, remembering the encounter from earlier in the day, then put his hands on his belly and chuckled.

The door to his shop was open and there were so many shoes everywhere that Jack wondered what kind of system allowed this man to keep track of his work.

"I never got the opportunity to thank you this morning, for, you know, showing me where the bathrooms are," Jack said, extending his hand.

Ahmed wiped his hand on his smock and shook Jack's hand briskly, happily. He smiled and snuffed out his cigarette beneath his shoe.

"My name is Jack and I guess we're neighbors."

Ahmed smiled, not understanding a word of it.

"I came here from New York and it's kind of nice to have someone to talk to after a day at the old grindstone," Jack sighed, trying to sound important. "Yep, I guess you may have heard but I run the airport over in town. It's not easy being so far away from home, you know, leaving behind family, friends, girlfriend. But this work, this work is very, very important. And I'm earning a pretty good paycheck here. I'll save and save all I can, know what I mean? I'll save and win Marci, oh, that's my girlfriend, back. I'll get her the best engagement ring you can get and it'll knock her right off her feet."

Ahmed nodded and continued smiling.

"How about you? Is there someone special waiting for you at home?"

Jack looked around and noticed a cot had been set up in the entranceway of the shop.

"Oh, well that's OK. I was single for a long time too. It can get kind of lonely but you find the little things to make you happy. You know what I used to love? I'd get a charge out of throwing my shrimp skins into the water after a basket of shrimp and fries down at Tony's Pier on City Island. The catfish would come up and start munching on them like they were going out of style. That's what I mean, the little things. Those are the things that get you through the lonely moments. I'd just try and find things that made me smile."

Ahmed smiled once more, lit another cigarette and pointed at the greasy white paper bag with Jack's dinner.

"Oh, just dinner," Jack said.

Ahmed pointed again and Jack opened the bag so he could have a peek. His eyes lit up when he saw the *baseema*.

"Ah, *baseema*," he said loudly. He made a thumbs-up sign and that was when Jack realized he had not understood a word of Jack's rambling.

"Hmm? *Baseema*? Oh, you must mean this coconut cake stuff. Is it supposed to be pretty good? It smells good. Here, I'll tell you what I'll do. The guy made me buy two pieces. He must have seen me coming from a mile away. Think I overpaid? So anyway, I think tonight I can make an exception and have dessert or sweet as they say over in London, before I have my dinner. Would you like to join me?"

Jack pulled out the two pieces of the flaky cake, getting powdered sugar all over his hands, and handed one to Ahmed. He bowed several times and then took Jack's hand and shook it. He motioned to the crate for Jack to sit down and the two men watched the moon rise while eating their sweet treat in silence.

EIGHT

THE ROOSTERS STARTED earlier than normal that night and Jack wondered how anyone in the country was able to sleep through the endless squawking. Once the roosters got going, some of the neighborhood dogs decided to put their two cents in and the yelping and howling followed.

Deciding to get up, Jack flipped the switch on the wall but there was no electricity. That's when he noticed that the fan wasn't working either. Jean Richard had told him that the electricity was spotty and that fuel for the generators—especially while people slept—was not always the best way to spend what little money they had.

Jack dug into one of his bags, a large duffel, and found his miner's style headband flashlight. He had to loosen the strap a bit to get it around his head before turning it on. He walked around the room a few times touching things indiscriminately before settling at the chair by the window. He reached his hand through, still amazed that there was no glass, and looked out at the sleeping city. It was incredible, he thought, that just a few hours earlier the square below had been bustling with shoppers, vendors, children, and the occasional goat. Now everyone was sleeping, except for him.

He leaned his head out and tried to see the dogs in the darkness but could not.

Not able to sit still for very long, Jack dug back through the duffel bag and pulled out a shoebox full of memories. He opened the lid and on top of dozens of photos of his mother was an 8-by-10 of Marci in an inexpensive frame.

She was beautiful, with short dark hair and light green eyes that looked gray like a wolf's. He stood the frame on the table so that she could greet him whenever he entered the room.

He held it up and moved the photo from side to side to see if Marci's eyes would follow.

He set the frame down gently on his bed as if not to wake her then grabbed the stack of photos of his mother. There was one taken at Jones Beach where Jack pretended to flex his little muscles and his mother smiled beautifully. Another was a close-up of her laughing, moving her hand up toward her mouth. He could almost hear her giggling. In another photo a petrified-looking Jack and his mother had just disembarked from the Monster Mouse rollercoaster at Rye Playland where she pretended to be on the verge of passing out from fear.

He stared at them intently trying to remember the moment but could not. There were photos of them at the Bronx Zoo riding atop an elephant, at the giant blue whale at the Museum of Natural History, and at the Macy's Thanksgiving Day Parade where Jack's dad would always pack egg sandwiches and a thermos of hot cocoa, something he did even when the trio became just a pair.

Near the bottom of the pile was a small stack of photos from a trip to Coney Island and the aquarium. His mother looked much skinnier in those and he did not want to remember her looking like that and so he thumbed through them very quickly. He stopped at one, taken with the famous and terrifying Wonder Wheel in the background. She was smiling, squinting slightly because of the sun and seemed very happy and content.

She did not look sick at all in that photo and he could almost hear his father proclaim: "Here she comes, Miss America."

Jack smiled and laughed out loud before realizing that he was actually crying. He turned the light off on his headband and put his head down on his pillow still holding the photo.

The next few days at the airport were spent learning everyone's name and responsibility. Jack started each day the same, by picking up trash that had blown onto the property around the perimeter of the fence. By the second day the entire staff had joined him and by the third day Jack started teaching them to sing "All my Loving" by the Beatles while they worked. He was surprised by how quickly they picked up the words and started improvising their own harmonies.

When it came down to business, Jack was faced with some hard decisions. The airport answered to investors and there was a bottom line. That embezzling Brit, Kennerly, had systematically stripped the airport of its general fund and emergency repair fund right out from under everyone's nose. Of course, Jack had no idea what a bottom line was and so he instituted a few changes to help raise that elusive bottom line. The changes went through much easier once Jean Richard had gone away on business.

The first thing Jack did was to color coordinate all the scheduled flights coming in and out of the airport by assigning them an odd or even number and a candy bar. For instance, the flights from Uganda were normally on planes that reminded Jack of Reese's Peanut Butter Cups. Since the cups came in packages of two, Jack decided that they should only be able to land on even-colored days. Flights from Egypt were on these very pretty multi-colored planes that reminded Jack of Mike and Ike candies. Jack once counted 57 pieces of candy in a small box and so assigned Egyptian planes to land or take off on odd-numbered days.

Jack also insisted on opening a very small hamburger grill at the airport, his very own version of McDonald's complete with fried potatoes and soft-serve ice cream. He ran the grill for the first few days, training Matthew and one other man to cook and prepare the burgers. He opened the small restaurant for about 90 minutes a day to the general public, not just those flying, and soon it became a money-maker for the small airport.

No one seemed to understand the rhyme or reason behind the new ideas but Jack was steadfast and soon everyone was murmuring about how this must be a business school technique, a proven strategy to save money and bring the airport back up to its former glory. That is, everyone except for charter pilot George White.

White, a mountain of a man at six foot seven inches from the mountains of Tennessee, didn't know exactly what to make of Jack but he knew one thing: the man was no business school genius.

White, who dabbled in photography, playing the banjo and growing bonsai trees, had his own little bonsai garden at most of the small airports he frequented throughout north and west Africa.

"I don't exactly get it," Jack said as George gingerly clipped the leaves and some branches from a tree that had been neglected for too long.

"Well, it's like this," George started and his big booming voice instantly reminded Jack of Baloo from the Disney cartoon Jungle Book, "you gotta clip 'em to keep 'em healthy."

"No, I mean how did you end up down here?" Jack asked, picking up a small potted bonsai that really was the tiniest tree he had ever seen.

"I think I could ask the same about you?"

"I asked you first."

George laughed.

"Well, I done a lot of jobs after getting out of the air force. Tinkered with journalism, gave banjo lessons, tried to make my way in Nashville, and did all sorts of stuff."

"Nashville?"

"Yep, thought I was gonna be the next big thing. I was in a band called 'G. White and the Bucketeers' and we thought country music was ready for us. Do you know what one music executive told me?"

Jack smiled and shook his head no.

"This guy has the audacity to tell me that I'm too tall to play the banjo. I give him this incredulous look and he says the instrument looks too small in my hands and it'll throw the fans off. Throw the fans off? I'll bet he never even gave our demo recording a listen."

Jack nodded and his eyes widened a bit.

"So I decided to get back into the sky. Plus, for me anyhow, there is no feeling in the world like flying. There's a freedom, a sense of purpose and almost a nobility in it that I have felt doing only one other thing in my life."

"What's that?" Jack asked and wondered to himself whether he had ever done anything that made him feel like that.

"Making music."

The two men stood in silence for a while as George continued clipping away at the dead leaves.

"So?" George asked, his booming voice cutting through the silence.

Jack looked up.

"Are you going to tell me how on earth you landed this job?" His look was not mocking just bemused.

Jack felt embarrassed and relieved all at once to be exposed for what he truly was.

"Is it that obvious that I'm a total fraud?"

"Well, I wouldn't say that, but you may want to tone down the safari gear." Then George let out a belly laugh and Jack joined in.

"I don't know why I got hired really. But I just got my first paycheck and if they want to pay me all that dough to do the things I've been doing then I'll be able to get home to Marci sooner than I thought I would."

"Marci?" George put down his bonsai tree and picked up another to examine.

"My girlfriend, or ex-girlfriend really. She has no idea that I'm even here. This whole thing has happened so fast. One day I'm at home about to be evicted and the next I'm here running this airport."

"Girlfriend? Well, is she or isn't she?"

"I am going to win her back," Jack tried convincing himself. "See, I took her for granted, us for granted. I didn't take care of her, myself, had no job, etc. I want to be able to buy her nice things and surround her with luxury."

"Is that what's important to her?" George gave a disapproving look, not surprising for a man who gave up life in the states to be little more than a bush pilot in North Africa.

"Yes, I mean no. I don't know."

Jack bent down and looked at one of the bonsai trees and gently ran his index finger over one of the tiny leaves. He stayed quiet for a few moments.

"I didn't mean anything, Jack," George said kindly. "Let's get back to your job. So you have no flying experience?"

"No flying experience."

"No business school?"

"Do I look like I went to business school?" he answered, feeling more like a phony than ever before. "The closest I've been to running an airport is fueling planes. You won't say anything, will you?"

"Of course not. It's none of my business and anyhow, they seem to really like you. You're very different from that Brit, Kennerly. He was such a stuffed shirt and he talked down to everyone, everyone that is, except me."

"Yeah, he'd have to be awfully tall to do that," Jack smiled. "Still play that banjo?"

"Sure do, keep it in my plane."

"Can you play 'All My Loving' by the Beatles?"

"Sure, Beatle songs are actually perfect for the banjo. Those tunes are right in my wheelhouse."

"Great."

Jenelle stood outside the chain link fence listening for a moment.

"Well, if it isn't a pair of farmers and their crops," she giggled.

"Well, hello there Miss Jenelle and Miss Cindy-Lou-Who," Jack said, hoping she would mistake his blushing for sunburn. The little girl held the teacher's hand tightly but her eyes were fixed on Jack.

Still kneeling by the bonsai, Jack turned and faced the little girl, her hair pulled tight with dozens of colorful little clips, ribbons, and braids. For a split second he thought he might have seen a smile. He spoke gently to the girl while Jenelle and George explained pleasantries. He stood up when he sensed a lull in their conversation and leaned against the fence, holding on with his fingers.

The sun was shining brightly on Jenelle's face.

"He's the farmer, not me," Jack laughed. "The only thing I know how to grow is mold, and actually I don't even know how to do it. Just kind of happens."

"Well, perhaps you'd like to give a science lesson on mold to my class?"

Before Jack could answer, Jenelle laughed loudly.

"I'm sorry, Mr. Hopkins. I shouldn't be teasing you. However, when you asked me the other day where my classroom was I was expecting you might pay a call."

George looked at Jack quickly.

"Well, I didn't want to intrude."

"Not at all. I think the children would find it fascinating to hear about your work here at the airport, plus any English they can be exposed to would only benefit them."

Jack knelt down again.

"What do you think, Cindy Lou? Do you wanna hear about airplanes?"

"Her name is Immaculee."

"Well. I think she kind of likes having her own special name from her crazy American friend. Isn't that right, Cindy Lou?"

This time he was sure she smiled before burying her face in Jenelle's long skirt.

"Perhaps you are right, Mr. Hopkins," Jenelle said with a smile.

"Can I swing by tomorrow?"

"Swing?"

"Can I stop by your classroom and meet some of the students?"

"Of course. Classes go from eight until about three."

"Sounds good. I will see you then."

"I'm looking forward to it, Mr. Hopkins."

"Oh please, call me Jack."

"OK, Jack," she smiled, said goodbye to George and turned away. Cindy Lou turned her head several times to see Jack waving every time until student and teacher disappeared into a crowd by the marketplace.

George collected his clippers and file and nozzle for the hose, quite content with how the mini-trees looked.

"Well, well, Jack. If I didn't know any better I'd say that you have made quite an impression on Jenelle."

But Jack didn't answer. Instead he remained leaning against the fence and staring out into the busy marketplace.

That afternoon Jack found another paycheck on his desk of his office. He opened it to make sure it was for the same amount and stuffed it into the top drawer.

No need to cash the checks, not when he lived so modestly and the small weekly cash stipend was more than enough to cover his needs.

NINE

THAT EVENING JACK spent an hour in the marketplace looking for two items in particular, and talking with his new friends, the vendors, who were quite sure he was mad—harmless but mad.

Many referred to him as "Safari Jack" because of the outlandish clothing he insisted on wearing. They were all friendly and happy to see him. It didn't hurt that he spent a ton of money in the market and never really bothered to haggle, often paying double or triple what others would. Eventually the vendors stopped taking advantage of him so terribly and usually asked only for double what they normally would.

The first item—a basket—was easy enough to find but only after Jack agreed to buy the thousand or so hot Sudanese chili peppers in the basket.

"The peppers are very healthy for men," the vendor said. It was a place Jack had shopped in before, trying all types of spices to bring back to the airport hamburger stand. "Be careful of the seeds. They will make your eyes water."

The vendor threw in a red scarf to cover the basket for the walk home.

The next item proved a little tougher to find and then much more expensive to purchase. This surprised Jack, considering the number of people that populated the streets on their bicycles or pushing their wheelbarrows.

Finally he found a bicycle pump sitting in the corner of a little greasy mechanic shop where the round owner couldn't speak a lick of English and who couldn't understand why someone would want to own their own pump when they could just go to his stand and use the pump for a nominal fee whenever they wanted to.

After what seemed an eternity to Jack, the man agreed to let him have it for the equivalent of 35 American dollars. Then Jack headed home, making sure to pick up dinner and two huge pieces of *baseema*. He nearly lost his load of goodies when a small herd of goats ran quickly past him and another time when a rogue rooster called out waking him from a daydream.

"Ah, Mr. Jack," Ahmed called out when he spotted his new friend and tenant coming around the corner holding his purchases. "I start worry."

Jack was amazed at how much English Ahmed had already picked up in a few short weeks, just by listening to Jack rattle on and on about the Mets or the Knicks. Jack had spent an entire evening going over the last Knicks NBA championship when center Willis Reed played the pivotal game with a broken leg and willed his teammates to victory. By the time Jack was done regaling Ahmed with these tales of heroism, his new friend knew that Walt Frazier's nickname was "Clyde" and Earl Monroe's moniker was "The Pearl."

"Come, my friend," Ahmed called out, proud that his neighbors could see he had an American friend. He pumped his chest out and kept his head high when he knew they were looking. "Please, my friend. Put down things and sit. You and me are friends, no?"

Jack was happy too.

"Yes, Ahmed, of course. You're probably my best buddy out here."

He greeted his friend with a handshake then pulled out the two pieces of sweet dessert that served as the origin and center for this friendship. As usual the men ate quietly and then Jack would tell Ahmed all about his day, some of the strange things he had seen in the marketplace or some eccentric behavior by someone at the airport.

"Today you buy lots of peppers?" he said in a half-question.

"Yeah, I needed the basket. Hey, maybe you can help me. I've got a project I need to do tonight and I think we may need to use some of your shoemaking expertise."

Ahmed could not have felt more important.

Jack stayed up after the first rooster started and went out to the well for a bucket of bathwater. Always one for long hot showers where he could sing Beatles' songs, Jack was surprised by how much he enjoyed a Sudanese bucket bath. There was nothing like the feeling he got when dousing his hot, dusty self with the cold water. It was invigorating, and he thought of incorporating the ritual when he got back to the states. Imagine how great it would feel, he thought, after a game of summer playground basketball with Chumbley and Lenny.

He set out with a bag over his shoulder and the creation Ahmed had helped him fashion under his right arm. It was still very dark so he grabbed his headband flashlight and set out to find the school. He had a general idea of where it was but wanted to give himself enough time in case he couldn't find it right away.

The marketplace was peaceful and Jack liked the calmness that he was feeling. It was that rare, small window of night where there were no dogs yelping, no roosters screeching, and no buses or cars driving through with mufflers from the 1950s.

He found the small campus with little trouble and entered the courtyard with a white statue of St. Jude at the center. The statue, nearly looking as if it belonged in the middle of an old Italian cemetery, looked as if it was new or had been freshly painted. The tall, bearded figure wore long flowing robes, as if he was in a hurry, held a large coin or medallion, and had a flame atop his head.

Jack stared for a moment, not quite sure what to make of it then placed his attention back on what he had carried to the campus.

It was perfect. Jack placed his creation on the ground and placed his bag on a bench and opened it. Then he got to work nailing the backboard and basketball hoop, or rather basket, up on the side of a tree alone in a small clearing to the left of St.

Jude. After he was done, Jack bounced the basketball a few times and was quite satisfied with the job the bicycle pump had accomplished.

He spent the next hour shooting free throws as the sun rose slowly to reveal the perfection of the newly minted St. Jude's Catholic School basketball court.

By the time Jenelle arrived at 6:45, there were four children playing basketball with Jack. She stopped near the statue of St. Jude and smiled. She was beautiful and the skin on her face was smooth and shiny and her large round eyes seemed piercing set against the purple flowers on her sun dress.

Jack smiled back.

"Ok, now, remember what I've taught you," he reminded the children. "There is really no defending a pull-up jump shot. If the defender is sticking too close then you just keep driving to the basket and take him to the hole. If he's playing off of you then just stop dead in your tracks, pull up and take the short jump shot."

He demonstrated the move several times and the kids marveled at how many times he was able to get the ball in the dried pepper basket with the bottom cut out. They fought each other to retrieve the ball every time he made a shot.

"I see you found our humble little school, Mr. Hop— Jack. I can't thank you enough this wonderful surprise. The children will love it. I mean, they already love it."

"I was hoping they would. I know how much we looked forward to shooting some hoops, playing basketball at recess when I was in school."

"OK, children. Please put down the basketball and find your places inside. I will be in momentarily," she called out.

"Wow, that is a good group," he said. "I don't think we ever listened to our teacher and obeyed as quickly as that. Of course we never had a teacher who looked like you either." Jack wanted to die as the words escaped his mouth, knowing what a blunder he had just committed. Not allowing a chance for a reprimand, he quickly pointed at the statute of St. Jude.

"So what's the deal here," he asked. "I mean he looks an awful lot like Jesus. I don't get that coin he's holding over his chest and the fire over his head."

Jenelle put her books down on the bench again.

"Are you a Catholic, Jack?"

"I'm not sure, maybe."

"Maybe?"

"Well, I remember going to church when I was very young, with my mother. I remember it being a pretty church, big, tall with lots of echoes. I remember statues and I think I remember the flames on top of some. That always scared me." He paused for a moment to laugh. "One that scared me the most was a statue of a soldier, or warrior. He was holding a spear or a sword and was stepping on the devil. He held the sword to the devil's face and I remember never wanting to look at it."

"That is a scary image, Jack. That sounds like it was a statue of St. Michael the archangel. He leads legions of angels in battle against the forces of evil."

"Leads?"

"Oh yes, leads. These battles continue every minute of every day."

Jack looked confused.

"Where?"

"In our hearts," she answered.

She walked to the front of the statue and looked admiringly at St. Jude.

"Why did you stop going to church?"

"My mother died when I was very young and my dad, well he was the best dad anyone could ever ask for, but he wasn't much of the praying type. You know what I mean? He said he didn't need a church to tell him that God was real. He said God was everywhere. But now I think it was just too painful for him to go to the places my mom loved when she was alive."

"He wasn't the only one in pain, was he?" she placed her hand on his shoulder and nodded. "So about our lovely statue of St. Jude: He is the patron saint of lost and desperate causes. The flame atop his head is the flame of the Holy Spirit. It is the essence of God in our everyday lives. I believe that the Holy Spirit is the thing in our insides, in our heart, that tells us whether something we are doing is right or wrong. It's the thing that tries to keep us from envying others and from spreading gossip. It is the feeling we get to do the right thing even if it is not the popular thing to do. The Holy Spirit is what allows us to recognize God, as your father said, in everyday things. It is the power that allows us to love our enemies and pray for those who persecute us."

Jack looked confused.

"I'm sorry Jack. I don't mean to sound preachy," she smiled. "But I have found strength and comfort in knowing the Holy Spirit. Now, about the coin or medallion that Jude is holding. Well, there is nothing in the bible about this. But there are some ancient writings that might give us a little insight. There is an ancient story, some would say legend, that says a king of a land called Edessa was suffering very badly from leprosy. He wrote a letter to Jesus asking that he come to his palace as his guest so that he might be healed.

"If you know any of the stories in the gospels, Jesus normally rewarded those who had faith like that. So Jesus, the story goes, sent one of his apostles—Jude—to visit the king. But before doing so, Jesus wiped his face on a piece of cloth or a rag and it left a perfect image of his face on the material. Jude carried the cloth with him and once the king saw the image of Jesus' face, he was healed. Jude became known as the apostle who carried a likeness of Jesus around. So later on, artists and sculptors turned the cloth into a medallion of Jesus' face."

"Wow, is that story true?"

"Well, we don't know for sure, Jack. Like I said, it's not part of the gospels but we do know for sure that Jesus was capable of miraculous things and I'm sure that many, many things like this happened that just didn't make it into the gospels for one reason or another."

Jack reached up and touched the statue.

"Is there a hell?" he asked her, sounding now like one of her students.

"I believe that being separated from Jesus is hell. But you can find many different theories on hell and what it is." She paused. "Jack, today is Wednesday and this is the day that Fr. Nguyen visits the school and says mass for the kids. Can you get out of work today and spend the day with us? The children would love it and maybe a good old fashioned Catholic mass will help answer some of the questions you may have. Of course, you'll have to listen very carefully during the father's homily."

"Yes, of course." Jack tried sounding serious.

"No," she laughed. "I mean because his Vietnamese accent is so thick that it can be difficult to understand what he is saying."

"A Vietnamese priest in Africa? Wow, now that's a story I'd like to hear someday."

Jack made a quick appearance at the airport to check in and make sure there were no emergencies then headed back to the school, where he tried unsuccessfully to blend in at the back of the class.

No matter how many times Miss Jenelle admonished, scolded, begged, or bribed her students to face front, they simply could not stop straining their necks, turning in their seats and staring at the visitor in the room.

Finally she gave up.

"Well, it is clear that I will not be getting any of my work done today," she said slowly in English. Jack looked up and motioned to her asking if he should go. She shook her head no.

"As you all can plainly see, we have a guest in our classroom today," she continued, pausing only when the class of about 40 children erupted in applause and laughter. "And since, and since he is from the United States and speaks English as other Americans do, I feel it would be a good idea to let him speak with you all for a little while about what he does. Mr. Hopkins has a very interesting and important position as the head of the airport here in town. So, without further ado, please give a warm welcome and then your full attention to our guest: Mr. Hopkins."

Jack stood up slowly, soaking up the applause and then stopped. Realizing this was the first time in his life he had people clapping for him he decided to really go for it. Getting down in a three-point football stance, Jacked yelled "hut" then ran around the room as quickly as he could slapping high fives with the kids who went from excited to frantic in a matter of seconds.

By the third time around the room, both Jack and the students began losing steam. He finished the second half of his last victory lap in super slow motion. He stopped at the teacher's podium and gasped to catch his breath. He looked up and the only person who wasn't smiling was Cindy Lou.

Still, Jack smiled and winked at her.

"Hello, class,"

"Hel-lo, Mis-ter Hop-kins," they responded slowly and in perfect unison.

Jack turned to Jenelle and smiled.

For a moment, Jack stood frozen, not sure of what to say and not sure of how much English the children would understand. But with help coming from no other sources but from within, Jack reached down and pulled out a story to tell.

He started to recount the tale of his old neighbor Bobby Payne who was the same age as he was. When both boys were 12, Bobby started playing drums and dreamed of being just like the Who's Keith Moon. That meant more than keeping furious beats and rhythms going but also drinking and taking drugs at a young age. Jack stopped going to Bobby's house but couldn't really tell his father why.

It turned out that Bobby became upset with his parents when they grounded him and in a fit of rage tied a belt around his neck and strapped it to the top bunk of the bunk beds he shared with his younger brother and sat there. It wasn't more than three minutes but it was enough for the oxygen to get cut off, causing major and permanent brain damage. That one selfish, impetuous moment cost Billy and his family everything.

Jack looked at the smiling eager faces and stopped the story well before the drugs and suicide attempt. Gotta think age appropriate here, he thought.

"Wait, wait," he said. "I have a better story to tell."

Jenelle had taken a seat now in the back of the class and Jack felt the pressure of impressing both student and teacher.

"Do you kids know anything about fishing? Do you fish around here?"

The children murmured and exchanged puzzled looks before Jenelle said something in a foreign language and they all understood. Yes, many of them had fished in one manner or another.

"Let me tell you about how silly and how sensitive I was the first time my father took me fishing with my uncle, may they both rest in peace, to a place called Captree, Long Island."

Some of the children liked the sound of Cap-tree and mouthed the word over and over.

"Well, we had to wake up super early in the morning and drive from the Bronx way out to Long Island while it was still dark. Once the sun started coming up, my uncle woke me. I had fallen asleep in the back of the car and for a moment I had no idea where I was. The whir of the car's engine was so soothing I could barely open my eyes.

"But when I did, my uncle pointed off to the grassy shoulder of the highway and motioned to the first wild rabbits I had ever seen."

Not sensing recognition in the children's eyes, Jack put his hands up over his head to show rabbit ears and hopped around in place a couple of times. The students erupted with laughter. By this time, an Asian man had entered the classroom and was seated next to Jenelle.

"I sat up, wide awake not believing my eyes. See, we don't get many wild rabbits in the Bronx. In fact, it was a big deal to see a squirrel in some neighborhoods. They chomped on the grass wet with morning dew and seemed totally oblivious to the 2,000-pound hunks of metal flying past them at 55 miles per hour.

"I instantly decided that I loved rabbits.

"That was the moment my uncle raised an imaginary rifle in his arms, took aim from the passenger side of my dad's Dodge Rambler and said 'If only I had my .22.'

"Later that morning, in an 18-foot skiff with a small outboard motor, I hooked my first flounder in Long Island Sound. If any of you have ever caught a fish then you know that excitement when you realize something's tugging at your line and it's not a piece of seaweed or an old boot or even just the current.

" 'Wait, wait, now set the hook,' my uncle barked from behind me.

"I jerked the tip of my rod upward and knew the fish was on there for good. I reeled and reeled and finally I could see flashes of white and brown through the green water. That was my fish, holy cow! It fluttered and jerked and I could feel my uncle's arms reach down beneath mine to help me lift the fish out of the water and into the boat.

"He took a pair of pliers and pulled the hook out of the fish's mouth and placed him carefully in a bucket on the boat that he filled with a few inches of sea water.

"I had caught the first fish on the boat. Woo hoo!"

The children laughed again.

"My heart would jump every time the fish did in the bucket and I kept looking over at it, not caring to catch another fish all day. But then something happened. The jumps became less and less frequent and my beautiful fish just kind of floated there, not doing much of anything.

" 'Is my fish dying, dad?' I asked my father as he cast his line.

" 'Yes, he probably is. He won't live too long in that bucket.'

" 'Can we put him back? So he'll live?'

"My dad smiled at me tenderly and looked at me in a way that he never had before. In fact, if I close my eyes tight I can still remember the exact look he gave me. It was a stare that said he was proud of me but at the same time wished he could protect me from how the world really is.

" 'We're not doing anything wrong Jack. We're going to take our fish home that we catch today. Your uncle and I will clean it and then we will fry it up and have a great dinner tonight. You know how much you love fried flounder with tartar sauce.'

"I looked down at my fish and he could see I was disappointed.

" 'There's nothing wrong with it, Jack. We're not going to waste the fish we catch. Some creatures have longer lives than others and as long as we respect life and never take it for granted then we should be alright. We have to love those and take care of those that come into our lives, even if they are only with us for a little while.'

"That was when I realized, even at that young age, that he was talking about my mother. She had died of cancer the year before and we both missed her terribly. It was those words, those fish, and that yummy dinner that night that helped me realize how lucky I was that my mother came into my life, even if it was for a short time. No one ever loved me and took care of me the way she did.

"I'm not sure exactly what it was about that day: the fish we caught, being on the boat, my quiet uncle with the steely eyes, my dad's words, or a combination of all of the above that made me feel OK about everything again. Don't get me wrong, I still miss my mom, even now as a full-grown man. I think about her every day."

He looked up, not sure if anyone understood a word he had said and could see Jenelle wipe her eye as she stood from the student desk she had squeezed into.

"Well, class? Before we all go to mass with Fr. Nguyen I think we should show our appreciation to our guest who not only came to speak with us but who also constructed that fine basketball hoop out there in the courtyard for us to use. How do we thank Mr. Hopkins for sharing his story with us?"

For the second time in his life and the second time that day, Jack closed his eyes and soaked in the applause.

TEN

THERE WAS NO organist or choir to speak of and so Fr. Nguyen did double duty leading the children in song as well as leading the mass. Two of the boys from the class participated as altar servers and sat up at the altar of the outdoor, makeshift church.

There were wooden benches under a shade structure and it was surprisingly cool.

Fr. Nguyen's voice was beautiful, and it was clear that he took great pride in it.

"He told me that he loves to do karaoke when he's back home in Vietnam," Jenelle leaned over and whispered in Jack's ear. The service was as Jack remembered, and it softly flooded his emotions with memories forgotten.

Fr. Nguyen raised the bible high up over his head and walked the circumference of the benches or pews before setting it back down on his lectern to read from the gospel of St. Matthew. Even when he spoke he made the words sound like a song. It took effort to understand the words through the accent but Jack thought the man made everything sound like a poem when he spoke. Even his movements, Jack realized, were graceful and slow.

"Jesus went through all the towns and villages, teaching in their synagogues, proclaiming the good news of the kingdom and healing every disease and sickness," Fr. Nguyen read from the gospel. "When he saw the crowds, he had compassion on them, because they were harassed and helpless, like sheep without a shepherd. Then he said to his disciples, 'The harvest is plentiful but the workers are few. Ask the Lord of the harvest, therefore, to send out workers into his harvest field.' "

During his homily, which was short—much like the attention span of the children—Fr. Nguyen spoke of the need for everyone to lift his plowshare and work in the fields of the Lord. He mentioned simple things like praying for someone, being kind, helping someone with a heavy load, and even teaching a child to shoot a basketball.

Jenelle placed her hand on Jack's at the basketball mention and left it there for the duration of the homily. It was a few minutes before Jack held it back.

"There is no act too small for God's eyes," Fr. Nguyen continued. "The harvest is so overgrown and so abundant that any help, any work, any love is welcomed."

Later, Fr. Nguyen went around to every student and shook their hand during the exchange of the sign of peace.

He prayed quietly during the consecration of the Eucharist, and a slight breeze kicked up some of the dust in the courtyard swirling it around like a mini, harmless tornado.

When it came time to administer the body and blood of Christ, Jack noticed the utter and complete joy in Fr. Nguyen's face. He led the children in song, stopping only to loudly proclaim "the body of Christ."

It was a hymn Jack remembered, though he was sure he had never heard it sung in English.

"Lord, when you came to the seashore you weren't seeking the wise or the wealthy, but only asking that I might follow.

"O Lord, in my eyes you were gazing, Kindly smiling, my name you were saying; All I treasured, I have left on the sand there; Close to you, I will find other seas."

Jenelle sang softly and Jack looked at her fondly. There was nothing pretentious or phony about this woman. She was the real deal, he thought. And he realized that he already admired her. She was obviously intelligent and educated enough to find work in a big city or even in another, more advanced country, yet she chose to work here in this tiny Catholic school teaching a handful of children.

He would later learn that the majority were orphans. Many were raised by grandparents or distant relatives that provided little more than the basic necessities to survive. Others lived on campus, in a building meant to be a pantry for food that was converted to accommodate at least a dozen children.

An old woman came by every day at the instruction of Fr. Nguyen and cooked a hot meal for the children who lived there. It was also practically Jenelle's second home as she hated the thought of the children staying there alone.

Jack hesitated when it was his turn to accept the Eucharist, knowing full well that he had not been to mass in many years. But Jenelle nudged him with a knowing nod and stood behind him in line.

"It's alright," she whispered. "You're a good man, Mr. Hopkins. I'm sure you and God can work out the details later."

Jack opened his mouth widely and Fr. Nguyen placed the host on his tongue. He walked back silently to his bench and for the first time in as long as he could remember, Jack prayed.

The kids spent the rest of the afternoon tiring Jack out by shooting baskets, though some were more interested in using the basketball as a soccer ball.

"Now that's a sport—soccer—that just hasn't caught on in the states," Jack said, breathing heavily and sipping from a glass of water Jenelle had brought him. Cindy Lou was holding her hand.

"It's big here, Mr. Hopkins, but I'm hopeful that, thanks to you, basketball may take off as well."

"Please start calling me Jack."

Jenelle blushed.

"And you know, the kids might be interested in knowing that the original basketball hoop was made from a peach basket. That's how the game received its name. This one is made from a pepper basket. So," he smiled, "it's practically authentic."

"We are very grateful."

"So you promised to tell me the story of how a Vietnamese priest wound up here in Africa of all places."

Jenelle smiled and Jack could not take his eyes from her as she spoke.

"Well, I'll tell you the story because I know that he is so humble he rarely talks about himself."

Without thought or hesitation, Jenelle placed her left hand in his and pulled him back over to the shade of the outdoor church. He allowed himself gladly to be led and tried to mask the excitement he felt at her touch.

The breeze from earlier had died down and the sun was directly above, making things dry and uncomfortable. The church could have used a large ceiling fan but the shade offered some relief from the heat.

Jack sat down first and Jenelle sat closely next to him with Cindy Lou plopped on her lap. She stroked the young girl's hair as she spoke.

"Fr. Nguyen, let's see, where do I start? Well, there are not many Christians in Vietnam, much like there are not many Christians here. So, even as a young boy, Fr. Nguyen was different from others and practiced a faith that others did not understand or even try to understand. In his culture, it is a very noble thing to follow the call of God and when he was still a teenager he knew that he wanted a life of holiness of service.

"So he traveled very far from his family, which lived in a small mountain village, to a seminary just outside the capital city of Saigon. He spent about six years there studying and training to become a priest. He described his life there as being very simple and humble, and I sense from our conversations that he was very happy there.

"Fr. Nguyen was very close to being ordained a priest when the communists came and took over the country. There was no room for God in the new leaders' vision of the country and so they systematically went around shutting down monasteries, seminaries, and all other places of worship not sanctioned by them. They told a heartbroken Fr. Nguyen to go find a piece of land, start a farm, and take a wife."

Jack listened intently and wished he was brave enough to place his hand back within hers. Cindy Lou was alternating glances between her teacher and Jack.

"Poor Fr. Nguyen didn't know what to do. He was too far from home to go back, especially with the uncertainty of the country and the fact that he had absolutely no money. So he took a job working in the rice paddies for the government with a few of his fellow seminarians. By day they were perfectly loyal communists, working hard for the good of the people. But by night," she smiled, "by night they would meet and continue their studies. They read the bible and whatever materials they had managed to salvage from the seminary about becoming priests. Fr. Nguyen told me that they would meet by candlelight in different locations and talk about Jesus. He said it was during those months that he felt very much like a true apostle. After Jesus was taken from them, the apostles had to meet in secret for a while as well.

"But after several months of meting like this, it was only a matter of time before they were discovered. Citizen-soldiers, another term for angry mob, found them and beat them with cane poles. One of Fr. Nguyen's close friends lost an eye in the attack.

"Two evenings later, still bruised and scarred, four of the seminarians pooled their resources and purchased a small homemade boat, nothing more than a raft really and set off to escape Vietnam."

Jack realized he was sitting there with his mouth agape.

"Holy cow, that is really something," he said nearly to himself. "But I still don't get how he wound up here." He looked over at Fr. Nguyen who was playing basketball with the children and laughing loudly at the crazy shots everyone was taking at the basket.

"The plan was to stay on the raft for only a few days and let the currents take them to Thailand, and make their way to a large seminary called College General in Penang, Malaysia. But of course, God had other plans. The raft drifted for days and days and the men ran out of food and water. They were basically stuck adrift in the open ocean with no hope.

"It was Fr. Nguyen's idea to take the last remaining piece of bread and give his first mass as a Catholic priest. The men, who were so weak and tired only moments before, came to life as they heard the prayers begin. They answered at all the right times and listened intently to their friend's first homily.

"He spoke of those who are able to recognize Christ in their lives, reminding his friends that the first person in the gospels to call Jesus a king was a thief dying on a cross next to our lord.

" 'Lord, remember me when you enter into your kingdom.'

"The man asked for nothing more than to be remembered. He didn't ask to be saved, to hold a special place or any other favors, simply to be remembered.

" 'I assure you, this day you will be with me in paradise.'

"Fr. Nguyen consecrated the bread and broke it into four equal pieces then handed out the life-giving miracle to the others. As the men chewed the bread, not easy to do when you've gone 24 hours without water, they heard it."

"Heard what?" Jack was now on the edge of the bench leaning forward staring at Fr. Nguyen play basketball.

"They heard the horn from a German freighter ship that had spotted them."

"Wow," was all Jack could muster, and he felt suddenly more inadequate than usual.

"Indeed, Mr. Hopk—, er, Jack. Wow. They were rescued. All four of them were very near death. To hear Fr. Nguyen describe it, he doesn't think they would have lasted one more hour on that raft. The four men were given asylum by different Catholic organizations. One went to the United States, another to Canada and Fr. Nguyen, well he wound up here with us. And that, to me anyway, is something of a miracle as well."

Jack stayed at the school for the rest of the day, leaving only for about 45 minutes for the airport where he bought hamburgers for the students when he realized they had gone the entire day without eating and probably did that every day.

The children sat in the shade of the outdoor church eating their greasy, salty delicious meals.

Jenelle surveyed the scene and couldn't remember if she had ever seen the children so happy.

Only when it started getting dark did the children begin to scatter to their homes and Jenelle helped settle the few who were sleeping there. Fr. Nguyen would be spending the night on the grounds as well and so she did not have to worry about them.

"What do you do for fun around here?" Jack asked her as they walked slowly, side by side, down the path away from the school and into the still-busy city center.

"Mr. Hopkins, are you asking me out on a date?"

Her response flustered him and he began stammering an answer when she laughed loudly.

"I'm sorry. I heard that line in an American movie once and always wanted to say it." She smiled and leaned forward to get a better look at his face to make sure she had not hurt his feelings. "Let's see. Fun is not really a luxury the people around here can afford. For many, life is so difficult and so tiring that really there is little room for anything else. The children, of course, like to play soccer, while the men gather sometimes to smoke cigarettes and talk politics or about their crops and the seemingly never-ending drought."

Jack stopped walking and took a deep breath.

"Yes."

Jenelle stopped and shook her head, not understanding.

"Yes." He took a second very deep breath. "Yes, I was, I mean I am. Yes, I am asking you on a date. Jenelle, would you like to have dinner somewhere tonight with me?"

She smiled and placed her soft hand in his.

"Come, I know a great little stand where we can get the best *shorba* and *maschi* in the entire city."

Jack felt proud walking with her, and she explained that for cultural reasons they should not hold hands in public. He understood, especially after she whispered "but I wish we could."

They walked far, to the north end of the city where Jack had not done much exploring yet. There were many roadside vendors cooking in the street and the sound of meat sizzling and popping in oil made Jack's stomach growl. Vendors were urging the couple to come and buy dinner from them but Jenelle knew exactly where she was going.

They finally stopped at a tiny booth where two women greeted Jenelle happily and spoke in another language about Jack and other things. Jenelle held two fingers up and gave instructions for their meal, then she and Jack sat down on a mat inside where she looked even more beautiful with the glow of a flickering candle providing the only light.

"Those ladies are widows, and I teach their children at the school," Jenelle said proudly. "They are the best cooks I know."

"I'm looking forward to it but I have to be honest, it's a little dark in here and I normally like to see what I'm eating. Despite my weight I am pretty particular. We're not going to be eating monkey brains or anything like that are we?"

Jenelle held her mouth up to her hand and giggled.

"First of all, Jack, it's obvious by how those clothes are hanging off of you that you've already lost a considerable amount of weight since coming here," she said. "I think you look perfect. Secondly, no, we are not eating any bushmeat, grubs, insects, or anything you might find distasteful."

One of the women brought in a tray of food and set it down in front of them.

"Perfect timing," Jenelle said. "It looks like we're starting with the *maschi*. These are dark red tomatoes stuffed with ground beef that has been cooked with cucumbers and eggplant. Oh and here, off to the side are tiny meatballs called *koftahs* made with beef, sometimes lamb and onion. You can dip them, if you choose, in this *shata*, a sort of hot spice that is very garlicky."

The food was delicious, matching the wonderful aromas of meat and spice that was wafting in from where the women were cooking out on the street. The dishes reminded Jack a little of eating from the street vendors in the Greek section of Astoria.

He could taste some of the same bitters and the lime juice as well.

The main course came out about an hour after they got there. The *shorba* looked like soup. The lamb dish was prepared in broth with peanut butter, rice, and lime juice. Jack had never tasted anything like it and was surprised by how filling it was.

It was very late when they were finally finished eating. They stayed and talked a little while longer before Jenelle recognized that the women had already cleaned up and were ready to close up for the evening. She spoke to them in another language and they seemed pleased at her words. They all smiled gently at each other, waiting as Jack tried figuring out the Sudanese money in his pocket. Finally he simply held out a bunch of small bills and large coins and let Jenelle pick out how much to give the women. They were very pleased at the amount and shook Jack's hand enthusiastically over and over.

"Hey, how much did I tip them?" he laughed as Jenelle and he walked back through the sticky air of the soon-to-be-sleeping city.

"Well, I'm sure the amount was less than what you spend for one of your McDonald's Big Mac sandwiches but to them, well let's just say they will be very happy to see you come by their restaurant again. Not many people can afford to tip here. But they expect it from foreigners."

When he was sure no one was watching, Jack slipped his hand gently inside hers and she clutched his tightly.

They walked back very slowly, never wanting the night to end.

"So let me ask you, why did you become a teacher and why here?"

"Jack, in my country it is very honorable to become a teacher. Those of us lucky enough to have been granted a chance at schooling, higher education, can either work for the government, work for foreign companies, or teach. It is very honorable to become a teacher. I grew up nearby in Jabra and my father was a teacher himself. He saved all of his money to send me to school."

"Sounds like a good guy."

"Yes, he was."

"Oh, I'm sorry."

"Don't be. He lived a good life and he was loved by many, many people." She stopped abruptly and kissed Jack lightly on his right cheek. She looked away quickly and kept walking, pulling his hand. "It's funny, all my years as a girl, growing up and going to school, I wanted nothing more than to leave this area and see the world. I dreamt of being a teacher for children of diplomats around the world, China, Europe, the United States. I wanted to learn all about other cultures and I envisioned myself as being a very cosmopolitan woman."

She laughed.

"Instead, look at me. My clothes are not very cosmopolitan are they?"

"I think you look terrific."

"I think you are very good for my self-esteem."

"So did you ever get a chance to travel, see the world like you wanted to?"

"No, that's what's funny to me. The second I graduated from the university I knew, I mean I knew right then and there, instantly, that I wanted to teach the poor children in my country. I know it sounds awfully idealistic and probably very corny to someone who travelled halfway across the globe to run an airport in a foreign land, but I wanted to stay and make a difference. Maybe one of the students I reach will one day become the first female president in Africa. Maybe another will find the cure for cancer. Who knows?"

"I don't think it's corny at all. I think it's pretty cool that you would stay and dedicate your life to them."

"They have so little."

"Well, now they have you, right?"

"Right, and a pretty nifty basketball hoop thanks to you."

"Are you trying to say we make a pretty good team?"

"Maybe, maybe."

They turned the corner when they reached the street Jenelle lived on and the cloud cover blocking the moon earlier had moved on and Jack swore he could see the moon beams darting in and around her eyes like some sort of dance. He had never seen anyone so beautiful.

Her home, the nicest on the street, was made of cinder block and had bars in all the windows and a reinforced front door with a barred gate in front of it. The bars made Jack feel good knowing she was safer than most in the city.

"I share this place with two older ladies," she whispered. "They are probably asleep."

Jack could feel his heart pounding with excitement and breaking with disappointment that the evening was drawing to a close. Without the usual hesitation—that he knew would paralyze him—he reached in and kissed Jenelle. Their lips grazed the other's and they locked together passionately.

Who are you and what have you done with Jack, he thought.

They kissed again once more before putting their foreheads together and pressing against each other until they had to laugh.

"Jenelle, I don't know what to say. Tonight was, well it was just terrific."

"Oh no, is this when you tell me you have a wife and children waiting for you back home?"

"No, of course not. My goodness, what kind of guy do you think I am?"

"Girlfriend?"

"No, no girlfriend either," he did not lie.

"Good. I had a great time as well."

"Will I see you tomorrow?"

"You'd better." With that she turned and unlocked the gate to her home before disappearing behind the door.

Jack walked home but not really. He was sure his feet never touched the ground but glided, floated past alleys and closed-up shops until he was back home. Ahmed was already asleep, and Jack felt slightly guilty that he missed having the usual sugary delights with his friend.

Only slightly.

Up in his room, Jack took the framed photograph of Marci from the table and placed it in his suitcase, then went to bed.

ELEVEN

THE ROOSTERS CAME at around two followed by the dogs but Jack slept through them, waking only when the beads of perspiration started rolling down his chest and off the sides of his belly. It was the deepest he had slept since arriving. He was surprised to see that it was already very sunny out, and he scratched his head sleepily at how quiet it was outside his window. The room was extremely hot.

He took a bucket bath, waved to Ahmed—who seemed preoccupied—got dressed, and started walking toward the airport. It would be Christmas in a few weeks and Jack imagined how wonderful it would be to have someone like Jenelle to share it with. He hadn't really heard anyone mention Christmas and wondered how big or small of a deal it was here. Either way he would have to think of the perfect gift to give her.

The one Christmas memory he had of his mother was one of her singing by the small nativity they had one year beneath the Christmas tree. She never liked any of the silly or commercial Christmas songs. Her favorite was a carol called "Bring a Torch Jeanette Isabella."

"Ah, ah, beautiful is the mother

Ah, ah, beautiful is her son."

Walking with visions of sugarplum and mistletoe and thoughts of scrounging up a Santa Claus outfit to wear at the school, he didn't really notice how less crowded the marketplace was or how there were very few groups of men gathered around smoking cigarettes, sipping coffee and discussing politics. The children were still out and about playing soccer or just running after each other, but they seemed not as loud as usual.

It felt like a holiday, maybe a solemn one, like a day of remembrance. And maybe it was—Jack would ask about it later. He was still high from the night before and bounced to work joyfully counting the minutes until he could sneak away to the school and see Jenelle. He wished he had not overslept. If he had the time he would have run to the school that morning to meet her, in part to make sure the previous night was not a dream.

By the time he arrived at the airport he had seen two different sets of families leaving the city with all their belongings, including furniture, animals, and clothing, and he found it odd. They didn't appear packed for vacation or pilgrimage. They were definitely leaving for good, packed with everything they had ever owned.

But things at the airport seemed normal, even if three of his workers—men who had not missed a day since Jack arrived—had not yet shown up.

He went through the usual ritual of cleaning around the inside perimeter but none of his men sang or whistled with him, not even Matthew, who was uncharacteristically quiet.

"What's going on today?" Jack whispered playfully. "Why does it seem like everyone is playing some sort of version of the quiet game?"

But Matthew shook his head "no" and held a finger up as if to say "not now, not here."

Slowly throughout the morning, things seemed to return to a sense of normalcy or at least routine. Children led large herds of goats past the airport to graze, and a pair of ranchers from the west arrived with a hundred head of cattle, the type with enormous twisted horns, to sell in the market. There had not been a trade as extensive as that one in months. Planes roared in and skidded to their stops on the runway as scheduled, and people from the city even showed up for some of Jack's famous hamburgers.

But not knowing what had happened or what the day signified gnawed at Jack all morning.

When he spotted Matthew finishing up loading small boxes of

cargo into a single-engine Cessna, Jack ran out to the tarmac to meet with him.

"Matthew," he was out of breath from the short run out toward the plane. "Can you talk? What was troubling you this morning?"

"I didn't want to speak in front of the others because I do not know how the others feel and where their sympathies lie. I mean, I am sure that we are all probably in agreement, but you can never know for sure."

He had piqued Jack's interest for sure now.

"Well, what is it?"

"There was news early this morning from Khartoum, not very good news. They have instituted Sharia Law throughout the entire country."

Jack nodded up and down in faux understanding before shaking his head from side to side.

"I'm sorry Matthew, but what does that mean?"

"No one is really sure. That is why it is best not to make any bold statements or proclamations. But Sharia Law is Muslim law that will force everyone, Dinka, Christians, the Animists to follow their rules regarding dress, worship, diet, everything. Our way of life will change completely if this happens here."

"They can't do that," Jack tried to laugh but couldn't.

"I'm afraid they can and they have."

Despite the news that changes were coming from the capital far away to the north, the mood in the city got closer to normal as it became obvious that any restrictive new laws would take weeks, maybe even months or years to reach this part of the country.

Wonderfully sweet and romantic visits with Jenelle continued as Jack spent less time managing the airport and more time teaching the children basketball and visiting with Jenelle. They did not speak of the coming changes and her demeanor remained as it always had been, though Jack did notice that they did not go out much together in public, instead spending time together on the campus or taking moonlit walks nearby. When they did venture away from the school it was normally to purchase what Jack loved to call "sizzling meat on a stick" at one of the nearby street vendors.

He was a regular at mass with her and the children whenever Fr. Nguyen was in town and everything really seemed exactly the same at the school and its grounds.

The biggest change was in Matthew, who went from a smiling, carefree spirit to one clearly troubled, talking in small groups with his fellow workers then shushing them whenever Jack arrived. He seemed angry, anxious, and the person most damaged by the proclamation made by government leaders in the capital city, even though Jack was sure nothing at all had really changed.

That was not entirely true. While activities in the city resumed like before the news, things at the airport slowed considerably. Flights from neighboring Uganda and Kenya had barely enough passengers on them to keep the planes flying. It was no surprise that Jean Richard paid a visit by the end of the week.

Still, Jack was startled when he walked into his office and saw Jean Richard sitting on his desk waiting for him. His first thought was that he was getting canned—something he was all too familiar with—and fear gripped his heart for a moment at the thought of being forced to leave without Jenelle.

Be quick on your feet, Jack. You can talk your way out of any trouble you might be in.

"Jack, you've done a fine job here, a damned good job actually."

"Oh, no."

"What is it?" Jean Richard stood from the desk and walked toward Jack who stumbled backwards into a chair, banging his funny bone on the armrest.

"I'm getting a pink slip, aren't I?"

"No, no, of course not. The shareholders are happy with everything you've done. I have to be honest, when I first laid my eyes on you I thought they had made a mistake. I hope you'll forgive me for thinking that way, but it's true. Clearly the powers that be that hired you, that brought you here knew what they were doing. I guess that's why they do what they do and I do what it is I do."

"Why do I feel like your sentence should be ending with the word 'but'?"

"That's one of the things I like about you, Jack." He gave a half-hearted laugh. "There are no false pretenses about you, no games, no hidden agendas, and no game playing. You get right to the point. What you see is what you get. Unfortunately that's not how the world works and certainly not how the Sudan works."

Jean Richard pulled a silver-plated flask from his pocket and poured a bit of Scotch whiskey into two Styrofoam coffee cups near the coffee maker. Jack's eyes widened—it had been months since he last caught the aroma of hard liquor.

"Drink up, Jack. Cheers."

"What exactly are we celebrating?" He was starting to feel uncomfortable. Exactly where was Jean Richard going with all this?

"Jack, what do you know of the history of this country?"

"Not a lot, I'm afraid."

"The British liked to divide and conquer, take what they wanted and then leave when the going got too rough. They controlled Sudan but kept the north and south separated for decades until nearly 1950. They would grant the Sudanese people their independence less than ten years later after unifying the northern and southern sections of the land. But they gave all the power to rule to a small, elite group in the north. This was a huge blow to the south, to people like my father, to the African Sudanese."

"The African Sudanese?" Jack sipped the Scotch and it burned the back of his throat and cleared his sinus passages.

"Yes. The people in the north are Arabs. The two sides have never gotten along. Sometimes it is as basic as identity. Is Sudan Arab or African?"

Jack scratched his head, trying to make sense of what he was being told. He finished his Scotch and had to keep his mouth open slightly in order to suck cool air in to alleviate the burn. He wondered if anyone actually liked the taste of Scotch—to him it tasted like cough syrup that had been soaked in an old sweat sock and wrung out.

"What I am trying to tell you, Jack, is that these last few years here have been good, peaceful. But that is never how it has been for long. Even before full independence was granted in 1956, the south formed an army, forming the Any-Nya rebel group. They fought until 1972 when a lasting peace deal was finally brokered and the southern leaders were given autonomy over their own lands."

Jack nodded his head and tried to look on intelligently.

"Now," he continued before Jack could offer any input, "it appears that the peace has been broken with the institution of Sharia Law."

"So," Jack was able to chime in, "the government wants everyone to become a Muslim? Is that what this next war is going to be about?"

Jean Richard laughed sarcastically, not so much at Jack but rather a bitter laugh at what was to come in his country.

"So many nefarious deeds have been committed behind the guise of religion, Mr. Hopkins. No, I'm afraid they couldn't care less what these poor country people practice as their religion. No, this is about one thing and one thing only, the one thing that drives men to do unspeakable things—greed."

He stood and walked over to the window where he held the blinds down with his hand and looked out onto part of the runway.

"You see, a few years ago oil was discovered in the south. It was an incredible find, one that gave many people of Sudan, including yours truly, hope, real hope for his people. This type of discovery is the kind of thing that can lift Sudan out of the third world. This would help make the country rich with resources coveted by the world. When I heard the news I instantly imagined schools being built, roads, bridges, infrastructure, technology, higher education, a better life for generations to come.

"Now that does not appear as if it will happen. The two sides could not come to an agreement on how to share the billions of dollars the oil will produce. President Gaafar Nimeiry covets the oil fields for the north. He is a puppet of the Islamic hardliners. Combine that with a growing radical Islam in the capital area and this is what you have—the makings of a civil war." He paused for a moment before muttering, "I wonder if the north would be so eager to share had the oil been discovered up there."

"Can't both sides continue to negotiate?"

"It's too late. The government of the north basically declared war on the south by instituting Sharia Law."

"Would Sharia Law be that bad?"

Jean Richard turned from the window and leaned toward Jack.

"I know we may seem like simple people to a westerner like yourself. But do you think we are that simple that we would abandon our beliefs and simply take on someone else's religion because they told us to do so? They will take the women out of schools and cover them up from head to toe. They will change what we eat, what we drink, how we pray, and who we pray to. Did you know that in the 1960s all Christian missionaries were expelled and all Christian schools closed down? Would Americans allow that?"

"No, I didn't mean—"

"I don't mean to snap at you, Jack. It's just that, well, it's over. This isn't religion coming down from the north. It is annihilation."

"What kind of army or weapons can they possibly have?"

"Actually they are well-armed thanks to the Cold War between your country and the Soviet Union. Both countries have thrown weapons, planes, tanks, and training at Khartoum. Then a few years ago, the Chinese got involved and have started supplying arms."

He paused and poured himself another inch of Scotch.

"Jack," his voice softened. "It has already started and is going to get worse. There is no question about it. Hordes of government soldiers and others are making their way southward, one village at a time. I have received very reliable reports and it is not good. They are killing the men who do not convert, raping the women and little girls, and forcing the boys to join in their band of monsters. They are setting fire to villages, defecating into the water supplies, slaughtering livestock. They are leaving nothing in their path. And they will be here sooner than later."

For the next half hour, Jack could hear the sounds coming from Jean Richard's mouth about scaling back the flights after the initial rush of refugees—the small percentage of lucky ones with passports and paperwork enabling them to leave the country—and about eliminating all inbound flights. There were warnings about people trying to rush to the airport to get out and about how it would be illegal to let them leave the country without proper documentation. Maybe it would be wise to hire a small security force, at least temporarily. He heard the sounds but processed none of it. All he could think about was Jenelle and the students. Surely they would be safe. Surely no one would bother with them.

He was snapped back to attention by a single phrase that also erased any peaceful sluggishness the Scotch had provided despite its taste.

"I've made arrangements with George White to get you out of the country whenever you wish and for safe passage back home through Cairo or Entebbe. You'll need to send us a forwarding address so we can send the remainder of your pay. We will honor the terms of the agreement even if the airport is forced to close before the deal is finished. The board wanted me to thank you personally for a job well done, and I would like to say that it has been a pleasure working with you."

He stood and extended his hand to Jack who shook it while trying to find the words to utter any form of protest.

"You've made a lot of people plenty of money during your short time here but all good things must come to an end, huh?

It's really a shame. I love this country. This is the land of my parents and their parents and so on. This, this right here is where we are from. This is where we belong but I am afraid it is not where we will always be. I love her with all of my fiber. It sickens me and breaks my heart to think of what is taking place and what is to come."

Jack again tried to protest but could only stammer out a few sounds.

"Jean Richard, are you sure you want me to leave?"

"You have no idea what is about to come down. You come from a place where things get done and changes are instituted by peaceful protest or legal elections."

"No, not always."

"Jack, this will not be a good place for someone who looks like you," he chuckled. "This will not be a good place for people who look like me. No one will be safe, unless they start kneeling five times a day toward Mecca and fool the marauders."

"What about Jenelle? Do you think she will be safe?"

Jean Richard looked straight into Jack's eyes.

"Does she strike you as the type of woman who would abandon her faith?"

"Of course not. Can I take her with me, if, I mean, if she has the proper paperwork to get out?"

"Does she strike you as the type of woman who would leave her children, her students behind?"

TWELVE

THE IDEA CAME to Jack the minute he saw Ti Burik gently touch down just clearing the row of tall trees bordering the eastern part of the runway. He had not seen George since the proclamation from Khartoum and it would be good to see a familiar face. He wanted to ask George about this Sharia Law thing. He'd been in Africa for a long time now and he'd be able to tell Jack whether things would get as ugly as Jean Richard predicted. He'd be able to tell Jack if Jenelle and the children would be safe.

Yes, he would definitely feel better after talking to the banjo-playing pilot from the mountains of Tennessee.

Only about half of the airport's workers were regularly showing up for their shifts and Jack was glad that Matthew was still one of them. There was something about him that Jack liked. He seemed honest and used to seem full of joy. Or maybe it was just his appearance. Maybe it was his brilliant white teeth or perfectly round face or the way his lips curled when he smiled, though there had not been many smiles lately.

Despite the change in personality, Jack felt very attached to Matthew and continued trying to engage the young man in conversation about anything from the proper way to dig out cassava roots to trying to explain to him the rules for the game of baseball. He was determined to break the barrier.

Finally he learned that all of his brothers had left home—when the announcement about Sharia Law was made—to join with the SPLA or Sudanese People's Liberation Army. They forbid him to go because he was the only one of them with any chance at all of one day continuing his education and making something of himself. But they bestowed upon him a great honor and responsibility, one he did not recognize. They chose him to look after his sisters and mother, an honor he was not all happy to be chosen for.

"I want to defend my land, my people," he admitted to Jack, who tried his best to convince him his brothers were right.

"You will, Matthew. You will. Someone has to protect the women. What is more important than shielding them from harm? Plus, I really don't think any of that trouble is going to make it this far south. Your brothers will be back before you know it and everything will be back to normal."

Jack tried to believe the words and though Matthew appreciated the effort, he did not believe them either.

He tried encouraging the others as well, reassuring them that nothing would happen to them or their families. He would speak, trying to sound sincere but the words always rang hollow. As badly as he wanted to, Jack could not believe them himself. But it was easier than telling them anything else.

So when Jack saw George's "little donkey" slow down and skid slightly on the runway before taxiing closer to the terminal, he was struck by an idea that might help lift the sinking morale among his workers. He still wanted to pick George's brain about the conditions and mood in the country and to ask him what he'd already seen but that could wait for now. There would be time to talk later.

"Staying long?" he asked his friend.

"At least until the end of the week."

"Good, got your banjo?"

"Always."

That afternoon, after selling the last of the hamburgers for the day and after the last flight from Kenya had arrived and gone, Jack rounded up the 15 or so workers left at the facility for a meeting. They gathered, albeit cramped, in Jack's tiny office and he knew right away that it would not work. The worn-down shag carpet combined with the low acoustic-tiled ceiling would not work, not work at all.

He glanced at George, who stood a full head taller than the tallest man, and he shook his head no, agreeing with Jack's unspoken assessment.

"Jack, what about the cleanest men's room in the third world?" George smiled. "Seems to me that might be a perfect place."

Jack had been totally underwhelmed when he saw the condition of the restrooms at the airport when he first arrived. In fact, he thought, the toilets at the 125th Street subway station on the No. 5 and 6 lines were cleaner and in better condition than these. The facilities looked as if they had never been touched by a brush, scouring pad or even a wet rag, ever.

"What's the first thing people want to do when they get off a plane?" he asked his workers during his first few days at the airport. "They want to go to the restroom. They either have to go or they simply want to wash their face, put on makeup, and simply feel refreshed. It can also be a place to finish reading a book—while taking care of business—or simply taking a few minutes to get away from an overly talkative wife or crying baby. Remember, traveling is very tiring and most people cannot wait to get off of an airplane, especially after a long flight. There is no way anybody is going to get off of an airplane here and want to do anything in these lavatories."

That's when he went creative and instituted the "Spotless John" contest, rotating weekly the worker given restroom cleaning duties and awarding the person who kept it the cleanest with a $25 bonus at the end of the month. It was Jack's own money but he was happy to spend it in exchange for a pristine place to go to the toilet. He would have spent $100 of his own money in this country for a clean place to go. He ordered new mops, scrub brushes, tile and mildew cleaner, Ajax, bleach, urinal cakes, and anything else he thought might help make the experience nicer.

The men took to the contest enthusiastically and Jack made sure a different staffer took home the extra $25 every month.

The men looked around quizzically and giggled as Jack led them into the spacious men's room.

"Ah, now this is more like it, wouldn't you say so, George?"

"No doubt about it."

Jack lined the men up in front of the bank of sinks in size order and for a moment daydreamed of sharing a bathroom with Jenelle. He pictured two toothbrushes on the countertop and a bin for all of her beauty products. Not that she needed to use any of them, he thought. The other bin contained his shaving kit and deodorant. Maybe they'd even have one of those fancy bathrooms with his and hers sinks. That way she would never complain about shaving cream left behind in the sink.

Bathtub or shower? Maybe both. I always wanted to have a shower with fancy doors on it instead of some mildew-stained shower curtain. I'm definitely a shower guy but we need a tub for her. I always found it weird to take a bath and lay in your own dirty water. Then there is the question of the feet. I wonder whether most people wash their feet with soap and water while showering or whether they just let the soapy runoff from their bodies do the job?

George opened the case to his banjo and the men giggled again at the site of this instrument they had not seen before. It made Jack happy to see that even Matthew was smiling.

"Now, I have written the words out for all of you to learn. It is a simple tune but, who knows, it may lead to other more challenging songs."

He passed out the sheets of paper with the lyrics to "All my loving" by the Beatles on them. Not embarrassed by his own mediocre, scratchy voice, Jack counted to four and he sang the tune alone with George plunking away on the banjo.

> "Close your eyes and I'll kiss you
> Tomorrow I'll miss you,
> Remember I'll always be true,
> And then while I'm away
> I'll write home every day
> And send all my lovin' to you."

They played the tune over and over, and the men joined in at their own pace enthusiastically, their improvised harmonies and counter melodies bouncing gloriously off of the perfect acoustics in the men's room. The high ceiling, tiled floor, and empty spaces helped provide reverb and chorus effects and after an hour the newly formed choir had mastered the tune. They even impressed George White, who was not one to throw around compliments lightly.

"That actually did not make me want to throw up," he laughed. "I would say it was even maybe pretty good."

Rehearsals became a daily ritual after the last of the airplanes had taken off, and the men were disappointed when George White flew out of town for a few days at a time but still met regularly to practice the song a capella, which sounded pretty good as well. George's quick picking and rhythmic tapping on the strings along with the flourishes he played really enhanced the sound and he was definitely missed when he had to fly. He had turned it into an almost reggae type of song with his rhythm. The men were amazed that an instrument that produced such a twangy nearly out-of-tune sound could also be so melodious.

Jack tried sharing the story of his new choir with Ahmed over their nightly *baseema* cakes but wasn't sure his friend understood even though he was picking English up very quickly. He told the story of the Beatles and their meteoric rise to stardom and how they shaped western music in the 1960s. He told him how some creep named Chapman stalked and then shot and killed John Lennon in cold blood in front of his apartment building.

Ahmed smiled a lot and was a good listener. If it wasn't for the cigarettes and the constant chain smoking he'd be the perfect companion to share cake and stories with after he'd spent the evening with Jenelle.

The stories would vary and Jack knew he was rambling most nights but Ahmed didn't seem to mind and he never complained.

He seemed to like hearing one story over and over again about how Jack and his childhood buddy Artie Morales went to a Mets game at Shea Stadium against the Pittsburgh Pirates. The stadium was 75 percent empty and after the third inning they tried moving down to better, unoccupied seats. There was this one usher, a hulking balding man with a thick Italian accent that made it his personal mission that evening not to let these two poor kids from the Bronx sit in any seats better than their Dellwood milk carton coupon seats had entitled them to.

He was a drunk and they caught him sipping from a silver flask every few minutes whenever he thought no one was looking.

They tried moving down from the grandstand to empty boxes down behind home plate, then along the first base line, and then the third base line and this bulging "seat Nazi" was there every single time to catch them and order them back upstairs. He swore at them, sounding nastier and drunker every time.

He was the only usher who seemed to care about it in the empty stadium of 8,000 fans and seemed to relish in catching them and being extremely mean about it. It was something that brought him happiness.

"If I catch you kids sneaking down one more time I am going to personally remove you from the stadium, fill your back pockets with packets of mustard, and sit your asses down so hard on the train that all your friends will think you had a bad case of the squitters when they see you."

That's when Jack and Artie hatched a plan that involved snatching dozens of mustard packets from the hot dog stand and finding seats in the mezzanine directly above the seat Nazi's station. By the seventh inning, the usher was loaded and sat down in an empty seat and started dozing.

From 50 feet above, the boys emptied 79 packs of Gulden's spicy brown mustard onto his blue usher's jacket, scoring direct hits on 99 percent of the packets. It was so thick that it seemed to plop down from above in slow-motion so as not to disturb his alcohol-hazed slumber. They hit and landed on each other, one after another creating this slow-moving avalanche of brown gooey mustard down his back.

There was so much mustard falling on him that eventually the fans began noticing and started cheering. It caught on and even the WWOR-9 television cameras focused on the sleeping usher covered in mustard. The crescendo of cheers grew and even the players on the field wondered what was going on. It had become a spectacle.

Finally the usher woke up, thinking he had missed a big play, only to receive more cheers himself when he stood up. He waved to the crowd happily before one of his co-workers, a cranky sort himself, pointed out his condiment-smothered jacket.

"He knew right away, Ahmed. He knew right away that he had been had by me and my buddy Art. He looked up and spotted us, his face turning beet red, lobster red, and then he came running up the stairs for us. But we were too quick for him. Twice I turned to look at him and our eyes met. I tell you, I have never seen so much hatred in someone's face. My buddy and I got out of the stadium and it was three years before we felt safe going back. The usher's picture was on the front page the next day of the *Daily News* and the *Post*. I'm sure he lost his job but we always felt like he might be there waiting for us anyway to take his revenge."

"What is this thing, spicy brown mustard?" Ahmed would always ask and the two men would burst out laughing.

Before George took off for a three-day turnaround in Cairo, Jack made sure to grab him for some one-on-one time. They went to the corner where Jack and Jenelle enjoyed the sizzling meat on a stick and gorged themselves one morning for an early lunch.

"I had a surprise visit from Jean Richard the other day, George."

"I know. He came to see me first," George replied, lifting the skewer away from his face to avoid getting burned by the hot grease.

"Right."

"And so you want to make a reservation or what?"

"I guess the 'or what.' "

"Ah, well in that case I am all ears, my friend. But I'll have to warn you. If I was you I'd probably make my reservation to get out sooner than later. I know you've had a good time lately singing with the boys and you've been spending time with that lovely school teacher but it's been my experience that these things turn pretty quickly. I've seen countries turn on a dime, none as fast as what happened in Haiti last decade, and people you think are allies and friends suddenly do an about-face. I'll stay for as long as I can and give you plenty of notice about my last flight out, but just start getting yourself packed and prepared to leave."

"Yeah, everyone seems to be telling me that. But I guess, I guess I just want your opinion about how bad this is going to get. I mean, seriously, those stories of rape, torture, and murder can't be true, can they?"

"Jack, I must have been from Missouri in another lifetime because I am definitely a 'show-me' kind of guy." George stopped and took a deep breath. "But I don't want to wait until they show me what they are capable of. If I'm hearing stories of rape, torture, and murder, then, well, I don't know what to tell you except let's get out of here before we know for sure."

THIRTEEN

REPORTS WOULD FILTER in every few days about a village or town that had been attacked and "converted." The people of Jabra would get up in arms and start bragging about how they would fight the invaders from the north and send them back home with their tails between their legs. But others, the cowardly or sensible, would quietly pack their life's belongings and disappear to the south or east with nary a word to anyone.

But there had yet to be a mass exodus and things, for the most part, seemed normal. There were some, like Jack, who felt the reports were overblown and that nothing like that could possibly happen. The world would never let another Nazi Germany happen again. They would not allow the systematic burning of villages and raping of women and children. Others had increasing faith in the formation of the SLPA and believed this newly formed local militia would protect them.

Regardless of Jack's personal beliefs, it was clear the airport would soon have to close. There was barely enough air traffic to justify staying open, especially when most of the small bush planes smuggling people in and out could easily land on the dirt strips outside the city near the river. Jean Richard had warned Jack to ensure that people leaving had proper documentation but his belief was that if a pilot was willing to risk it then he had no business interfering. Let the country on the other end of the journey worry about documentation, he thought.

There was really no reason to stay open and so Jack and even the most loyal of workers were getting antsy to leave their jobs. Jack was determined that once George returned from his latest flight he would get the boys together for their one and only performance.

Whenever George—all six foot seven inches of him—walked through the streets of Jabra, he typically drew stares and even followers. Now, walking with his banjo in his hand and followed by Jack and 15 White Nile International Airport employees holding makeshift drums and tambourines, he was truly a spectacle.

At first it was dozens of children who joined the quick-moving parade past the spice dealers and food vendors—often described by Jack as the closest thing the city had to a food court. But before long people were hastily closing their shops and following Jack's choir through the twists and turns on their way to St. Jude's Catholic School. There were more than 100 followers by the time Jenelle could hear the commotion still several hundred yards away.

Her heart quickened and she ran out to the courtyard to seek Father Nguyen. Had the attacks already started so soon and without warning? He was already standing out by the statue of St. Jude looking on stoically.

The children waited in the classroom working on their assignments oblivious to the noise and danger their teacher sensed. She clenched the small wooden crucifix hanging from a string around her neck.

Before seeing George's head high above everyone else's, Jenelle could hear the joyousness in the crowd. This was not a lynch mob at all. This was something good and exciting. She yelled for the children to come out of the classroom to stand by her in the courtyard. They bolted from the classroom as if she had announced early dismissal or the first day of summer holiday.

She could not believe her eyes when she saw George and Jack come around the bend leading scores of villagers onto the property. She covered her mouth and laughed though her eyes teared up at the same time. She didn't know if the tears were from jubilance or relief.

Jack smiled at her and set the choir members in place to the right of the altar in the small outdoor church. George plunked a note and then men found their key. Then, without warning or opening words, the choir broke out in a rousing version of the Beatles song they had been practicing so faithfully. The men went above and beyond, breaking off into traditional Sudanese rhythms and harmonies that Jack was sure would have made Lennon and McCartney proud.

Jack stared at Jenelle the entire time and mouthed the words to her personally. He thought she looked incredible in a plain blue dress, not unlike one a nun would wear.

She could not take her eyes off of him.

The villagers danced and cheered wildly as the men played the song a second time. They then broke off themselves singing African folk songs that often ended in some sort of riddle or good-natured joke. Before long vendors, whose cooking stands were on wheels, arrived and the school grounds took on the look of a county fair. Jenelle had never seen anything like this in the city and felt very proud that Jack was responsible.

He walked over to her and they held hands while listening to the people singing. George tried keeping up on the banjo but gave up after a while and was content to sit on a large rock by St. Jude letting dozens of little children climb all over him and strum and pluck at his banjo.

Everyone was singing or laughing or smiling, except of course, Cindy Lou. She wore the same emotionless expression she normally did, her big baseball-sized eyes staring blankly at the goings on around her.

Jack tried making eye contact with her but she stared right through him.

"Jack, you are one amazing person. Do you know that?"

"Uh yeah, I think I know," he answered seriously before laughing loudly.

"You are so easy to love," the words came out before she had a chance to filter them.

"A-ha!" he proclaimed loudly. "So you do love me. And really, who can blame you? I mean look at this fine specimen."

He stood tall, held in his gut and flexed his non-existent muscles like Popeye.

"I never said I loved you. I simply said you were easy to love."

"Well, that doesn't make sense. If I'm easy to love then one can only deduce that you love me."

"Not necessarily," she smiled coyly.

"Oh brother, OK, if you really insist on me being the first to come out and say it then I will. Jenelle, I love you."

She smiled but said nothing.

"I'm waiting," Jack persisted, suddenly feeling a bit exposed.

"Well, I'm thinking."

"Why do you love torturing me so?"

"Because it's so much fun."

"Are you going to make a grown man cry in front of all these people and children?"

"They are having so much fun I don't think anyone would even notice."

"Oh, brother."

"OK, OK, only because I can't stand to see a grown man cry. I love you, Jack Hopkins. I have loved you for quite some time now and I'm pretty sure you have known it. So there, you have it, out loud and official."

His heart bottled her words so they would never be able to escape and he wanted to lean close and kiss her. But that sort of display would not have been acceptable and so he smiled gently at her and said nothing for a few minutes while the people continued to sing.

They walked away from the crowd together, closer to the classroom, in silence. Jack knew that one of them would have to finally acknowledge the proverbial elephant in the room and he knew it would just about kill the euphoria of hearing Jenelle profess her love. He ran his hand over the smooth wooden wall on the outside of the classroom and peered inside to see some scribbling on the chalkboard.

"The children?" he finally broke the silence.

"Yes. The children know what's coming," she said slowly, quietly measuring her words. She stopped, not offering more and slightly frustrating Jack.

"What are you doing about it?" he asked, trying to sound gentle and not heap anymore responsibility on her.

"I am teaching them to run, to hide, and to pray."

The words hit Jack like thunder. *Was that it? Was that really the only option? No orphanages or other safe places of refuge?*

"Prayer can be very powerful," she added, perhaps sensing his concern. "When you have lost everything, you always have God."

"Will you teach me to pray?"

She smiled and took his hand, making the sign of the cross with it. "Well, for me personally, I like to pray the Hail Mary."

"Why?"

"Well, I know how difficult it is for a son to deny a request from his mother. So I ask Mary to intercede."

"Show me."

Jenelle knelt down onto the red clay dirt and Jack followed.

"Hail Mary, full of grace,

The lord is with thee,

Blessed art thou among women

And blessed is the fruit of thy womb, Jesus."

They stayed kneeling for a while and Jack committed the words to memory. Their concentration was broken only when little Cindy Lou came over and knelt with them, slipping her hand into her teacher's.

"Immaculee, my precious. Don't you like the music?" But the girl did not answer. "Come, let me take you over there with the other children. It's not healthy for you to only want to spend time with me."

She stood from her kneeling position.

"I'll be right back. I think we probably still have more to discuss."

Jack nodded and breathed in deeply taking in all that Africa had given him until now. The air was dry and smelled of charcoal and dust, a combination he had come to love. The sun was relentless but gave him the appreciation of finding a bit of shade. The people were clean and friendly and generous, nothing like he had expected. They laughed all the time and the women seemed to be bathing their children all day long. This was a place where the people respected him and his ideas and he would be content to stay for a long time.

He looked down at the red clay stains on his pant legs and he hoped they would never come out.

"I worry for that girl," Jenelle said, coming back and shaking her head. "I had hoped to get through to her at some point."

"Well, don't talk about it in the past tense like it's hopeless."

Jenelle gave a small smile and sighed.

"She still hasn't spoken to you?"

"No, I'm afraid not," she said, putting her hands up to her face as if she were about to cry.

"You were going to tell me one day about Cindy Lou and what happened to her. Is today one day?"

"I guess it is."

They walked over to the statue of St. Jude and sat on the base side by side. George White had put down his banjo and was demonstrating how being six foot seven inches tall was an unbeatable advantage when playing basketball against 10-year-olds. He waved at Jack and banked another basket in.

"I do not understand the Cindy Lou reference. Her name is Immaculee and I have known her for about three years. She was born in this village, a few years before I arrived, into a very good family. They were well respected. Her father was a very hard worker I am told. He worked way down south in Zambia, a country that used to be part of Rhodesia, in one of the European-owned copper mines. He would work several months and then come back for about six weeks before going back. It is grueling, back-breaking work but it provided a good income for his family.

"His wife was absolutely stunning. They were both born and raised here themselves and had Dinka ancestry. Anyway, these mines make tons of money for the European owners and so they like to keep the men happy when they are away from home for so long. They provide them whiskey, gambling, and of course women. Well, from what I understand, these prostitutes they provide really get around and many have gotten the men sick.

"Have you ever heard of AIDS, Jack?"

"Yes, yes, I have heard of it. But I thought it only afflicted, um afflicted men who, well, men who like to be with other men."

"Well, that's not the case here. People don't know much about it and they don't even like to call it by its proper name. People just call it the sickness. They break out in these terrible festering lesions, their eyes turn yellow like they do when they get malaria and they just lose the will to live.

"Well, Immaculee's father caught this dreaded disease from one of the women supplied by the copper mine owners and unwittingly brought it home to his wife. When he began to display the signs of the disease, he was let go, sacked, by his employers and sent back home to Jabra. They told him his services were no longer needed. He returned home to the villages in shame, 40 pounds lighter than what he had normally weighed. The terrible tragedy is that he blamed his wife for giving him this death sentence of a sickness.

"He accused her of being unfaithful to him while he was away working. He said she brought shame and a curse upon their family. She pleaded and insisted that that was not the case. She told him that he was the only man she had ever been with but nothing she said would convince him even though he knew that he had infected his wife with the disease as well. When both of them started to get sick, the people of the village said they were cursed and they became ostracized. No one wanted them around. No one came to visit to help care for them. This once wealthy and proud family was now just a blight, a terrible cursed tragedy waiting to happen."

Jack shifted on the base of the statue and shook his head.

"That poor little girl. So her parents died in poverty and shame?"

"Jack, I'm afraid you have not heard the worst of it. With little or no money left for food. Immaculee's father decided to sell the only thing of value he had left and that was a machete that he had purchased at the airport in Johannesburg on his way back home from one of his stints working in the copper mine. It was a beautiful, handcrafted piece that was very valuable. But he found no takers for it in town. In fact, most of the shopkeepers did not even let him enter their store. They chased him away and threw stones at him to keep away.

"He arrived home in a fit of rage and started screaming at his wife, calling her a whore and all types of other derogatory names that I'd just rather not mention."

She paused and wiped her eye then stood up to stretch. Jack stood as well and they walked slowly down the path to the entrance of the campus where it was very quiet and found shade under a large mango tree that gave more than a hundred mangos the previous May.

"Jenelle, you don't have to tell me any more of the story if it's going to upset you."

"No, I think you need to know. It's important that you have this information, even if it is painful.

"So, in his rage, he is cursing and screaming obscenities at his poor wife, simply a victim of his poor choices. She is crying and pleading with him to stop when he starts hacking her to death with the machete. It takes a long time to kill her, neighbors said, who watched from outside their homes. He hacked and sliced at her until she was literally in pieces. Then even after she was dead, he continued his onslaught until really there was little left than a massive pool of blood on the ground. And all this was done only inches away from poor Immaculee, who sat crying on the dirt floor of their home in her diaper. Her father then collapsed on his sleeping mat and spent the next several days crying, just moaning and wailing day and night until his heart stopped beating, making his one and only daughter an orphan.

"He never paid one bit of mind to this poor little girl who was forced to witness this massacre and who was left to wallow in her mother's bloody remains for days with no food.

"Finally, when the smell of the two dead bodies became too much for their neighbors to tolerate, an old woman entered the home and discovered what had happened. Immaculee was near death, motionless, listless, and her breathing was very shallow."

Now Jenelle was openly weeping and not bothering to wipe away the tears that came streaming down.

"Fearing that the curse of the family would be passed onto this poor young baby, the woman took Immaculee and placed the child in a pile of rubbish, a trash heap, at the side of the road. It would be better for everyone, she thought, if this baby just died. Plus, no one would be willing to take in another child, another mouth to feed.

"But this little girl, this child who will probably never smile again due to the horrors she has seen, this little miracle of life was not quite ready to give up her ghost. No, three days after being left for dead in the trash, she was still making gurgling sounds." Jenelle's voice rose in excitement now. "That was the very day that Fr. Nguyen was coming to town for the very first time to bless the school and give mass. I wasn't here yet. He heard the baby and scooped her up out of the trash. He took her back and tended to her, calling in a doctor from Juba to help bring this child back to life. She has lived here ever since."

Jack looked over toward Fr. Nguyen and smiled.

"Someone must have been praying for that little girl, Jack. For her to live in the trash for three days after being left for dead is nothing short of a miracle. But then, to have this man of God passing by just at the right time, at the exact time she made enough of a sound for him to notice something in the trash is really nothing less than the hand of God himself coming down and touching the earth. That little girl over there, the one who has never spoken and who is way too small for her age, should not be alive. There is no medical or scientific explanation as to her survival. But I will tell you one thing. She was saved for a reason."

FOURTEEN

JACK WAS DREAMING of planes, of one in particular.

It was the Cessna Skymaster push-pull plane. It was always his favorite even though he joked that it looked like half of an airplane and that someone at the factory had made a gross mistake by putting a propeller in the rear. The twin engine had a prop in the front and one in the back.

In the dream it flew very low to the ground and the pilot kept circling as if getting ready to land but never did. Jack stood there waiting on the runway with his luggage and bags of souvenirs for the children of the neighborhood. Jack waved to the pilot, signaling that he was ready for pickup. He flew the Skymaster lower and lower until it was nearly touching the ground but it never reached.

He stared at the plane and after a while he was able to make out Cindy Lou waving from one of the passenger windows. There were no words exchanged but somehow, in the dream, Jack knew that he was her father and he needed to be reunited with her in the air. He tried jumping up and down to reach the plane but couldn't.

The engine seemed very loud and even though he was watching from the ground, he had to cover his ears every time the engine backfired.

The banging and knocking continued, but it wasn't until Jack could make out the words "Are you up?" did he realize someone was banging on his door in the middle of the night.

"Yes, yes," he muttered, his eyes still closed as he tried rubbing them awake, and for a moment he sat in the bed, dazed, not knowing where he was at all.

"Jack, Jack, are you awake?" The knocking had stopped but there were still loud bangs in the distance.

"Coming, coming." His heartbeat slowed when he recognized Ahmed's voice at the door.

He tried the light switch and was amazed that there was electricity at that hour. He stared at his wristwatch for several seconds until his eye adjusted. It was 1:13.

The door was swollen with humidity and it made a loud noise when Jack finally pulled it open.

"Jack, I am sorry to come to you so late."

"Ahmed, is there something wrong?" The words hurt Jack's exhausted brain as they came tumbling out and his heart raced with worry at the late-hour visit.

"I wanted to come and say goodbye."

"Goodbye?"

"Have you heard the Antonovs tonight?"

"Antonov?"

"The Russian planes our government is using to bomb the villages in the south. You can hear them dropping bombs somewhere very far away, maybe even Juba. Many changes come soon to village and it is best for me to go."

"Wait a second, wait a second now." Jack pulled Ahmed inside his flat and swung the door partially closed behind him. "I don't understand. Aren't you Muslim?"

"Yes."

"The non-Muslims have been the ones leaving, Ahmed. You will be fine if you stay. I don't think the fighting will come this way. No one cares about this little town. It has no military or strategic significance.

"Do you think that really matters to them?" He smiled sadly at Jack. "No, I think people here will be very angry once the fighting stops. They will not like Ahmed very much and will have vendetta against me for what the others will do to them. Everything here is going to change. This village, everything you know of it, will become a terrible lie."

"No way, not the people around here. They know you. You've had your shop here for many years. Everyone here knows you wouldn't be responsible for what the government is doing."

"People will change. Trust me. I know how this is going to turn out. It is going to be bad and people will blame me. I must go." He sounded very much like someone who had decidedly made up his mind.

Jack rubbed his eyes and listened for more bombs in the distance but there were none.

"Your English has gotten much, much better," he finally said softly and with a smile, realizing he would never see his friend and building-mate ever again.

"I have you to blame for that and for the extra ten pounds I have gained eating *baseema*." Both men laughed. "You are the only American I have ever met and you were not what I expected."

Jack waited for an explanation but none came and so he took it as it was meant, a compliment, a confirmation of deep friendship.

"Are you sure you have to go?" Jack rubbed the last little bit of sleep from his eyes and felt a pang of sadness in his gut. .

"It has started and will get here soon. Yes, I must go. I will take my things, right now, so no one sees, and go north. I have many cousins in villages scattered about. I will see where it is safe and try to open a shop there. It will be difficult to leave here and start over but sometimes things are just difficult."

Jack held out his hand but Ahmed held open his arms and the men embraced warmly.

"Good luck Ahmed. Please be careful."

Then the two men shook hands heartily.

"I will miss you and think of you often," Ahmed said before turning to go. But he spun around as he reached the doorway and handed Jack a small package wrapped in newspaper.

"These are for you," he said. "I think they are the finest I have ever made."

Jack never really got back to sleep that night though he tried. He tossed and turned listening for bombs and half-expecting one to come crashing straight down through the roof and onto him. He rose early and made a decision that was unexpectedly energetic.

He bathed and dressed quickly, skipped his morning coffee and hustled into the airport. There was smoke in the distance, at the far end of town, and he wondered if one of the bombs had hit Jabra.

Grabbing two of his paychecks from the drawer in his desk, Jack quickly left the airport and headed to the bank—really more of just a moneychanger—in town who offered Jack a horrible rate of exchange, but it didn't matter. It would be far more money than he would need. The man shook his head realizing that he could have gouged even more money from him.

Jack stuffed the fistful of cash into his pocket and ran out to the jewelry district in the town. A hot, dry wind had picked up and it was swirling red dust around like mini harmless twisters. He was stunned to see how many shops had not opened and how many looked as if they had been abandoned. In fact, the one place he had in mind, with the shopkeeper that teased him and Jenelle whenever they walked by, was gone, his shop abandoned.

Could this really be the end, time to go?

He rushed around and behind a smoky grill that was overcooking a large slab of meat, Jack found a vendor that was sticking it out for as long as he could. The man, with greasy hair and a long pointed nose, was all alone and seemed almost to be waiting for Jack. He did not look African and he did not look Arabic either. Jack thought he looked like a Pakistani. All of his belongings were balled up in a "ready-to-leave" position by the entrance and his wife and children had already gone on ahead. His eyes greeted Jack with a look that said "Ah, I've been expecting you."

He motioned to Jack to sit down on the mat on the floor and offered his some tea. Jack politely declined and made a motion with his hand of putting on a ring and taking it off.

The man with the greasy hair and pointed nose held up a finger as if to say "Ah," and disappeared into the rear of the shop for a moment. The smoke from the cooking meat came into the room and made Jack hungry. The man returned with a brightly-colored orange scarf and opened it carefully on the mat between them. A few of the neighborhood children, some of them wearing nothing at all and none of them wearing shoes, poked their heads in to watch but the man spoke harshly toward them and they left before Jack could protest.

There were about a dozen rings, some of them men's and some used. One stood out immediately to Jack who held it up high and looked at it in better light.

It was a thin, golden band with a green stone set atop and little carvings all around. The light came through it beautifully and danced off in a hundred different directions.

Jack stared at the tiny separations of light for a few moments and followed the particles of dust that floated in the room. He wondered if each band of light carried with it its own set of dreams and its own set of realities.

"This is the one I want," he said proudly to the man, who smiled approvingly. He took the ring back and polished it with a fine cloth, not unlike one you'd shine your shoes with. He held it up in the light to admire it as Jack had done and smiled. Jack knew the man was simply trying to drive up the price but he didn't care. It was a beautiful ring and certainly by Sudanese standards, Jack was a very wealthy man.

Jack stood up and asked the man how much money he wanted. The man started speaking rapidly and continued polishing the ring. Jack was in a hurry and so he made sure they came to a price quickly. He peeled off several large bills and the man's eyes widened. He placed them in the palm of the man's hand, put the ring in his pocket, and then turned to leave. But he returned to give the man a little extra when he took notice of the tattered belongings by the entrance that represented this man's entire life's earnings.

The children the man shooed away were still outside and Jack gave the street vendor a few bills and instructed the man to cut up the entire slab of meat and distribute it among the children who were there. The man, tall and very black with a shaven head, took the money but protested about giving all the meat to the children so Jack waited around until the man did as he instructed.

"Come on, buddy. I didn't give you all that money for nothing. Get that knife out and start cutting this meat up now."

The man yelled something back that Jack did not understand but he refused to be intimidated. He stood there waiting for the man to do as he had asked. Jack fingered the ring in his pocket over and over again while he waited.

He knew exactly where he would get down on one knee and propose to Jenelle: the base of the St. Jude statue, the patron saint of impossible tasks and lost causes. He would wait until classes let out later that afternoon and it wouldn't matter if Cindy Lou was there clinging to her teacher's hand.

Jack would drop to a knee and Jenelle would have seen enough American movies to know immediately that he was about to ask for her hand in marriage.

"I love you Jenelle. I have loved you since the day I first laid my eyes on you. I want you to be my wife. I want to grow old with you. I want to walk hand-in-hand wearing matching windbreakers on the beach when we are both senior citizens. I want to take you on the Dragon Coaster at Rye Playland and take a ferry up the Hudson all the way to Poughkeepsie in the fall to watch the leaves changing color. I want to take you for the best hotdog you've ever tasted at Papaya King, where they toast the bun for you as well. I want to take you to the Rose Hill campus at Fordham University where Keating Hall looks like it belongs in some King Arthur movie. I want to take you to meet Old Man Dukes, Mikey Morgan, and the Sullivan boys. Of course, there are also the museums. My favorite is the Museum of Natural History. My dad and I would go in there and spend entire rainy Sunday afternoons staring at the exhibits. He liked the ancient artifacts while I preferred the dinosaur bones.

"We'll spend warm spring days at Shea Stadium cheering for the worst

team in baseball. In the summer we will wake early every Saturday and drive to Jones Beach or Robert Moses State Park as long as the green flies aren't biting. Then there's Broadway. We can get discounted tickets for all the shows at Times Square. Oh, the shows we'll see. Have you heard of 'Cats?' or 'Les Miserables?' They are supposed to be wonderful. We'll go together and discover the magic ourselves.

"What's that? You love me but you couldn't possibly leave Cindy Lou behind? Well, that's no problem, no problem at all. She has no one to take care of her, right? Why don't we adopt her? We'll be an instant family. Oh, I know what you're thinking, but people back home are much more accepting of inter-racial couples these days. That wouldn't be an issue at all.

"So, Jenelle, what do you say? Will you make me the happiest guy this side of the Bronx and marry me?"

It will be perfect, especially when she accepts.

More and more children arrived and the man slowly sharpened his knife and finally started carving and serving until all the man's food was gone. Some adults wandered over as well to locate the founder of this charity and some started asking Jack for money or food. Others tried to take food from the children and for the first time in Africa Jack started feeling uncomfortable. He wanted to help these people but at the same time he knew that if he gave one person even just a dollar he would likely be overrun with people in a matter of moments. Instead, Jack focused his attention on the food vendor and every once in a while he shook his head no at someone who came up begging. Jack started to regret having stopped to commit this kind act of feeding the children.

The street vendor kept shaking his head and Jack could practically read his mind about good food being wasted on begging street children.

But despite the attitude, the man continued as instructed. Then Jack gave him another bill and the man was extremely grateful. He turned off the kerosene, waved his hands at the grill, and started packing up for the day. Never had he been able to leave his post so early, and with such a profit.

The jeweler was also leaving, hauling the large balled-up sack of his belongings. He waved at Jack and headed down the street, heading south.

FIFTEEN

WHEN JACK FINALLY arrived at the airport, which was eerily quiet, Matthew sprung up from a chair near the entrance of the locked gate to greet him.

"I have been waiting for you," he said as he clumsily tried forcing several different keys into the huge padlock to let Jack onto the property.

"What is it, Matthew?" Jack looked around and saw no one. "It's very quiet here today, no?"

"Just about everyone else is gone. I did not want to leave without first seeing you and saying goodbye."

"Leave? I thought you were going to stay and watch over your family members."

"They left last night for the border to meet up with some of my aunts and uncles who decided to leave as well. I think they plan to go to Ethiopia. Things have started happening. I met a friend of mine in town this morning who told me that they have already started raping the women of Jabra."

Jack's heart tightened at those words and he reached into his pocket to feel the ring he had purchased.

"I thought everything was still weeks away." Jack tried changing the truth with his words.

"Did you not hear the Antonovs last night?" Matthew's voice started rising in anger at the invaders. "Some of them are already here doing what they are doing and so I have decided to join my brothers and fight. I will be a member of the SPLA and we will fight these devils until the end."

Jack absorbed the words and admired Matthew's heart but at the same time he wondered how they could go eagerly against an enemy that had superior weaponry, manpower, and Russian bombers.

"Wow, Matthew. I don't know what to say. I am truly sorry this is happening to you and your people."

"You are a kind man, Mr. Hopkins," he said over Jack's automatic protestation to call him Jack. "I have enjoyed my time working here very much. Maybe one day we will meet again, if not here then maybe someplace better, someplace finer."

He then lifted the plain wooden cross on a thin leather strap from around his neck and placed it around Jack's.

"Here. Jesus taught to love our enemies and pray for those who persecute us. But I have chosen to fight instead," Matthew said, shaking his head sadly. "I don't think it would be right to shoot at men while I have this around my neck. Please, I want you to wear it. May His love protect you and serve as a reminder of better times here. May His love work on eliminating the anger and hatred of those that hurt and kill my people. Maybe you can remember to pray for me when you can."

"Yes, of course. I will."

The cross was around his neck before Jack could offer any sort of fuss. He held it in his hands and thanked Matthew for his generosity.

The two men embraced and Jack knew that he would never see Matthew again, anywhere.

"Matthew, please be careful."

The young man started walking away through the gate and then smiled looking back over his shoulder.

"Let's go Mets."

There were still about five or six men left working and Jack instructed them to abandon all duties now except security. Of course they were unarmed but someone looking to do mischief would think twice after seeing half a dozen people at a locked gate. He also knew that the men would be gone at the first sign of trouble. The airport was definitely not worth dying for.

From his office, where Jack contemplated his next move, he could see George's plane circle once then come in smoothly, landing on the runway. It gave him some peace of mind to see the little donkey again.

Jack had spent the previous hour consolidating paperwork and supplies. Five packed suitcases, four with clothing and one with souvenirs for the old gang in the Bronx, were propped against the back wall. The apartment only contained a few of the necessities Jack needed to keep it going.

Eager to see his friend and desperate for news, Jack ran out to greet him.

"Jack, I was thinking we still had about three or four more weeks before we had to leave for good, but things are happening fast. It's already started and reports are that they are worse than we anticipated."

The words stung Jack's ears and it took him a moment to process what George was trying to say.

"You mean they will be in Jabra soon?"

"No, I mean they are already in Jabra." George climbed down off the plane and proceeded to tie everything down. "Jack, I mean to fly out of here today. I mean for good. My only responsibility left is to get you to safety. But I don't think I can do that after today."

Jack nodded.

"Can you be ready in, say, three hours?"

He nodded again.

"Jack, are you alright?"

"Yeah, yeah," he whispered then cleared his voice, reaching into his pocket to feel the ring. "Three hours?"

"Yes. Is that going to be a problem? No one has flown in for days, have they?"

"No, no. It's not that. Let me ask you something." The two men were now walking in toward the main building where George would freshen up and maybe be able to sneak in an hour of sleep before taking off again. He stretched his long arms way up over his head as they walked.

"What is it?"

"Would there be room on the plane for Jenelle?"

"Why, you sly old dog," George laughed a great big old belly laugh, pulling back his long white hair. "Sure there is, as long as she's got the right paperwork. Everyone is cracking down now about taking Sudanese refugees. They will lock me up for human trafficking and a litany of other charges, confiscate my aircraft, and send her right back here. No one gets served doing something like that at a time like this."

"I'm sure she has papers," he lied, not knowing at all whether she did. "I'm pretty confident that she's done some traveling." He tried thinking hard whether she had ever mentioned leaving the country for any reason, whether for school, training, or pleasure.

They felt the ground shaking before hearing the two far-off explosions that interrupted the conversation. The ground continued to rumble beneath their feet. The trembling and the low roaring lasted for nearly a minute. For the first time Jack noticed dark black smoke rising from dozens of locations in the city and knew immediately that they could not all be from the bombs.

"Antonovs," George said, shaking his head. "Those sounded like they dumped their payload at the north edge of the town. I don't get it. This would be a decent town for them to have. I'm not sure the plan is to bomb it entirely. Maybe they were just getting rid of their ordinances before going back. Let's just hope they don't decide to start putting holes in this runway, at least not until after we take off. The South Sudanese have no fighter planes or anything like that here. Once we're up in the air I don't care what they do to it."

Jack didn't care to hear as much about the Antonovs as he did about the mayhem everyone else was worried about.

"What exactly have you heard, you know, about what is happening, about what they are doing?" He strained his neck to look up at George and make eye contact. "Is it just bombs for now or more?"

"The long and short, plain and simple of it is that villages are being wiped out. They are making them disappear, taking them right off the map, burning them to the ground, and eliminating the population," George said. "I spoke with someone who said he heard that they had chained dozens of people together in one village and set them on fire. I heard that observers with some human rights group or even the African Union took photographs of the remains, just charred skeletons, still smoking, all chained together at the ankles. People who leave proof of atrocities without care that the world would see them either truly believe what they are doing is right or are the worst kind of barbarian."

Jack clutched his head as George's words seem to build in volume once inside it.

"These animals are using rape as a weapon," George continued. "They are trying to limit the news that leaves the country. They have taken down all the radio stations except for the state-sponsored station. But you can't keep atrocities like this a secret for long. I'm sure once our government hears about this they will get involved. The United Nations will be forced to do something as well. There is no way we are going to sit back and let this happen."

Jack nodded in agreement, wanting to but unable to speak, and wondered how many villages would disappear before that happened.

"I'll be back," he finally muttered. "Wait for me. I need to go get Jenelle at the school."

"Jack," George reached out and grabbed him by the shoulder, forcing him to turn around. "I'm leaving in three hours."

"I know."

"I'm serious,' he reached out again and held Jack in place in order to look him in the eye. "Whether you're on the plane or not I am getting out of here in three hours. Understand?"

"Yeah, I know," Jack said not able to mask the frustration of being spoken to like a child. "I've got it."

Jack walked away slightly resenting George's tone.

What was he trying to imply? Was he saying that Jenelle will not want to come and I'll spend hours trying to convince her? That girl loves me. It will be terrific, if not altogether romantic. Of course with bombs falling nearby, I may have to cut short my proposal speech.

He chuckled to himself.

The air was very still and extremely hot and Jack felt as if he couldn't pull enough oxygen into his lungs. It wasn't so much like asthma. It felt more like walking into greasy Nick's Pizza place on Gun Hill Road in the Bronx in the middle of a sweltering August day and just getting smacked in the face by the heat from the ovens. He pursed his lips into a circle to breathe, fooling himself that he would get more and cooler air into his lungs that way.

Jack had a better understanding of George's words when he left the immediate typically quiet neighborhood surrounding the airport and found himself in the center of town at midday, only a few hours after he passed through earlier.

There was no one anywhere.

He stopped in the middle of the square, where the spice vendors typically set up their colorful goods in baskets perfectly aligned. It looked as if a bulldozer had gone through and changed the entire landscape. Several booths and stores were charred black and still smoking. Others were completely destroyed, pulled apart and smashed, perhaps by large sledgehammers.

Jack lost his breath at the horrible site. Only a few hours earlier there had been people shopping and performing their day-to-day activities. One vendor had even taken him by the arm to try and get him into his shop.

Someone or some group had come in and deliberately destroyed everything these people had worked for, what they stood for.

Jenelle!

He started running, jumping over wooden beams and smoking sheets of wood that used to hold the marketplace together. There was no one around, giving Jack the sensation of being in some apocalyptic dream. Not seeing any sign of life— not even a bird overhead or a hornet darting in and around the shadows—Jack wondered if the vendors and merchants had enough time to at least pack their goods and take them or whether they were stolen, looted by the invaders.

Hopefully they all just decided to pack up and go.

All the fires seemed to be out, except for one, which he could still hear sparking and flickering up around the corner from where he would buy his nightly *baseema* for him and Ahmed to share.

He ran faster toward the corner to see what was burning when he was stopped in his tracks by the jolt of rifles being fired.

Blam! Blam!

He clutched his heart and held his breath knowing that one more step would likely get him killed. He looked down and could see that the sudden stop had forced him to twist his knee in an awkward position and it was already swelling up.

Again the rifles went off—*Blam! Blam!*—and Jack jumped as if being awoken from one of those falling nightmares that jar you to reality in that one split-second before you make impact. This time he gasped out loud before quickly cupping his hand over his mouth and could not help but to peek around the corner and gaze upon the worst thing he had ever seen.

There were two of them, boys really, not older than 15 or 16, firing their rifles into a massive heap of burning bodies. There were wearing shorts and sandals with military-styled jackets. They laughed at how poorly they shot, taking turns announcing their targets before taking aim.

Jack crouched down and through the visible heat, smoke, and fire he could make out some of the faces of those in the blaze. He even recognized some from his daily walks from the airport to the school. He stared and there was some relief when he recognized no one from the school.

His heart was beating so loudly and he was breathing so heavily that he was sure the two government soldiers would hear him and add him to the 10-foot-high pile of corpses.

A ragged, rusted jeep rambled down the street noisily toward them and an older man, wearing military clothes yelled at them angrily is short staccato sounds. He waved his ancient-looking rifle high over his head and continued barking at them. The two boys put their guns down sheepishly and got into the back of the jeep that sped off around the burning funeral pyre.

Jack waited several minutes to make sure they were not returning before he slunk out from behind the corner and took in fully the small mountain of burning people before him. There was still no wind and the smoke rose straight overhead.

He fell to his knees and wept, shaking his head no. This can't be real. People just don't do things like this. He was thankful not to see any chains and that it appeared as if they had already been slaughtered before being set ablaze.

Finally he found the strength to stand and touch the ring in his pocket. It felt tiny and warm and it was the only thing that kept him focused enough to actually get up and not allow him to fall completely to pieces.

My God, please let Jenelle be alright.

He walked slowly past, so close that the heat singed the hairs on his left forearm, staring into the pile and fully expecting to wake up at any moment from this horrendous nightmare.

But much to Jack's dismay, if not his surprise, the waking moment never came and he continued on, no longer running but sticking to the shadows, moving slowly toward his destination.

SIXTEEN

THE WALK TO the campus of St. Jude's Catholic School was as scary as anything Jack ever dreamed of doing. The rambling, rusting jeep continued racing in and out of the alleyways searching for more potential victims. The riders had a crazed, sadistic look in their bloodshot and bulging eyes and sporadically shot their rifles into the air and laughed heartily.

Every time they passed, Jack was lucky enough to be close to a collapsed wall or overturned table that he could duck behind. The jeep was loud enough that it gave him ample warning to hide. It was all he could do to keep from throwing up every time he heard them pass.

Finally after an excruciating 33-minute walk for what should have lasted only 10 minutes, Jack found himself on the short, winding pathway leading to the school. The path was cool, covered almost entirely by tall palm trees used for their oil by some of the school's neighbors. Jack suddenly felt safe, like the comfort that comes with seeing the first familiar landmark near home after a long, exhausting trip. He took a deep breath with his hands on his knees then continued up the pathway quickly. It was one of the few hills he had seen since being in Sudan.

By the time he had neared the top of the path, he half expected to hear the children playing basketball or one of their many chasing and hiding games. He expected to hear Jenelle imploring the children to calm down or to take their seats.

But he heard none of that.

Maybe they are in mass. Yes, that's why it's so quiet. It's a perfect time to pray, to ask for God's help.

But the first thing Jack saw was the makeshift church with

outdoor altar and there was no one there. Like the town below, there was no sound, no sign of life.

He walked slowly toward the altar and the classroom to the far end of the campus waiting, hoping to hear Jenelle's familiar voice chastising him for waiting so long to get her out of this place. But the only sound was that of his own breathing.

Then he spotted something he did not immediately recognize. It was a brightly-colored green fabric fluttering lightly on the ground behind the altar and Jack ran over to see Fr. Nguyen's lifeless body. He was wearing full vestments and smeared with dried blood where the bullets ripped his flesh. At his feet was one of the younger children, his stiff little arms still clinging to Fr. Nguyen's right leg.

Jack lost his breath and fell to the ground, his tears bouncing on the hard, dry red clay.

"He was ready to give mass," Jack gasped aloud, to no one in particular. "This man did not have a mean bone in his body. He was a man of God. He sacrificed his entire life just to help others."

Then he stood defiantly, but rose too quickly and nearly passed out from being light-headed.

"What kind of people would kill a priest?" he screamed, with large tears now welled up in his eyes refusing to be released and his nose running. "He was here to help teach your children."

Jack whirled around pointing at the air around him. A palm frond came tumbling down from one of the trees and Jack spun quickly to face it. The tears made everything blurry.

"He was here to help make your country better, not his. Why would you do this? He was just gentle, that's all, just a gentle, gentle person and you murdered him."

Dizzy from whirling in circles and screaming, Jack collapsed on the ground next to the fallen priest and little boy.

"And who kills a child?" he whispered, having no energy left to speak, and a deathly sleep came over him and he had to fight not passing out. He stroked the little boy's head. "This is no revolution. This is no government action. This is murder."

He crawled up to Fr. Nguyen's face and was surprised at how peaceful he looked despite his violent end. He put his hand on Fr. Nguyen's cheek. It was no longer warm.

"You survived the elements and being lost at sea for days, my friend, but you couldn't survive people."

He stood and was certain that Jenelle and the bulk of the children had made it into the nearby woods behind the classroom while Fr. Nguyen held off the killers for as long as he could.

She taught them to hide and pray.

Jack walked into the darkened classroom and it took a moment for his eyes to adjust. It was stifling in the room and he could see wafting particles of dust suspended indefinitely in the narrow streams of sunlight that were coming through the closed shutters behind Jenelle's desk.

The little benches and small plastic chairs with metal legs were in disarray. He continued on slowly to the front of the room, stepping over the chairs and books, not making a sound. Again the heaving of his chest increased and he could hear the blood rushing through the temples in his head. He rubbed his eyes and wished he could see better in the room. He was able to make out something on the ground by the teacher's desk. He stopped and peered trying to see what it was.

The classroom seemed so much larger in the dark.

He ran when he recognized Jenelle's black leather shoe and collapsed hysterically upon her body, kissing and hugging her as if somehow his love could bring her back to life.

Both her shirt and her long blue skirt had been ripped open. Her hair was no longer tucked neatly into the tight bun and there were bruises on her thighs and on her neck.

"Shh, shh," he said as he lifted her onto him, cradling her face, his tears falling onto her cheeks. "It's OK. I'm here now, my love. I'm here. These men can't do that to you again. They can't hurt you again. Oh God, I'm here now. God, God, God, please let me wake up, please God. I'm begging you, please; I'll do anything you want. Just please let me wake up. Let all of us wake up. Oh my Jenelle, my love."

He rocked back and forth weeping aloud, wailing, repeating her name over and over.

"Why did I wait?" he rebuked himself quietly. "Why didn't I come for you yesterday? Why did I wait so long?"

He kissed her mouth tenderly and was positive that he would never be able to stop crying.

He took the ring from his pocket and held it up in one of the streams of light just as he had done earlier. It was still beautiful and still made the streams of light dance through the stone. He closed his eyes and tried to smile before lifting her left hand gently and placing the ring onto her finger.

"There are so many things to say," he whispered to her. "This wasn't how it was supposed to go. You'd laugh if you knew how much I agonized over having this talk and how much I practiced it. Now I can't even remember one word of it, except the part where I tell you that you are the best thing in my life, that you have become the part of me that makes me a better person, smarter, funnier, more likeable, and friendlier. And, of course, the part where I tell you that I want to spend the rest of my life with you."

He kissed her again and stared lovingly at how the ring looked on her hand.

"Oh, Jenelle, I wanted you to meet Felicia, my cat, and Old Man Dukes and the rest of the boys. Boy, I could just about see the expression on their faces when they see me walk into that bar with the most beautiful girl they had ever seen. They would love you instantly. They would see how kind and how generous you are and most of all they would see how much you love me. I wanted to take you to Tony's Pier on City Island for fried shrimp and French fries. There is a little Mexican guy behind the counter who makes the best piña coladas in the Bronx.

"Oh, and how I wanted to take you to Shea Stadium. Maybe the cameras would have caught us kissing and embarrassed you totally by projecting it up on the giant scoreboard.

"I wanted to take you to the Empire State Building and to St. Patrick's Cathedral in the city. Oh, you should see how they do up New York City around Christmas. There is this giant crystal snowflake suspended over an intersection and then there are all the shop windows with their moving figures. And nothing, let me tell you, nothing at all beats going downtown to see the lighting of the tree at Rockefeller Center. You can even go ice skating there. You can't get much more Christmassy than that. Oh, Jenelle, I've already lived out the perfect life with you in my head, in my dreams."

Jack was startled by a muffled sound in the back of the room and he rose with a fury.

Can I be lucky enough to find one of these cowards still here? Oh, please let me be lucky enough to find one of these raping murderers still here, hiding like the cowards they are. Hmm? Did you hide when you saw me coming?

He grabbed one of the small hard plastic chairs used by the children in his left hand and walked a few feet from where he left Jenelle on the ground. He waited for a moment and there it was again!

The shuffling sound came from a thin supply cabinet at the rear of the classroom close to the door.

I'm coming for you. Are you ready to pay for what you did here?

The blood was boiling in his arms, chest, and head and he stood waiting outside the closet door for confirmation, for one more sound.

Something moved inside and Jack felt sick inside with anxiety and hatred. Something had broken deep inside him and its poison was spilling out.

I'm going to make you suffer for what you've done.

Jack raised the chair high up in the air with his left hand and clenched his teeth tightly. He reached for the loose wooden door handle with his right hand and placed it firmly between his fingers without making a single sound. He surveyed the classroom once to make sure no one was creeping up behind him. Then he counted to three slowly in his head before ripping the door open with all of his might and screaming fiercely.

He brought the chair down with all his might in a crushing, punishing blow and stopped it just before making contact with Cindy Lou and two little boys who stared at him wide-eyed. There were dried salty trails of tears on their cheeks.

Jack fell to his knees and sobbed loudly gathering the petrified children in his arms. They could barely move and seemed almost stiff with rigor mortis. They cried silently, stifling their sounds and limited their movements.

"Oh my God," he cried and laughed at the same time. "You're alive! You're OK. It's OK now, I'm not going to hurt you. I'm sorry."

For the first time since Jack had been in Africa, the skies darkened and it started to rain.

It came down very hard for only a few minutes and made everything smell fresh and clean. Jack hadn't realized until then just how much he missed the rain. It was the kind of downpour that hits you twice, the first on the way down and the second when it splashes back up off the ground. He hugged the children, not wanting to let them go, and even after the rain stopped the water dripped down rapidly from the sagging palm tree branches cutting narrow canals and ruts into the red clay.

"Thank God you are alive. Are there more? Are there more of you hiding?"

But the children were still too much in shock from what they had seen to answer. They stared at him blankly. The two boys looked like brothers with one looking about 10 years old in his face but he was very small and thin.

Jack stayed with them, comforting them until the last of the drops came down from the trees and the scorching sun made its return. The entire storm lasted less than 10 minutes.

"I'm not going to hurt you. No one is ever going to hurt you like that again. Do you understand? I'm going to take care of you. I am going to take you to a safe place. Can you understand me?"

The small, thin older boy nodded his head yes and Jack nodded and smiled.

"Good, good. Now listen. I have a plane waiting for us that's going to take us far away from here to a safe place where people do not do this to each other. Now, you two stay here for a few more minutes," he addressed the younger boy and Cindy Lou, then looked at the older boy. "Can you speak? We have something very important to do."

The boy breathed deeply and answered "yes."

"Come with me."

But as Jack stood to go, Cindy Lou clutched his leg tightly not letting him go.

Jack dropped to knees again and kissed her tenderly on her forehead and then atop her head.

"Oh, my little Cindy Lou," he tried speaking without crying. "No one has had the life you've had and seen the horrors that you have, my poor little baby. I know I don't have the right to ask you this because you have already used up more bravery than most grown men do in their entire lives. But I need you to be brave for just a little while longer. Can you do that? Can you do that for me? It will take only a little time and then we will go far away from here. What I need to do is very important to me."

She did not answer and Jack couldn't be sure she even understood a word but eventually she loosened her grip and sank back into the closet with the other little boy.

Then he turned to the older boy.

"I need your help. The quicker we do this, the quicker we can get to a safe place."

The boy nodded and started to cry.

"It's going to be alright," Jack tried to sound convincing and strong though his broken insides hurt like hell. "What is your name?"

"Raphael," the boy whispered and tried his best to stop crying.

"OK, Raphael, do you know if there are any shovels here on the grounds?"

The boy took off quickly, and Jack felt the ground in numerous places and was disappointed that the rain had not softened the ground up any more than it did. This was not going to be easy.

Raphael returned with two shovels and watched for a moment as Jack tried unsuccessfully to dig a grave in the hard earth by the statue of St. Jude. He reached out and touched Jack's arm.

"I know a better place," he said and led Jack to a small vegetable garden that was in the shade behind the small, modest office that doubled as Fr. Nguyen's sleeping quarters when he visited. There were only a few plants left and Jack and Raphael pulled them from the ground and threw them to the side. There were two huge mango trees, no longer dripping from the rain and the sun had moved behind the building giving it the shade.

Jack reached down and felt how soft the ground was.

"Raphael, this is perfect." He patted the boy on the shoulder.

The boy struggled to help him carry over Fr. Nguyen's body and the little boy who he died protecting. Then Jack took a deep breath told Raphael to wait there and went into the classroom alone to get Jenelle.

He knelt down beside her and kissed her face repeatedly.

"God, I'm trying to be angry with you but I can't be because I know how much she loved you. She wouldn't want me angry with you even though everything inside of me feels broken. Please God, love her back, please look after her now. Please never let her suffer again." Then he caressed her face. "I am so sorry, my love." He began crying once more and lifted her light body off the ground. Her arm dangled loosely and as he carried her the sunlight tore through the ring's stone and the beautiful light shot and danced majestically all over the school's courtyard.

SEVENTEEN

CINDY LOU CLUNG tightly to Jack's hand as they left the school grounds. He was completely dazed, exhausted. He noticed dozens, if not hundreds, of black vultures circling over the town ahead and shook his head.

They wouldn't be able to touch Jenelle.

Any and all evidence of the rain, fierce though brief, had long dried. The road before them looked as though it had not seen a drop of water in years. That's when Jack noticed how low in the sky the sun was and a pang of apprehension shot through his heart.

He wondered if there was any way George would still be waiting at the airport and how long past the three-hour window he had taken.

They stopped at the bottom of the hill and Jack knelt in front of them.

"Raphael," Jack patted the boy on his shoulder. "Do you know where the airport is?"

"The one owned by the British?" he answered in a very quiet voice.

"Yes, well kind of, it's owned by British investors, but yes. That is where we are going. The tricky part is that we are going to go there and we can't let anyone see us. There are bad people out there, as you know only too well. They want to hurt us. I'll need your help with the younger ones. We need to keep quiet and we need to make ourselves invisible."

The boy's eyes widened and he nodded. Jack wondered if it was a mistake to share this information with the children at all. The last thing he should have done was add any more anxiety for him but it was too late to take the words back now.

"If anything happens that forces us to separate or run, I want you and this other little boy to stick together and meet us at the airport. But you would need to be very careful that no one sees you and you must try and do it quickly. Do you understand?"

"Yes."

"OK, good. Do you know this other little boy at all?"

"Yes, he is my little brother."

"Perfect. What about your mom or dad. Have you got parents? Is there someone who might be looking for you to come home?"

"No, we lived at the school," the boy shook his head.

"OK, what is his name? Your brother?"

"Emmanuel. It means 'God is with us.' "

"Let's hope so."

Jack picked Cindy Lou up and was surprised to feel that she was as light as she was tiny. He reached down and held Emmanuel's hand, who in turn grabbed his brother's as they started into town. He knew it would be nothing short of a miracle if they made it to the airport and George's airplane was still there.

Things were quiet and smoky in the town and Jack figured that all the fires had gone out during the downpour. There were still a few traces of smoke rising, a few streets over, and he realized they must have been recently set. He didn't think any smoldering embers would have been able to reignite after the downpour.

They're still here.

But any thoughts of retribution were washed away by the need and the promise he made earlier to keep these children from further harm. Cindy Lou's arms were locked around his neck so rigidly that he did not have to support her weight at all. They stopped every few yards and Jack listened for gunshots or the distinguishable rattle of the jeep, or any other vehicle.

They passed the corner where only that morning Jack had purchased the ring he thought would forever change his life. He hadn't noticed that morning how close it was to the street vendor they started buying food from regularly once Jenelle had convinced him to try some of the street foods, specifically the sizzling meat on a stick.

"Now, isn't that yummy?"

"I do have to admit that it's pretty tasty," he said, not bothering to wipe away the juices from his lips or chin.

"See, you had nothing to worry about," and she playfully patted his belly. "The food is very safe for you to eat."

"Well, the only thing is—"

"What?" she smiled and her teeth were perfectly white.

"Well, I like to know what it is I'm eating. I'm funny that way," he raised his eyebrows.

"It's bird meat, some sort of bird."

Jack took another bite, raised his eyebrows and laughed loudly.

"Well, that's a start but could you narrow it down a little. I mean are we talking chicken here or pterodactyl?"

"Pterodactyls were not birds, Mr. Hopkins!" She covered her mouth to laugh and shook her head in mock disbelief. "Plus, you'd have to think that any pterodactyl meat would have gone bad by now. After all, it has been several million years."

Jack smiled.

"They weren't? Well, they had wings and they flew around. Where I come from that makes it a bird. So, if we can eliminate pterodactyls and other flying reptiles, then that narrows things down considerably. What about vulture meat?"

She laughed again.

"No, no I'm serious. You think I'm joking around because I'm just this charming, funny, dashingly handsome fellow who constantly makes you and the children laugh. But I am being totally serious."

"Vulture?"

"Vulture. Why not?"

"Jack, that's disgusting."

"They get a bad reputation. They are seriously one of the better birds out there. Look at the service they provide."

"Service? They are disgusting, vile-looking birds that feast on the dead."

"A-ha. You just made my point for me."

"What point?"

"Imagine how much more disease we'd have to worry about if vultures weren't around to take care of the dead. There would be bugs everywhere spreading bacteria and viruses to all of mankind. Vultures are like a free sanitation crew that keeps everything neat and tidy. An animal gets hit by a truck in the middle of the night and by the sun's first light they are hard at work clearing the road. Yes, I admit they may not be much to look at, but then again neither are chubby, middle-aged construction workers who would be forced to get rid of the carcasses."

"Well, I guess if you put it that way." She pursed her lips.

"But who would have ever known?" Jack took a big bite of the meat and had to keep his mouth open a bit to cool it off in his mouth.

"Ever known what?"

"Just how tasty and delicious they are. This is really good."

She playfully punched him in the gut.

"You are terrible. You love to get me, don't you."

"Not really, it's too easy," he smiled. "Plus, I've already got you."

They continued walking and Jack could not have been prouder of his tiny traveling companions. They had stopped crying, were quiet as falling snow, and kept up with him when he picked up the pace. Jack remembered the street where the massive funeral pyre had been and avoided it purposely. There were many more vultures in the sky.

Sticking to very narrow and little-used streets, Jack led the children to the airport as clandestinely as he knew how. They turned down one street, where there had been a sort of antique shop, and Jack knew right away that it had been a mistake.

There was broken glass and debris everywhere and every step sounded like thunder against the backdrop of the silent city. It slowed the walk considerably, but they maneuvered the broken glass, shattered plates, and hundreds of bullet casings with the deft and grace of Kung Fu masters walking on rice paper without leaving a mark.

Jack carried both Cindy Lou and Emmanuel during one stretch where there was simply no avoiding stepping on large pieces of mirror. Luckily, one of the Russian planes blared overhead at the same time and Jack was sure no one could have heard them.

But as they turned the corner out of their own personal minefield, Jack froze when he saw the Jeep stopped in the middle of the next street. He moved back slowly out of sight and pushed the children back against the cinder block wall of an unfinished structure. There were lots of houses and buildings at various stages of completion littered throughout the city. Someone explained to Jack when he first arrived that people build their homes in stages as they had money to afford building supplies and laborers. Many of the homes belonged to families whose fathers worked in Saudi Arabian oilfields or in South African copper mines. They would send money back to family and after expenses were met and bills paid, any leftover money would go buying rebar, blocks, sand, and cement.

He wondered how many never got finished.

Jack moved the children back into the unfinished home against the far wall inside the home where it was darkest and they all knelt down. A blue tarp fluttered above them though there was very little breeze. There were no soldiers with the jeep and Jack thought that perhaps it had broken down and the men left the area using another vehicle.

Cindy Lou began to tremble slightly and Jack kissed her atop her head.

"It's OK," he whispered. "There's probably no one there. We just want to be careful."

But as the final words escaped his lips, they could hear the crunching sound of shards of glass getting pulverized beneath a soldier's boot. They tensed and Jack held a finger to his lips though there was no real need to.

The crackling sound of the glass moved closer and there was absolutely no place for Jack and the children to go. Yet they moved backwards and would have squeezed into the cinder blocks if they were able. Jack slipped back on a cut piece of rebar, rolling it ever so slightly but making a noise nonetheless, and the soldier stopped immediately on the street. Raphael let out a little gasp.

Damn. Please do not come in here.

Cindy Lou began trembling again and Jack could see that she was crying. Emmanuel and Raphael were crying as well. Raphael's chest heaved up and down as he tried suppressing the tears.

They could hear the soldier moving again and the children became more panicked. They started trying to move but there was no place for them to go. Jack embraced them all tightly and closed his eyes to think of Jenelle.

"I'm teaching them to run and I'm teaching them to pray."

"I know," he answered. "But to me that sounds kind of helpless."

"Don't underestimate the power of prayer my love."

"But is saying the Hail Mary or Our Father really enough? I mean, shouldn't we then actually ask God for help? Should we beg him not to let anything bad happen or just to steer these people away from us?"

"I never like to ask God for anything too specific," she answered and smiled knowingly. Then she pointed upward with her index finger. "Trust me, He already knows what you need. He knows what you need even before you do. So I like to thank Him and praise Him."

"Even when things are not going that great?"

"Especially when things are not going that great. Have you ever thanked God for giving you the ability to see or hear or taste? Have you thanked him for your life or your friends or for the precious little time you had with your mother? Plus, I figure so many people are asking him for stuff that I'm sure it must be nice for him to hear a prayer every once in a while that is simply a 'thank you.'"

"How did you learn all this stuff?"

"I was just born wise." Jenelle raised her hand to cover her laugh, then reached over and kissed Jack on the cheek.

The soldier was stepping more carefully now and not making as much noise as before. His pace was slow and measured. If it had not rained they would likely have been able to hear every step whether there was glass strewn about or not.

"Children," Jack whispered urgently, "close your eyes with me for a moment. Do you know how to pray? Maybe the Hail Mary? After all, what son is capable of truly denying his mother's request?"

They nodded and started in unison.

"Hail Mary, full of grace,

The lord is with thee,

Blessed art thou among women

And blessed is the fruit of thy womb, Jesus."

The soldier was right outside the unfinished building and Jack could see his worn and muddied boots through the uneven streams of sunlight. He was debating whether to go in and search or to keep walking. The soldier listened for signs and sounds of life.

The solider took a step inside the structure and tried adjusting his eyes to the darkness. He lifted the tip of his rifle and it reflected sunlight up onto one of the walls. Jack held his breath as the rifle rose slowly and entered in, searching, poking in the darkness like the flickering of a snake's tongue.

It was at that exact moment when Jack became sure they would all soon be dead.

Please God, take these children into your arms peacefully. Please let it be quick. I know, I know I shouldn't ask for things, but I'm not asking for myself. I just don't want them to suffer. Welcome them, Lord, into your kingdom.

He kissed each of the children once on their foreheads and clenched his tearing eyes shut until they hurt. He recited the Hail Mary in his head over and over again. Like a machine-gun of prayer, the words came firing out of his brain in rapid-fire succession trying to vanquish any foe. The true miracle was that, as the words flew silently through his mind, Jack was no longer afraid.

He could not distinguish whether he recited the prayer a dozen times or five hundred times because he got so lost in the words and the pleading for the children that he totally lost track of reality. Maybe it had happened and this was the feeling that comes with death. But it stayed very quiet and the gunshots that never came finally caused him to open his eyes slowly, half expecting to be staring down the barrel of a gun or to see a bullet approaching in slow motion. But there was nothing.

No one.

The children's eyes opened once they felt Jack ease the pressure with which he was holding them.

The whir of the Jeep's engine trying to start startled them to attention once more, but soon the engine kicked over and the only sound was of the danger driving away. The dust from the tires lifted up and floated past them as they stayed crouching in the darkness.

EIGHTEEN

All sense of time was lost but Jack was certain of one thing as the sun lowered in the deep blue sky and they were within sight of the airport gates: he had taken more than three hours and there was no way George White would be waiting with that beautiful "little donkey."

Still, going to the airport was really the only option and maybe they were due for a miracle and George would be there.

From across an open field of four-foot-high elephant grass, Jack could see the gates firmly shut, chained, and locked. There was no one in sight and he was sure that his men had worked their last minute at Jabra International. He was only mildly surprised that it wasn't under military control yet, or at least didn't appear to be.

Maybe the government did not want to draw unneeded international attention and they knew the private airport was owned by foreign investors. Maybe it was that there was no resistance at all in this town and that the southern city of Juba, with a public airport and certain to have resistance fighters, would be a better place to land and launch the Antonovs from. In any event, the first miracle seemed to have taken place: the airport looked safe.

The only problem now was how to get inside.

Jack and the children ran single file crouched down low through the tall golden grass, stopping every 25 yards or so to listen for any sounds of danger. When there were none, they would stand slightly and continue on.

Finally they risked being seen by running the final 100 yards of cleared land to the front gate. Jack pulled but knew it was locked. He stood for a moment then started scrambling on his hands and knees around the bottom of the fence that encircled the 95 acres of the airport, reaching down to touch the bottom of the fence.

"I go around this thing picking up trash every single morning," he explained in a frantic voice to the children who looked at him as if her were crazy. "I know there is an opening. It has been on my 'to-do' list to fix ever since I noticed it. Maybe we can all squeeze through it. Come on, stay with me."

Not the quickly eclipsing seconds, nor the oppressive heat, nor his broken heart were capable of slowing Jack down as he scrambled on all fours like a caged gorilla desperately looking for a way out. He was manic and knew it, but he also knew that these children would end up dead if he could not get them to safety.

He pushed with his hands and kicked with his feet and knees at every single inch of fencing around the deserted airport, stopping only once for a second to catch his breath.

Raphael imitated him and started kicking at the fence on all fours as well. His little brother followed as well but realized that he was unable to keep up with them if he continued. Cindy Lou simply walked closely behind Jack, not sure what to make of this new game. There was no longer a fear of making too much noise and being discovered. That had gone out the window the minute they reached the sanctuary of the airport. The only fear now was to be on the wrong side of the fence when George's plane revved up and left Sudan without them—if he hadn't already.

Finally at the very opposite end from the airport gates, Jack kicked the fence and found the opening.

He laughed hysterically.

"Oh, my God, this is it," he yelled loudly to the children who looked like they were more than ready to wave the flag of permanent defeat. They were completely dehydrated, were covered in dirt and dust, and forever scarred by having witnessed their teacher get brutally raped and killed as well as seeing their only father figure, a gentle man from Viet Nam who spoke with a funny accent, get killed before their eyes. Yet they continued on.

Jack, moving with the quickness of a person who knew to avoid all-you-can-eat Chinese buffets, jumped to his backside and kicked at the fence with both feet. He held his legs there creating and holding an opening that the children, even the older and slightly larger Raphael, could quickly and easily scamper through like lizards.

No one was there to hold it for Jack, so using his hands to keep the sharp edges of fencing from his face, he struggled to get through. The jagged pieces of metal ripped his shirt and dug into the soft flesh of his belly. He slithered, snakelike, through the very small opening and the only significant injury was when a piece of metal fencing went deep down into his right thigh, causing him to cry out in pain.

"I'll need a tetanus shot for that I suppose." He laughed silently to himself, even as his shirt filled with blood. Then they started out for the administrative building and Jack was surprised at how badly he was limping. They were only about fifty yards into their walk across the steaming tarmac when Jack noticed Cindy Lou turn and look at him suddenly, urgently.

He stopped them all, put out his hand for them to be quiet, and listened.

She had heard it first, but now they all did. It was the sound of propellers churning loudly and rapidly. His heart leapt with joy and the pain was gone from his thigh.

"Follow me," Jack yelled to the children and then proceeded to run with all the strength he had left and with Cindy Lou still clinging to him with her arms around his neck. They needed to get up to and past the administrative building before they would be able to see George's plane.

"Oh, God, please let him wait. Please let him wait. I recognize that sound, it's George. It's definitely George. Do not fly away just yet."

Jack and Cindy Lou ran ahead of the two boys and Jack was sure they would turn the corner just as George's plane was lifting off the ground.

But there it was, revving, buzzing loudly with George still

outside the cockpit removing the wooden chocks from behind the plane's tires. He looked up in disbelief and threw his hands in the air as Jack fell to his knees in pure exhaustion. He reached into the plane to turn off the engines and ran over to greet Jack, who was on one knee trying to lift himself up.

"Jack! I thought you had bought the farm. Oh man, I am glad to see you. I was sure I would never see you again. I waited and waited. It's been more than six hours. You have no idea how many times I started that little plane over there to leave this place. But every time I did, I don't know, something just did not feel right. This was really it. It will be dark soon and I needed to be up in the air before nightfall."

"It's a miracle you are still here." Jack was badly out of breath and everything hurt.

"I heard a few more Antonovs drop their bombs and I kept seeing plumes of smoke rising up all over the place from the city. They destroyed this place in a matter of hours. What is it like out there?"

"It's a wasteland." Jack looked down and fought to keep from tearing up. It was the first moment he had to actually take in all that had happened that day and it was too much. He fell to his knees once more.

"Jack, I'm sorry. Do you need some water? Or better yet, I have a bottle of Gordon's Gin on the plane."

Jack shook his head no.

"Jenelle?" George asked already knowing the answer.

Jack shook his head no, this time raising his eyes to meet George's.

"Oh, my God, Jack. I'm so sorry." He looked over at the children. "So what's your plan exactly?"

"My plan?" he nearly laughed. "My plan is to get out of this hell hole as fast as we can. I have my bags packed in my office."

They walked toward the plane before stopping just outside the door.

"No, Jack. I mean with them." He pointed with his chin over

at the children who were crouching on the ground in a tight circle of three.

"I'm taking them out of here."

George stiffened and Jack sensed his hesitation immediately.

"They got papers?" George looked away and pretended to examine something on the wing. The sun was setting quickly and the heat finally started to let up slightly.

"Papers? George, do they look like they have papers?" He couldn't believe they were about to have this conversation. "They don't even have shoes for crying out loud."

"Jack." George turned slowly to look at him.

"George, don't even say it. Don't you even dare try to say it. Not after all we've been through." His voice shook with anger and felt that he was about to cry. "Not after what these children have been forced to see today. Not after all we had to do to get here. Those murderers are out there hunting people. These kids wouldn't last a minute out there. So don't you dare say it."

"Jack." He walked over and tried putting his hand on his friend's shoulder but Jack shirked him away. "Jack, you know very well I cannot take these children up onto that aircraft and out of this country, at least not without proper documentation. Come on. You know I can't."

"Can't or won't?"

Jack looked past him and got the children up onto their feet. He tried leading them up onto the stairs leading to the airplane's door but George walked over and blocked their path.

Jack sighed heavily.

"George, get out of the way and let these kids onto that plane."

"I'm sorry. I can't do that."

"Let me buy their way on. I have dozens and dozens of uncashed paychecks in my desk. Don't worry, they are drawn on a British bank. I'm wealthy now. Whatever you want, name your price."

"Come on Jack, it's not about money."

"George, are you going to make me beg you? Do you know what they have had to witness today?" His voice was cracking and shrieking. "They have absolutely no one left in the world. They are refugees in the town they were born in, the only town they have ever seen. Leaving them here is as bad as turning them over to those monsters out there."

"Jack," he said in the most soothing of tones he could muster. "They are not refugees yet, at least not technically, not as far as the international community is concerned. No one knows yet what is happening here. They've got a tight lid on the amount of information making its way out of this country. But you and I, we can leave here and tell the world what is going on. Let me walk you through what will happen if I attempt to take these kids out of here. The first thing is that wherever we land, the authorities will take the children—or anyone without papers for that matter—and detain them for a short period before sending them back here. They will then confiscate my aircraft, and trust me, I would never get it back from any of these surrounding countries around here. They're more crooked than a three-dollar bill. They don't operate on the same standards that you might be accustomed to. I've saved the best for last though. They will arrest you and I for human trafficking, yes, that's right, and judging from the ages of the children will likely accuse us of being pedophiles as well. Have you ever spent time in an Ethiopian jail cell, Jack? I haven't either and I have no intention of ever spending time in one. So, please, give these children some food, some blankets, wish them well, and let's get the hell out of here before the government starts landing planes here and we never even get the chance to leave."

Jack did not move from the landing of the stairs but he knew that George would never let the children on the plane. His mind was racing, trying to come up with some sort of "plan b."

"Leaving these children here is a death sentence, George. Don't you see that?"

"I do. It's a terrible time right now. I feel awful about it. It's not something I want to do. But we, I, have no choice."

"We always have a choice, George, always." Jack shook his head and came down off the stairs. "There is always a choice."

He walked down slowly from the plane to where the children were seated on the ground. They did not understand the conversation or the reasons why, but they understood that they would not be getting onto that airplane. Jack sat with them and immediately Cindy Lou jumped into his lap and put her arms around his neck.

George looked away and continued prepping the craft for flight. Finally, after several minutes of no movement by either side, he came down off the plane and crouched down near Jack. Again, he tried putting his hand on Jack's shoulder.

"Are you saying goodbye?"

"Yes."

"Good, we need to get going."

"No, I mean, I'm saying goodbye to you."

George shot up on his feet like a tightly coiled spring and pulled Jack up along with him.

"Jack, you can't be serious. What are you doing? Think about it."

"George, I am not leaving these children alone here to die." His words were icy.

"If you're bluffing, it's not going to work. There is no way I can take these children on the aircraft."

"This is no bluff, no game. I'm staying with them. I will take them to safety myself."

"Jack, there is no shame in leaving. And there is nothing noble about staying."

"Isn't there?"

"Not if it means you get killed and can't protect them anyway. You can do more good by living and telling the world what is happening."

Jack noticed that George would not look at the children directly. So he walked over and stood behind them.

"I am staying. I will get them to safety in Ethiopia or even

Kenya, anyplace where they are not raping women and slaughtering children."

That was the moment that George realized Jack was being serious. The sun was starting to set and he needed to get his plane up in the sky before long. He walked up onto his plane and came down holding a laminated map and a compass.

"Is there anything I can do to change your mind?" George tried sounding friendly and tender. "I wish you wouldn't do this."

Jack turned and was no longer angry at his friend.

"If I don't do this for these children, who will?"

"You're a better man than me."

"I know," Jack answered and both men laughed.

"Do you know how to use a compass?"

"Come on, George, do I look like the kind of person who knows how to start a campfire, use a compass, or how to pitch a tent? We didn't have the option of Boy Scouts where I grew up."

"Here, let me show you."

They walked over to the wing of the plane and George pulled two plastic Dellwood milk crates from the cabin for them to stand on. He laid the map open and put the compass down next to it.

"OK, this is where we are," George pointed to a blank part on the map northwest of Juba. It struck Jack that the town of Jabra was never even on this map and now it will never be on a map. It is gone, forever.

It also struck him that perhaps he was making a huge mistake, a deadly mistake. He began to have doubts. *Maybe the children would have a better chance of survival without me. What do I know of the land or how to get around without being seen?* A sick feeling rose in his stomach and reached the back of his throat and he wanted it to go away. He could hear George's voice but he wasn't able to make out any of his words. The fear rising up to the back of his throat tasted like acid.

"Jack, Jack, are you with me?" George scolded mildly.

"Yeah, I'm here. What was that last part again?"

George pointed at the map and explained how the compass always points north, making it simple to determine how to find southeast, which is where he needed to go.

"Remember, if you're facing north, as per the compass, then east is to your right."

"Got it."

Then he proceeded to point out sections of the map that he would avoid altogether, mainly busy roads and populated towns.

"Now at some point you're gonna have to cross the river," George said while rubbing his chin and tracing his finger up and down the Nile on the map. "Now, of course, we have to assume that the soldiers will have already taken control of these major crossing points. But these here," he pointed at spots on the river, "are only used by locals and have no strategic interest for them."

"What if we run into the good guys, the Sudanese army of the south?"

"They will probably take you and the children prisoner and try to turn them into child soldiers. The oldest one over there looks like he might be able to handle a small rifle. Your best bet will be to stick to the wooded areas and avoid people altogether."

"Once we get to the border?"

George had already folded up the map but reopened it once more.

"Jack, this trip will take you weeks, if not months."

The sick, acidic feeling rose in Jack again along with a deathly sleepiness. All he wanted to do was to crawl in his bed and close his eyes and not think of any of this. But he knew the second he closed his eyes he'd simply remember that he spent the bulk of his day burying the woman he loved, the one he planned to propose to that very day. Still, even with that knowledge, he had a difficult time keeping his eyes open even as George spoke.

"I will fly to Ethiopia and Kenya and let the NGO's, or non-government agencies, know what's going on. I'm sure that in no time they will start seeing people trickle over the border. They will likely set us some sort of refugee camp. I will distribute information about you and ask them to contact me. I will check every day until you make it across the border."

Jack yawned loudly.

He looked down and all three children had fallen asleep on the tarmac. He wished he could as well.

"OK, thanks, George." The sleepiness had evaporated any residue of hard feelings and Jack was resigned to the fact that this could very well be a suicide mission. Still, it wouldn't be right to die without first getting to sleep. That was all he could think of until George mentioned lions.

"Now, stay with me for just a little longer. You never know which snakes are poisonous so it's best not to mess with any at all. I saw a Black Mamba once and I wouldn't have been able to distinguish it from a simple Black Racer. They say one bite and you're done for."

"No need to worry about that," Jack yawned again. "I'm from the Bronx, so my snake-handling experience is very limited. I'd probably run the other way even I was sure it was 'only' a Black Racer, yech."

"OK, OK, that's good." George folded the map and handed it over along with the compass, which was much heavier than it looked. "Scorpions and any other bugs you don't recognize should be avoided as well."

"Once again, I'm from the Bronx where the roaches have their own area codes." He shook his head vigorously to keep awake.

"OK, good. I guess that's it. I need to get out of here and you need to go get a few hours of sleep in."

They hugged, and the kids, sensing an end to the conversation, began stirring from their sleep. George held onto Jack for a while and patted him on the back. He whispered another apology to him and offered some words of encouragement. Finally they let go and Jack started leading the kids back toward the administrative building where they would be able to sleep for a few hours in his office before hitting the road before sunup.

But the battery acid fear came rising up again with every step he took away from George and the plane. Every fiber in his body told him to turn around and get on that plane, that it wasn't too late, that he could sleep while George flew them to safety. But he continued walking, turning only when George called out a final time.

"Do you know about the lions?"

With that, Jack spun slowly on his heels and walked back toward George. They met halfway.

"Lions?"

"Yes, obviously you want to avoid them."

"Lions?"

"Jack, I'm being serious."

"Don't tell me there are tigers and bears also."

George tried masking his frustration.

"Jack, please listen to me. I don't know if this is some old wives tale or African folklore nonsense or what. But they say that if you start to hear a lion, never, ever run away. They say the only thing to do is to run toward the roar."

He realized the words sounded on the silly side as they came pouring out of his mouth.

"Sure, that makes a ton of sense." Jack started to turn back around.

'No, no, wait. I'm serious. The thinking is that if a lion has picked up your scent, he doesn't really need to see you to know where you are. He's already got you pegged. If you start running away from the roar, he will keep tracking you and then finally pounce on you without you ever having even seen him or where he was coming from. Plus, running away from the beast will only kick in his natural hunting instinct and it will attack in a heartbeat."

"Wait, how do we know it's a male lion," Jack laughed.

"I'm being serious. Come on, focus. They say if you run toward the roaring, or at least walk, you'll be able to always tell where it's coming from, pinpointing the lion's location."

"Why on earth would I want to pinpoint the lion's location?"

"So you can ultimately avoid him, or her. You'd have a much better chance at surviving if you know where the lion, or lioness, is at all times."

"I'd rather totally avoid that scenario entirely."

Jack yawned loudly again and this time added a roaring sound.

"Agreed. I guess I wouldn't worry much. The word is they prefer gazelles to humans any day of the week."

NINETEEN

JACK SET THE children up quietly and cozily on the carpeted floor of his office. He spread out some of the clothes he would not be taking with him for them to lay on. He remembered a moving blanket that was left behind by the contractors hired to construct the hamburger stand and found it easily enough and covered them with it.

The sun had already set and with the lights off in the building, it was very dark. Jack put on his miner's flashlight and went scouring for supplies while the children slept. He returned thirty minutes later with several rolls of toilet paper, two gallon containers filled with water, several bags of stale hamburger buns, four empty tin cans that once contained ketchup for the burgers, a few books of matches, and a spare flashlight with dying batteries. He spread the bounty out before him on his desk and decided to also take the letter opener.

The children slept soundly and Jack smiled sadly when he heard little Cindy Lou snore loudly. He hoped they were having sweet dreams.

It was closing in on 9 p.m. Jack had it all figured out. He would sleep for about three hours and they would leave the city at about midnight and travel until they were safely away from any towns or villages. Then they could properly rest and set out again. He had no way of knowing whether they would be able to travel in the daytime or whether they could only move under the cover of darkness. He didn't like the idea of moving through the woods at night but it beat the alternative of having the government soldiers find them.

He took off his shoes and leaned way back in his leather chair, propping his feet up on the desk. He was nearly delirious with sleep and the chair felt as good as the finest bed he ever slept in. His right hand was involuntarily trembling and he grabbed it with his left hand to stop the moving. He was asleep within moments and dreamt of Jenelle.

He was awakened back in his bed in the Bronx, in the apartment he was evicted from, by Felicia rubbing her furry face onto his.

"I don't know if I should be jealous of that cat or not."

Jack opened his eyes and Jenelle was in the kitchen making coffee, wearing a blue road Knicks jersey with the name 'King' on the back of it. She smiled at him. The orange trim was vibrant and it hurt to look at it. He couldn't remember where she had purchased the jersey and didn't know she was such a big Bernard King fan.

"Jenelle?"

"Yes."

"Is it really you?"

"Of course, silly boy. Who were you expecting?"

She poured two cups of coffee and walked over to the bed where she sat down on the edge. Jack reached and took the cup after propping himself on his elbow. It smelled strong and hot, like African coffee, and he took a careful sip after blowing on the side of the cup. He rubbed his eyes with his free hand.

"It's just that I, I don't know, I wasn't expecting this," he said. "Aren't you—?"

"Shh," she interrupted. "Let's not talk about that now. I'm here. Aren't you happy to see me?"

"Am I ever." He placed the coffee down on his night stand and reached over to kiss her. She felt real. "I don't understand."

"Stop trying to analyze or understand everything," she scolded him lightly. "Can't we enjoy the moment?"

They drank coffee and the traffic rumbled by outside their window on Bruckner Boulevard. Jack looked around the apartment, amazed that absolutely nothing had changed. There were even baseball caps stuffed into coffee mugs on the countertop. There was evidence of Jenelle everywhere from her shoes by the front door to the thin vase holding flowers atop the console television set.

"I love you and I'm glad you're here."

"I love you too, my precious Jack."

"What should we do today?" He swung his legs over the side of the bed to sit up next to her. He had never before felt so alive. "Maybe the Knicks have a home date at the Garden tonight? Bernard King will be playing."

"I think I'd like to be outdoors. It's so beautiful outside."

She walked over to the window and from his vantage point on the bed, Jack could see that the busy highway was gone. Everything was green and lush and he could see little Sudanese children kick a deflated soccer ball back and forth in the distance. There were a few mud huts, and he could see some of the older boys herding goats gently with long sticks and mothers out front sweeping with straw brooms. He thought it was strange but said nothing.

"Well, I suppose we could go to Central Park and take a rowboat out. Then maybe we can go to the Central Park Zoo. We haven't done that yet, have we?"

"That sounds lovely, Jack," she laughed. "I know how much you love those little baby elephants with the hairy heads."

She continued staring out the window. He walked over to her, sipping his coffee with each step, and Africa vanished and the highway reappeared as he neared. It was loud and roaring by the time he put his arm around her by the fire escape. Felicia climbed up onto the window sill.

"That's strange."

"What is?"

"Nothing." He smiled and hugged her tightly, suddenly realizing that this might not be as it seemed. She felt differently but he wanted desperately to keep things as they were. "I don't know if I have ever been so happy."

"Then stop worrying about every little thing," she said. "I'm here with you now."

"You are real, aren't you?"

"Yes. I'll always be with you, right here." She placed her hand over his heart.

"Right here?"

She nodded.

"Here in my heart and nowhere else because you are, you know, you're—" He couldn't bring himself to say the word.

"I wish you would stop with that talk."

Things began to change as he considered her words and a deep, thick sadness entered his heart, making him ill. The orange on the basketball jersey began to fade and things looked dingier, gray, in the apartment. The flowers were gone as were the shoes by the door and his heart began to ache. He turned around to look out the window and the sun had vanished completely and the sky was sad and dark like it was right before the snow.

From the corner of his eye he saw something or someone scurry across the living room floor to the bedroom or the closet. He couldn't be sure. There was a muffled sound overhead, like the roar of a wild animal and Jack looked up. There was a slight thin, winding crack in the ceiling and a fine stream of plaster began falling. Some of the dust and sand landed on his face and he had to spit some out of his mouth. It tasted badly. Everything was deteriorating.

Jenelle looked down and was now wearing the blue dress that he buried her in. She said nothing. A sick feeling came into Jack's throat and he wished that he hadn't kept pressing the issue and ruined everything. Just a few moments earlier it had been perfect. But now it was destroyed forever. He knew that.

The lion roared again but this time sounded as if he was in the apartment. It was so loud that it hurt Jack's entire face and caused the wall to crack behind Jenelle. This rip in the plaster was wide and looked as if someone had taken a side in each hand and just pulled it apart.

The child scurried from the back room to Jenelle's arms. It was Cindy Lou and she cowered behind her teacher's dress.

"Come, it's OK," she called out over the lion's terrifying grumbling, and Raphael and Emmanuel came running over to her as well. She held them tightly and wept as she comforted them.

Jack tried to walk toward them but the lion's roars caused the ground to shake beneath their feet and he fell to the ground.

"Do not underestimate them, my love. They will do everything they can to rip you apart, you know."

"Who? Not the children?"

*"No, silly Jack. The lions. They want you dead and the children too."
Then she turned toward a dark corner in the room as the roaring moved
closer. "Stay! You have no power here. Now go!"*

*She held up her hand, and it was sunny once more outside and the light
came in and reflected brilliantly through and off her engagement ring. There
was no more roaring and the danger was gone.*

*"Jack, you must listen to me carefully. Trust no one right now. They will
do whatever they can to rip you apart and the children too. They are against
the notion of life. Trust in God and in the love you hold for me."*

He began to weep.

*"You've got to be strong for the children and for my sake. There are more
people counting on you than you know. Please never give up until they are
safe and you are safe right back in the states where you belong."*

*"I wanted to show you so many things here. I wish I hadn't ruined the
dream."*

*"You couldn't ruin anything. How could you even think that? You're
my wonderful Jack. And you will still get to show me everything you hold in
your heart for me."*

*He smiled—not wanting to disappoint her—but could not stop the sick
feeling of despair that was deep inside him. Despite her words to the contrary,
he still blamed himself for how the dream turned badly, and he wished above
anything else that he could make it all go back.*

*"I will love you always, my Jack. You are the best person I have ever
met. You are truthful and noble and I will be with you always until the end
of time."*

Jack's heart was breaking once more.

"I never got to ask you to marry me."

"I already have."

Jack woke with a start and though it was pitch black in and out
of the office, he knew that he had slept much longer than three
hours. Feeling very unhappy at having overslept, he scrambled in
the darkness to find a light and his watch. He was incredibly
groggy and knocked several things from off his desk while
searching.

He clicked on his flashlight and he felt sick to see that it was after two in the morning. Making matters worse, he felt no better after the sleep and desperately wanted to close his eyes and try to find Jenelle again. He was still deathly tired and his temples throbbed as if he had spent the night drinking.

"I don't even have coffee to make," he muttered and wished he at least had some chewing gum to get rid of his morning dragon breath. "This is not going to be pretty."

He stood slowly from the chair and stretched himself awake before rousing the children.

TWENTY

They walked slowly, sleepily in the darkness and shivered themselves warm.

They were no more than a few miles outside of Jabra by the time the sun came up, and Jack could still see rising pillars of smoke from the burning town behind them. They stuck very close to the main road leading south on walking trails barely visible in the thick vegetation. There was never any sense of anticipation or novelty at going on this road trip. This was only about one thing: survival.

Jack carried Cindy Lou until he could no longer and placed her down gently to walk sluggishly alongside Emmanuel. Raphael kept pace with Jack and was good about finding walking sticks. Earlier Jack had given him the sandals Ahmed had made for him and although they were several sizes too big, the boy wore them proudly. He tried explaining to Jack that nobody had ever given him a gift in his entire life but he wasn't sure Jack understood.

Jack barely used the compass that first day, checking it two or three times only, as the road they paralleled was going in the direction they wanted. Only once was there a sense of danger as a long caravan of government trucks and soldiers barreled past. It was easy to hide in the thick brush until the last of the vehicles blurred by them.

They saw no one else for the duration of the day.

Jack was very proud that the children never asked, not once, to be able to stop and rest or for something to eat. They never even complained about the non-stop walking. When they stopped for the night they climbed deeper into the woods and completely out of sight from the road. Jack laid out the moving blanket and poured generous amounts of water that the children drank eagerly. As he watched them slurp it down, along with the hamburger buns he scavenged from the airport, he wished there was a way he could have taken more water.

They fell asleep easily but the nighttime air was cold at times and the ants and other biting insects never stopped feasting. They rose—eagerly escaping the insect-infested area where they slept—before the sun was up and restarted the journey. Their arms and faces were covered with bug bites, and Jack urged them not scratch but it was nearly impossible.

Midway through the second day, the path veered further away from the road and Jack continuously checked the compass. It was fine. The path was now heading southwest, away from the atrocities and the horrors, to a land of safety.

The path widened late in the afternoon and before Jack and the children had a chance to seek cover, they found themselves walking with dozens of other south Sudanese refugees fleeing their own land. Many of them were boys, walking barefoot, with dead looks in their faces. The majority of them were very thin, sickly thin. One boy, who looked as if he had not eaten in weeks, looked especially pathetic. His head looked too big for his body and his neck hardly seemed able to support it. His ribs were visible and there was a yellow crust covering one of his eyes.

The fellow travelers approached them only once to see if Jack and the young children had any food to spare. But they did not and so they all kept walking in silence. Jack suffered through the painful blisters he could feel developing and swelling on his feet. He and Emmanuel were the only two walkers lucky enough to wear shoes. Still, a hot soak or an oatmeal bath would be wonderful and soothing he thought, and before he could force the thought from his mind, other luxuries popped in like cold beer and a day at the ballpark or bodysurfing the waves at Jones Beach or playing basketball down in the schoolyard.

He tried not to think of Jenelle.

That night Jack built a small fire to keep warm and to keep the bugs away. There were several little campfires lit and some of the other travelling boys cooked up little bits of cassava root or rice. Jack was rationing the bread so it would last a few more days but he wished there was some protein to go with it. The bread was hard, like a cracker, and the crumbs that fell from the children's mouths were scooped up fervently by some of the other boys who noticed Jack and the kids eating.

There was only enough bread for one more day of travelling and Jack knew there wasn't enough for these other children. Still, watching them scoop up tiny crumbs of stale bread from the dirt and greedily put them into their mouths made him cry bitterly. He slept atop the backpack of meager supplies and when he finally got to sleep he dreamt of Jenelle.

He lay there for a long time trying to get to sleep. He thought they had walked many miles over the last two days but the looks of hopelessness on the other children's faces told him they had not yet made a dent in the journey.

This dream was more like watching a movie than an actual dream. It was fuzzy and surreal, like a flashback scene in a romantic movie. The only thing missing were the crashing waves in the background. He remembered no talking or anything else really—other than her smile—when he woke. Just that he had dreamt of her and while it was still dark he pulled her photo from his bag and stared at it in the darkness for a little while until it was time to wake the children and restart the voyage.

They each drank a small amount of water before the sun was up and then began walking once more.

The third day was the worst of the journey so far. The trail led out to open areas and then vanished completely leaving them to create their own walking path in the wilderness. There was high grass, thick brush, thorny bushes, and even swampy areas to maneuver through that morning. They lost sight of the other refugees early on and Jack continuously worried that he was going in circles.

Emmanuel and Cindy Lou were both losing strength and walking much slower than they had the first two days. Of course, they all had to walk very slowly when the ground turned from dry to muddy to a swamp.

Jack picked up both of the little children and worried that the extra weight would sink him down permanently into the mud.

"No! Mr. Jack, look down!" Raphael called.

Jack did and there were half dozen snakes sunning themselves on the one stretch of high ground he was about to step. One coiled up immediately and struck out at Jack's foot but did not penetrate his shoe.

"Oh, my God," Jack said loudly. "Let's back up slowly away from here."

He stepped back and the snake struck again, getting stuck for a moment on the rubber around Jack's shoe. A second snake lunged higher and barely missed his pants. Cindy Lou began crying loudly.

They backed up, sloshing into knee-deep pools of water behind them, and eventually the snakes stopped pursuing them. It didn't make Jack feel much better to be walking so deeply in water that might have other exotic, strange, and dangerous critters swimming or floating around as well. But at least nothing was actively attacking him.

"I don't know if those were Black Mambas, Raphael, but man, I think you just really saved me, saved all of us really."

The boy said they were indeed Black Mambas and Jack took him at his word. It made the child feel proud that Jack acknowledged his help.

"If you want, I can look out for dangerous animals that might do us harm," he said once they were out of the water.

"I think that would be a perfect job for you, Raphael. It suits you just fine."

Jack smiled at the child but felt increasingly angst-ridden about their chances of making it through this. There seemed to be no end to the journey coming any time soon and he was tired, hungry, lonely, and feelings of desolation started creeping up into his heart.

The sun was incredibly close and hot that afternoon and they had to stop several times in what little shade they could find just to try and recoup some of their energy. Jack considered sleeping during the searing heat of the day and travelling by night but even though he had a small flashlight, he decided it would be too dark, too treacherous to do.

That afternoon they came across a small abandoned village where little plots of land had been raided by soldiers or refugees or both to take what little this land would yield. But Raphael, empowered by his new position, walked up and down the short rows of upturned plants looking for anything they could use for food.

Jack stayed in the shade of a large Acacia tree and let the little ones sleep in his arms. He could have slept too. Even though there was no movement in the air at all, the shade gave the illusion of a breeze and Jack had to fight off the coming sleep. He checked his compass a few times, ignoring the churning of his stomach, and it seemed as if they were still headed in the right direction.

A little while later, Raphael returned with a wide smile on his face. Jack had never seen the boy smile and it took away his sleepiness and gave him life. He stood to meet the boy who was bounding toward them with his hands full.

"What have you got there?"

"Lunch," he smiled. "I have found us lunch."

The boy explained that he went through all 24 of the small houses and found enough spilled grains of rice on the ground in each to fill half of an empty tin can he held. Then, going through the fields, he found several very small cassava roots that were likely too small when the earlier scavengers pillaged the land.

Jack made a small fire, allowing the younger children to continue sleeping, and happily prepared a tiny dish of rice and the starchy root vegetable. Raphael showed him how to mash the cassava once it was soft enough to mix with the little bit of rice. There was enough for about two spoonfuls of food for each of them.

The vegetable was bitter and tasted like the ground but it was life-giving and something different from the stale bread they had eaten for the last few days. They welcomed it happily and that tiny amount of food was enough to get the young ones going again.

"You are really an invaluable part of this team, Raphael," Jack told him after they were done eating. "I think tomorrow I will put you on the task of finding water for us."

The boy stood and pumped his chest out. That's when the first bullet went flying just past Raphael's head and into the tree where they rested. Jack was startled by the sound of the flying bullet and the "thwack" against the tree a few inches above his own head but it took a few seconds to register that someone was shooting at them.

"Thwack."

A second bullet struck the tree and Jack threw the children down on the ground. Lying there, he scrambled to shove everything back into his backpack. He could hear several people shouting but he never looked up. A third bullet whizzed past his ear so close that he could feel the air displaced followed by the intense heat.

"Run!" he yelled to Raphael, who was flat on the ground, paralyzed by fear. "They are coming for us. Please, Raphael, get up and run."

The boy did as he was told, running with all his might away from the shade of the acacia tree, through a small field of tall golden elephant grass and into a thick wooded area littered with many fallen trees and limbs on the ground. He tripped on a fallen branch he didn't see and tumbled hard onto the ground, skinning his right knee.

More bullets were fired and Jack was sure he'd be hit if he stood. But he also knew he was sure to be killed if he stayed there on the ground clutching the two little ones.

"OK, OK, I've got to do this," he said aloud. "Come on, Jack. OK, OK, on the count of three."

He breathed deeply and counted out loud as more bullets flew by over head, badly missing.

"Oh my God, they must be running this way. One— two— three—"

He stood with Cindy Lou and Emmanuel in his arms in one abrupt motion and started running through the elephant grass. It was easy to follow where Raphael had gone before them, leaving a trail of bent stalks of grass in his wake.

Jack knew it would be even easier for the soldiers to follow them as well. But nothing mattered now except to get to the cover of the brush. The children were silent and still in his arms and felt lighter than normal.

Jack made it to the edge of the forest and turned around to see how close the assailants were. He couldn't see them through the grass but could hear their shouting, which had grown much closer. Not able to get a visual on their targets, the soldiers stopped shooting, conserving their ammunition for now.

"Raphael, are you alright? Where are you?" He was certain the boy had not been shot. "Raphael."

He heard a muffled cry several yards deeper into the thicket and he climbed in further. His heart sank when he saw the boy on the ground clutching his bloody leg. He dropped down on the ground beside him.

"Did they get you?"

The boy shook his head no.

"I fell."

"Thank God. I thought they shot you. Thank you, thank you God. Can you walk? You must try. They are getting closer. We've got to get into this mess of trees and hide. Try and stand."

They could hear the taunts of the soldiers.

The boy let out a muffled yelp of pain as he stood. The outer layer of skin was completely gone from the knee leaving behind a soft, exposed mass of extremely sensitive flesh. Blood dripped slowly down Raphael's leg and he started to cry.

"We'll clean that up," Jack assured him. "But right now I need you to muster up even more courage than you've shown. And believe me, Raphael, you are absolutely the bravest person I have ever met. There is no shame in crying, no shame at all. I feel like crying right now as well. But I look so ugly when I cry that I'm afraid I might frighten the young children."

The child tried to smile through his pain.

"I know you've already used up a lifetime of bravery these last few days. Dig deep and see if there is a little bit more to get us all to safety."

He nodded and started limping deeper into the woods.

It was very thick with vines, trees, fallen limbs, and mosquitos. The bugs were everywhere, interrupted only by clouds and clouds of hungry gnats. Waving a hand to keep them away only seemed to spur their appetite further. It was very difficult to maneuver through and Jack hoped the terrain would deter the killers from following too deeply.

The bugs were relentless, coming in hordes, clouds of blood suckers punishing them for seeking refuge in their forest. Cindy Lou slapped at them but Emmanuel seemed too tired or weak and just let the insects exact their fee.

After walking and pushing their way through an extremely dense area, they climbed over a thick tree that had fallen and was soft with rot. Large mushrooms had sprouted all along where the trunk met the ground and they were wet with slime. The trunk was enormous and difficult to climb over. They finally made it over and Jack thought it would be a good place to hide. Plus, there was really no place further to go in the forest without a bulldozer. He placed Cindy Lou to his left, Emmanuel to his right, and Raphael to his far right.

They were all breathing heavy and Jack put his finger to his mouth. He also motioned to them not to slap at the mosquitos.

The area of forest in front of them was so closed up with growth that it looked impassable without heavy machinery or at least a machete. This was it. They could go no further, not really. The woods were silent. It was a fine place for a last stand, Jack thought.

They sat in silence, letting the bugs feast on them and waited. It was a strange bit of forest. There seemed to be no birds, no lizards, no life except for the weary travelers and the parasites. The canopy allowed very few streams of sunlight to come through. Otherwise the entire area was gray, like a stormy day.

A little while later the shouting started again, much closer than before.

"What are they saying?" Jack turned to Raphael.

The boy listened for a moment and his eyes dampened with tears.

"They say if I join them they will let you and the 'babies' leave unharmed."

"Join them?"

"They say, they say they want to make me a soldier. If I agree then you will be safe."

"Absolutely not. I will not allow that kind of sacrifice or trade. They must be nuts if they think I'd ever let you go to them."

"But, I could save my brother."

"No buts, Raphael. I, we, we will all save your brother. We will never give into them. They are murderous and evil. Now stop talking and keep hiding."

The boy smiled and closed his eyes.

Jack put his head back, not caring what crawled onto him from the soft, rotting tree trunk and tried hard to remember something Fr. Nguyen had said during mass.

"Better is one day in your courts than a thousand elsewhere; I would rather be a doorkeeper in the house of my God than dwell in the tents of the wicked."

Jack closed his eyes too and waited. He prayed silently to himself, rattling off the Hail Mary a few hundred times until he drifted off to sleep.

They woke sixteen hours later, as the sun rose again. The bugs and the soldiers were gone.

TWENTY ONE

BOTH CINDY LOU and Emmanuel could not walk on their own after the fourth day without food. Raphael did not speak and Jack became so lightheaded that everything seemed funny as they walked further into the valley of the shadow of death.

"Maybe we should stop and call a cab," he said as they sat and rested for a while on a large rock. The water they had found a day earlier kept them alive but was not agreeing with any of their digestive systems. "That water is cutting through me like a sack of belly-bombers from White Castle after a night of drinking. That's what Old Man Dukes would say anyhow. Lucky we still have some of this toilet paper."

He pointed at clouds and said they looked like some of his elementary school teachers, and then he would get sad thinking about Jenelle. Everything he saw was funny and just about everything reminded him of something back home. A fallen tree was a motorcycle, a rock was a tortoise, and the road sparkled with diamonds. The children were not listening and at some point Jack realized that he was making no sense. And like the person at a party who realizes they've had one too many he tried to keep his comments to himself.

That is, until he saw what reminded him of a small mud hut up ahead with a small plume of white smoke. He stared hard at it to see what it really was but couldn't make it out. He squinted and realized that he couldn't really focus on anything without it all being blurry. He put Cindy Lou down for a moment and slapped at his face a few times to try and rid himself of the blurriness. She looked up at him sadly.

He pointed on up ahead and said "What is that? It looks like a mud hut with some smoke above it, right?"

Raphael had plopped down onto the ground when the pitiful caravan came to a halt. But he looked up with joy at what he saw.

"It is a mud hut. Maybe there is food. I think someone is cooking. Can this be a dream?"

The four weary travelers were no longer too concerned with being taken captive or killed by northern soldiers. They were starving to death and Jack knew it. His legs felt heavy, like in a dream. They wanted to run but no one really had the strength and so they continued their quiet, steady pace until a woman at the hut began yelling at them. Jack did not understand what she said but through her hand motions he could tell they would not be welcome there. He tried calling out to her, to try and explain, but his throat was too dry to make a loud sound.

The woman continued to yell as they came closer and finally Jack told the group to stop. She kept yelling and gesturing even though they were coming no closer. She was very angry.

Jack sighed deeply and thought once again of approaching her and begging for something but could not take being rejected. It's funny what you can and cannot take when you're in that state, he thought. He was alright with getting shot but was sure he would crack mentally if this scenario continued any further. The children showed no reaction and Jack could see that they looked very dull compared to just a day or two earlier.

Carrying the young ones, Jack started walking again, in the same direction but away from the mud hut slightly so the woman would stop yelling.

He had only taken a few steps when he was startled by the yelling of a man. It sounded scary at first until Jack decided it was different, not angry. The man sounded as if he was pleading and so Jack turned his head to look. The man, wearing little more than a wrap around his privates, was waving at the group to come closer. He admonished the woman when she tried to yell over him. He raised his hand as if to strike her and she finally cowered backward in fear and fell silent.

The man used both hands to wave them over and so Jack carried and led the children to the hut. There were a few chickens pecking at nothing in particular on the dry, dusty ground.

He was thankful there was no mirror there at the hut. He could tell from the looks given to them by the man and woman that they must have looked terrible. He could almost feel the dark circles around his eyes, his sun-scarred skin, and the thousands of little reminders left behind by hungry mosquitos. It could also have been that he was the first white person they had seen in their lives. After all, this was a pretty remote stretch of country.

I wonder if they think I'm a ghost.

The man had been sitting on a straw mat but barked an order to his wife—who argued back but finally acquiesced—to bring out a large colorful blanket that he helped place over the straw mat. He motioned to his guests to sit at the edge of the blanket. It was shady on the mat and provided a much-needed escape from the ferocity of the sun.

The man stood and went away only to return a few moments later with a bucket of clean, fresh water. There was a cup tied to the metal handle of the bucket and Jack filled it one at a time for the children.

The transformation was nothing short of amazing. The life-giving water did just that. It put a glow, a life, back into the children's eyes and instantly gave them animation. Jack was relieved to see Cindy Lou moving around better, more freely, though she eventually plopped down onto his lap and lay her head on his chest again.

Jack was the last to drink and the cool, clean water burned his throat at first before soothing every part of his being. He could almost feel the fire being quenched as the water raced through his body. It was life itself that he was drinking.

The man motioned for them to have as much water as they wanted and Jack repeated the process, serving the children a second round of drinks before taking a second cupful himself.

When they were done drinking, the man tried speaking with them, most likely asking for an update on the government's actions but spoke a dialect that Raphael could not understand. That did not stop them from trying. They both spoke, trying to make each other understand and Jack even got into it, speaking English and using hand motions and gestures to explain what they had been through. The man understood really only one thing: Jack holding his hands in the shape of a gun and firing off several imaginary rounds. Then, using two fingers, he showed people running.

When they were done talking, the man yelled at his wife, who once again did not do his bidding without an argument. She went to the rear of the hut, where the smoke was still spiraling up to the sky, and brought out a pot of boiling mush made out of beans with some natural vegetation mixed in. It smelled thick and rich and earthy and the children started salivating.

Jack could hardly believe his eyes. The man handed them each a spoon and motioned to eat. The children looked at Jack before digging in and he nodded. Jack tried standing to thank the man but the man would hear nothing of it. He insisted Jack sit and scoop out some of the food.

It was delicious and not nearly as bitter as Jack anticipated. The beans were soft and smoky and tasted a bit garlicky. The children each took a spoonful and ate slowly, not knowing if they would be allowed a second go at the filled pot. But the man was generous and motioned to them to eat as much as they could. The sauce with the beans was delicious. Jack could not pinpoint the spices used but it bordered on being spicy. He thought of the trick his father taught him to leave some of the sauce on his lips to use for later and smiled to himself. He could not help but to think of his parents, of Jenelle and become a bit melancholy, if not downright morose.

He tried snapping himself out of his brief encounter with self-pity and focused on making sure the children ate enough to continue the journey.

They each took four or five spoons full of the thick bean stew and were quite full. Jack was proud of how polite they were, thanking the stranger over and over and waiting for him to motion toward the pot of beans after every spoonful they finished. Jack ate plenty as well and made sure that there was plenty left in the pot for the man and his wife to eat later.

The woman sat off away from the mat and looked bitterly at the people eating her food. Jack smiled at her and nodded a "thank you" but she just looked away.

When they were done eating, the man tried continuing the conversation from earlier. Jack could only guess that he wanted the information see if it was necessary for him to pack his meager belongings, close down his small home and field where it seemed so dry nothing could grow, and leave like others already had.

Just about all meaning was lost in the attempted conversations and it left them all a bit frustrated. At one point the man motioned at the wooden cross around Jack's neck and then pointed up to the sky. Jack nodded and the men smiled gently at each other.

They took more water and then Jack realized the man could help him more than he already had. He zipped open his backpack and pulled out the map that George White had given him. He spread it out on the map and pointed at the border they were trying to reach. The man studied it carefully and Jack wondered if he had ever seen a map before but there was finally a look of revelation in the man's eyes. He lit up and pointed at a spot much closer to their destination than Jack expected.

This won't take months. Jesus, we'll never make it if it takes months. This looks like days, maybe a week. Please God, let it be only days longer that we have to endure this.

Jack felt certain the man was telling him that the terrain would get much harsher and pointed at a spot where they could cross the river. Jack nodded and shook the man's hand several times. The man laughed every single time.

Before they stood to go, the man's wife softened and came over to join them. She seemed to be ashamed of her behavior and now acted proud to have such a husband. Jack stood and shook her hand too though she was not sure of what he was doing. She smiled and insisted through words and motions they stay and rest a while longer. There was plenty of food left but everyone had eaten their fill.

Jack refilled the water containers and knew they could go on walking much longer as long as they had water.

The woman looked at Raphael's knee and though it had scabbed over, there were areas of white puss that she did not like and she retreated into the hut for a bit. When she returned, she gently cleaned out the wound and dressed it with the very same bean stew they had just eaten and a few additional spices that did not smell very pleasant. She packed it with care on the knee and blew gently on it. The warmth felt good and Raphael, braced for pain, felt none.

"Look at that, Raphael. They feed us, water us, and mend us. It's one-stop shopping for the hopeless."

The boy smiled, not taking his eyes from the new dressing on his leg.

After a long while sitting and resting in relative silence, the revitalized band of pilgrims stood and said their goodbyes. Jack had never met such generous people and he felt his gratitude was inadequate. He hugged the man and kissed his cheek.

"If you're ever in the states, New York: the Big Apple, look me up," Jack gushed. "I'll take you guys to all the sites. There are buildings there you just won't believe. Forget the Twin Towers, I'm talking about marvels like the Chrysler Building or Grand Central Station too."

He paused for a moment, hoping to see some recognition or reaction from them. Seeing none, he continued.

"And the food, whoa the food is something, well, you'll just have to experience for yourself. Ever have Chinese? I'd say it would be a safe bet to say you've never had Chinese food. Well, I know a tiny little place in Chinatown, looks like a dump from the outside but oh the food! It will ruin you forever from eating egg foo young anywhere else on this entire planet. It is to die for."

He stopped for a moment and quieted his voice. "I'll repay the favor. I promise, I'll repay your generosity one day."

The man smiled and pointed to the sky as if to say that was where they would meet one day.

"Right you are. At least I hope that's where I wind up," Jack smiled. He felt re-charged and wondered just how close to death they were before the fresh water and warm meal. "I'm working on it, that's for sure. But I have a lot of making up to do."

Jack reached around his neck and pulled off the cross that Matthew had given him a week earlier. The leather was damp with Jack's sweat. He pulled it off gently, reverently, and walked over to the man. With two hands clutching the leather, he placed the cross around the man's neck.

Elated, the man clutched the gift in his hand and spoke rapidly pointing to the heavens. His wife smiled and he held it out for her to see. She reached out and touched if softly as if trying not to break it.

Not exactly sure why, Jack felt compelled to get behind the man and take his right hand into his and show him how to make the sign of the cross.

The man's hand was warm. Jack touched the man's hand to his forehead, chest, left shoulder, and right shoulder. Then he repeated the motion on the man's wooden cross so he would understand what he was doing.

"In the name of the Father, Son and Holy Spirit," Jack said.

They practiced it several times. The man couldn't get the words right but that was OK. Out of the corner of his eye Jack could see the woman doing it as well. He walked over to her and showed her how as well. She was very grateful.

Cindy Lou, revived by the food and water shared by the perfect strangers, was the most animated she'd been in days. She tugged eagerly at Jack's arm and jumped up and down to gain his attention.

"What is it, my darling?" He knelt down on one knee to make better eye contact.

She made the sign of the cross on herself and smiled. Her eyes were bright and alive.

"That's perfect! You are the cutest little thing. Do you know that? One of these days you will let me hear your voice, won't you? That is the thing I want most in this world, well, besides, getting us all to safety. I know you'll talk. I know you've been through a world of hurt. But now you have people round you who love you."

She continued making the sign of the cross and the smiles turned to giggles. Raphael and Emmanuel started making the sign of the cross over and over again as well.

It had been a perfect day and neither Jack nor the children wanted to leave. But they knew they couldn't stay and so as the sun began to drop slightly in the sky and the scorching temperature broke just a little bit, they started their journey once more.

TWENTY TWO

"WAKE UP, YOU sleepy heads," Jack whispered. "Don't you know what day this is? Good gravy! I think he found us. Don't ask me how. Somehow or other he found us. Wake up."

The children, startled at first, were put to ease by the tone of Jack's voice. They woke slowly, rubbing their eyes, and were shocked at the site before them.

They were two days removed from another encounter with the government soldiers that made them take refuge under the bank of dirty, slow-moving river.

Jack held on to roots jutting out below the water's surface and the children clung to him silently as the soldiers yelled, taunting them, teasing them. No one had seen them but Jack was sure the soldiers knew they were in the area. Perhaps they had seen smoke or the remains of a small fire. Perhaps they were the same soldiers tracking them from the previous time. There was no way to really know. It didn't really matter. The kids and Jack were terrified and stayed in the murky, muddy water most of the day. Jack did not allow himself to think about the creatures and organisms in the water that might be a danger to them. At least he didn't think too much about it.

He hadn't seen any crocodiles but was more concerned with the microscopic parasites he had heard about that cause blindness or even find their way into certain parts of the body he definitely did not want invaded by a parasite.

All they could do was continue their journey and hide when they had to.

The very next morning, after drying their clothes by a fire most of the night, they were awakened by the sound of something rustling through the forest very close to them. They could smell the foul odor of the lion way before they ever spotted him. It smelled like a barn that had not been cleaned out in weeks.

The stench hung over them as they sat in silence and when the beast let out a terrifying roar, Jack ignored the advice given to him by George to charge the animal. They stayed completely still but the lion moved closer, preceded by his stink, until it permeated everything in the area.

The animal roared again and the children began crying, even Raphael. At that point Jack knew that they couldn't just sit there and become breakfast. But he also knew—from watching Mutual of Omaha's Wild Kingdom—that male lions rarely do any of the hunting. This guy was probably in heat and marking his territory. The stench was intended to keep other males away and draw in the females. That little bit of knowledge, gleaned from the television, gave Jack the tiny smidgen of bravery he needed.

He scrambled to his feet before the lion made any move to attack and found two heavy branches. He handed one to Raphael and held on to the other. He shoved the younger children between them with his feet. They continued to cry.

"I am very sorry, Mr. Lion, but we are not going to be today's entrée. You see, we have traveled very far on a very difficult road and we are not going to let an overgrown pussycat stop us now. I know this probably contradicts your plans for this fine morning. But I must tell you that we are not backing down." Jack's voice rose in volume with every determined word. "We will not back down and we will hurt you if you come near us."

With that, the lion's gigantic head—the size of a tremendous medicine ball—came snarling out of the thicket. Its nose was glistening and drool escaped the corner of its mouth. The animal was mangy and dirty and looked nothing like he deserved the title of king of the jungle. It let out a loud sound that was a combination sneeze and sneer. A mist of lion mucous wafted over them and was cold.

"That has got to be the last straw," Jack said as the lion approached the group slowly, not sure what to make of them. "I will absolutely not die in this jungle covered with lion snot."

Then he roared at the lion as loudly as he could and waved his stick at the brute. The lion raised a paw and barked something back.

"Go on, get away from here!"

The other children began yelling as well and the lion looked confused and suddenly disinterested.

"Come on now," Jack yelled as he got closer to the lion, poking at it with the branch. The lion raised his paw again and squinted its eyes. "Get out of here this instant. You smell very badly and you have covered us in snots. Now get out before we have to get nasty. You don't want us. You're looking for a girlfriend."

The lion turned and trotted off into the forest without making another sound.

Jack and the children stood frozen in their positions for several moments trying to take in what just happened.

They knew the lion had not returned. Jack's voice and the absence of the disheartening stench were proof enough. What they did see when they opened their eyes was a small tree, replanted in the ground in the middle of their camp, decorated with papers, paperclips, and other miscellaneous items gathered from the bottom of Jack's backpack.

Cindy Lou smiled at once at the marvel before her. Beneath the tree were three small objects, wrapped in sections of the map Jack did not need anymore that included northern Sudan and Egypt. The children did not know what to make of it. Emmanuel was still very sleepy and climbed up onto Jack's lap and rested his head on Jack's chest.

They've never received a gift in their lives.

"Don't you guys realize who visited us last night?"

Their faces were blank.

"Santa Claus! Today is Christmas Day, or at least I think it is. Anyway, it's got to be getting close," he laughed.

Only Raphael responded with any sort of recognition of the name Santa Claus when he squinted his eyes tight and cocked his head to the side.

"Santa Claus?" he repeated.

"Yes," Jack said. "He's that jolly old elf, a big elf really, sort of fat, maybe even obese. Anyway, he spends all year running a workshop of elves making gifts for little children around the world. Then in one magical night, Christmas Eve, the night Jesus was born, he loads all the gifts onto his sleigh and delivers them. I think he has the power of time travel because really, there is no way he could deliver them all in one night."

"A sleigh?" Raphael laughed. "There is no snow here."

"His sleigh is doesn't need snow because it flies. There are eight magic reindeer that can fly and so they pull the sleigh all over the world. And when it's really foggy out he has a special reindeer whose nose lights up like the high beams of a tractor trailer." As the word came out of his mouth, Jack wondered how he ever fell for such a preposterous story.

"What is a reindeer?"

"Hmm, I guess it's like a small antelope. Do you understand?"

The boy nodded but Jack felt the need to explain further.

"Look, I'm certainly no replacement for Fr. Nguyen or Jenelle, but I'll give it a shot. You see, Mary was pregnant with the son of God. Her husband Joseph was jealous at first but then decided to go along. They had to go to Bethlehem for a census but when they got there they couldn't find an empty room anywhere."

The children had moved closer to listen to the story, sitting with legs folded beneath them.

"Normally this wouldn't have been a problem. They could have camped out, sort of like what we have done for these past few weeks. But, you see, Mary was really pregnant. I mean, she was about to have a baby. So one innkeeper felt sorry for the young couple and told them they could sleep in the manger, where the animals were. It was stinky and disgusting, but it was out of the wind and cold so it was better than nothing.

"Now, Mary and Joseph didn't know it at the time but there was a star, the brightest star ever, shining in the sky right over the stable. And people from all over were following that star because they had read in some ancient scrolls how the new king of kings would be born. The old writings told them to follow that star.

"When she had the baby, when Jesus was born, angels came down from heaven and began to sing. Shepherds in the fields, strangers, and people in town for the census came to see the newborn king. Some of the people following the star included three kings who came to give Jesus gifts. I think that's why Santa Claus chooses Christmas Eve to give out his gifts, to remind us of what God did for us, and maybe to remind us that we should all try and live like Jesus."

Jack put Emmanuel down on the ground and knelt over by the little tree. He picked up one of the three small packages in his hand. He shook it by his ear, weighed it in both hands, and then smiled at Raphael.

"Why, this one is for you, big boy. It says 'To Raphael, love Santa.' "

The boy tore open the flimsy wrapping paper and found the compass hidden inside. He held it in the palm of his hand and determined which way was north. He smiled proudly.

"Raphael, I don't know if we would have made it this far without you. You have proven yourself to be much more than a smart little boy. Your bravery has saved us many times already. I know that when I was your age there was no way I would be able to do the things you have done. You are a leader and a navigator and everyone knows that a navigator needs a compass."

"Thank you, Mr. Jack," he said softly. "Thank you very much."

Jack reached down for another of the gifts. He repeated his actions from earlier—weighing and listening to the object to see if he could guess the contents.

"Ah," he exclaimed loudly and excitedly. "This teeny-tiny little present is for none other than Emmanuel." He was using his Michael Caine English accent. He put the present on the little boy's belly and the child opened it in a hurry.

It was a little wooden cross that Jack had made during the night. It was crude and unfinished but it was clearly a cross. The boy kissed it over and over again causing Jack to tear up slightly.

"Emmanuel, ever since you joined our little traveling party, I have known the truth in your name. I've known that God is with us. That's why I wanted you to have the cross. You can be our spiritual navigator. Keep that cross with you always, OK?"

The little boy nodded and smiled and kept kissing his cross.

"Let's see," Jack said continuing to use the English accent that was getting zero attention from the children. "Tough crowd, tough crowd, this accent usually brings down the house. Hmm, we've got one more present here."

This one was flat and Jack shook it by his ear and then held it sideways and put it to his eye as if examining some sort of secret document. He held it up to the sky to see if he could decipher what was inside.

"This one is for Immaculee, or Cindy Lou," he said happily. He stood up and put his hand above his eyes as if he was searching far off in the distance. "Now where is that girl?" he continued doing so until she tugged at his pant shorts.

"A-ha! That's where you are. Here you go, my love. Merry Christmas."

He placed the flat index-card sized present onto the palm of her hand.

She opened it excruciatingly slow and was careful not to rip any of the packaging. When she finally got it open, her eyes widened and she pulled the photograph close to her heart. Then Jack heard something he had never heard before.

Cindy Lou was laughing, laughing with pure joy in her heart.

She closed her eyes and clutched it tightly. Jack leaned over and kissed the little girl atop her head.

"Merry Christmas, sweetheart."

She stared at the photograph of Jenelle and the rest of her classmates and started shedding tears of joy. It was the only memento of the only woman she would ever remember as her mother. There were no memories of her real parents. She put the photograph over her heart and smiled.

"Merry Christmas, Mister Jack," she answered softly, uttering the first words she had ever spoken aloud.

It took Jack a second to realize that she had spoken. His eyes widened and he lifted Cindy Lou high up into the air. She giggled loudly as he tossed her up and caught her again.

"You spoke! Did you hear her, Raphael? She spoke, she spoke. What a beautiful sound. Cindy Lou can talk! I have to be honest. I had given up all hope that she ever would. Wow, this is like a Christmas miracle."

The children laughed at Jack's ravings and relished their gifts as if they were toys they had always dreamed of having.

"Cindy Lou. Can you say it again? I just want to make sure that I'm not dreaming."

"My name is Immaculee. But I like when you call me Cindy Lou," she said in a small voice and Jack shrieked with delight.

"I couldn't have asked for a better Christmas gift," he told the little girl. "I have wished for you to start speaking many, many times."

She leaned up on her toes and planted the sweetest kiss he had ever received on his cheek.

Jack sat back and watched as the children played with one another and showed off their new gifts proudly. He wouldn't rush them this morning to continue their improbable trek out of Sudan and away from the violence. The truth was he didn't know how far they still needed to go and letting the children rest one morning wasn't going to affect their exodus much anyhow.

He felt the pain of yet another Christmas without his mother and now of one without the love of his life, but only for a little while. Oh, the Christmases he wanted to spend with Jenelle. He imagined showering her with gifts and taking her to see the tree in Rockefeller Center. Maybe they would have even gone ice skating on Christmas morning. He wondered if she had ever eaten anything close to the Christmas feasts he was used to having, turkey, gravy, sweet potatoes, and pumpkin pie. But he didn't want to think of food. So he kept picturing the perfect Christmas with Jenelle in his arms. They would see the Rockettes at the Radio City Music Hall and then go home and feast on exotic cheeses and dried sausage in bed as they watched as many versions of "A Christmas Carol" as they could on television.

He loved the version with Albert Finney, the musical. He had seen that one for the first time with his father at Radio City and there was pure magic in watching Finney's Scrooge transform from a miser to a philanthropist. After that he made it a point to try and see all the other versions in black and white. He also especially liked the version with Reginald Owen as Scrooge. He wondered which version Jenelle would like the best. Maybe she had even read the story. He convinced himself that someone as intelligent as Jenelle would definitely have read the story.

He looked up at the sky and whispered "Merry Christmas, my love."

He didn't want the children to see him crying on this special day and so he tried his hardest to stop thinking about the things that made his heart hurt. He forced a smile onto his face until it became real. This really was a special moment. Jack shook his head and chuckled. He still couldn't get over the fact that Cindy Lou was talking, making this maybe the most magical Christmas he had ever experienced.

The pain finally passed, allowing him to enjoy the children, who for this brief moment, were distracted from the genocide and the fact that they would likely never make it to the border and away from the horror.

TWENTY THREE

THE JOY OF celebrating Christmas lasted a few hours but dissipated under the scorching sun and the endless road.

Jack always hated the letdown, the emotional hangover of the day after Christmas. This year it came sooner than ever. The week before Christmas was always the best week of the year. The day after, December 26, was always the worst.

They all walked in silence, like they had on most days. Today Raphael was out in front with compass in the palm of his hand.

They had stumbled upon a dirt road heading south and they decided to try and stay on it for as long as they could. It wasn't the safest or smartest bet but they were all pretty weary from trudging through forest and were sick of battling insects and snakes. There was no one anywhere. Though they had heard government troops a few days earlier, which caused them to hide in the river, they had not seen a single person since eating with the man and his wife outside of his mud hut.

Jack doubted the government troops had come this far south.

He couldn't get Jenelle and the thoughts from earlier out of his mind and he allowed the pain to seep back into his heart where he kept it protected like his own Christmas present. He decided to keep it this day and he would not try and force it away before the next sunrise.

His stomach hurt from hunger.

Jack was sitting on a large boulder at the bottom of the hill that led to the school grounds, waiting for Jenelle. It was one of those rare days where there was actually a breeze and the boulder at the bottom of the hill in the shade was as perfect a spot as he had ever been. He had watched a woman, who could not have been more than 30 years old, spend the previous 40 minutes ankle deep in the tiny stream that trickled by the western-most part of the town.

She was very beautiful and looked to be very tired. She held what appeared to be a two-year-old child in her arms and an infant was strapped on her back. Jack watched carefully as the woman continuously dipped a glass Coca-Cola bottle into the water. It was one of those old-fashioned glass bottles, very thick, that Jack had not seen in years. Every few seconds she would lift the bottle and look at it. She was methodical in her actions and showed no emotion in her face.

He stood and stretched to see if he could get a better look at what she was doing but he could not figure it out. At first he thought she might be washing the bottle or trying to get a clear batch of water to drink. But that clearly was not the case. At one point he even climbed atop the boulder for a different vantage point. It did not help. She simply was dipping her soda bottle into the water over and over again.

Jenelle came running down the hill.

"I'm sorry I'm so late." She was a little out of breath and little beads of sweat had formed on her nose. "I didn't mean to keep you waiting. The children misbehaved so much this afternoon that the lesson took longer than I had hoped."

"It's no problem, my love. Was it anything serious?"

"No, no, just children being children."

"Well, you look beautiful as always. You never let them fluster you too much. And really, those children are amazing. I have never seen kids so eager to learn and so eager to impress. Look at you. Who wouldn't want to impress someone so gorgeous?"

"You must get your vision checked the next time the doctor comes to visit the school," she laughed and playfully punched him in the arm.

"If only you had a mirror," Jack replied. "Then you'd be able to see what I see."

"I don't think anyone sees what you see." She was blushing. "And that is because you are certifiably insane, Jack Hopkins. Now, on to more important things, where are we going to dinner?"

"Well, I feel a craving for a hot pastrami sandwich on rye bread with mustard and a big kosher pickle on the side with maybe some cole slaw or a knish with a Dr. Brown's cream soda. I prefer the potato knish but the meat-filled versions are not so bad. Then for dessert I would love a large chunk of raspberry cheesecake followed by a small cup of espresso, maybe with a drop of anisette for good measure."

She raised her eyebrows not having a clue as to what he was talking about.

"But," he continued, "since I doubt very much that we will be able to find that here in Jabra, then I suggest you make the dinner recommendations. I have enjoyed thoroughly any and all of the places that we have tried so far."

"Hmm, well let's head down this way and see what they are making tonight at the café. I know you don't like the goat very much but maybe they are cooking chicken tonight."

She slipped her hand into his and they kissed gently, lips barely touching.

As they turned to go and started walking, Jack stopped her and pointed at the woman in the stream.

"I meant to ask you. What on earth is that woman doing?"

Jenelle squinted her eyes and stared for a moment, before taking a step or two closer to the stream.

"It looks like she is getting dinner for her children."

Jack shook his head.

"I don't understand. What are they eating? Is she collecting stream water?"

"Not exactly."

Jenelle called out to the woman who turned and answered politely.

"She said she is fishing. She wants to put some sort of meat, some fish, into her soup. So she has taken just a little bit of cornmeal, a very small amount that she can spare and put it at the bottom of that bottle. Then she dips the bottle gently in the water and very small fish, minnows, swim in to eat the cornmeal."

"She is catching minnows to make soup with?" Jack shook his head and felt great pity for the woman and her children in his heart. "The minnows in that stream are much smaller than the ones I use as bait on City Island to go fishing with? That's terrible, just terrible."

"I know, Jack. I love that you have a big heart. She is poor and that is the best she can do for her children right now. It will be enough, for tonight. They will get the little bit of protein that they need to live another day."

Jack wanted to say something, to come up with some sort of solution but could not find the right words. He wanted to help this poor woman but did not know how. He continued shaking his head as they walked down the hill, hand in hand, toward the center of town for dinner.

Jack did not realize it but tears were streaming down the sides of his face as he walked. He felt a little hand creep into his and looked down to see Cindy Lou.

"Why are you crying?" she asked in her soft wisp of a voice.

The sound of her voice made everything better.

"I was just thinking of Miss Jenelle and how much I missed her."

"I miss her too. Will we ever see her again?"

Jack stopped and knelt down in front of the little girl whose first words he had heard only a few hours earlier.

"I hope so, my precious. I'm pretty sure we will, someday."

Raphael had stopped walking out front and walked back to see what was the matter.

"I hope we don't see her too soon," he said and then smiled at Jack.

"Yes, Raphael, good point. Hopefully we will meet again in the future some time. But not today. We've come too far and too long for that to happen now."

The next few days were more of the same and they were very weak without food. The water had run out now as well and any green in the land they had travelled through now gave way to dry, brown land. It was as if someone had set everything on fire and nothing had ever grown back.

Things turned slightly green as they approached the river they would eventually have to cross. In one patch of trees they came across a mango tree that still had a few mangos in it. But none of them could climb the tree or shake the trunk sufficiently for the fruit to fall.

Jack tried with all of his might to climb the tree but his legs and his arms were too weak. Raphael tried as well and could not even get off the ground. That's when Jack realized that they were slowly starving to death.

They slept there that night, under the mango tree, with the hopes that in the morning they would find the strength or see that some of the fruit had fallen during the night.

Jack awoke early the next morning to the sound of an airplane. The hum of the motor and the roar of the blades sounded familiar. He was sure it was Ti Burik and that George White was out there looking for them. He pulled all the strength that he could gather and stood out in a clearing waving his arms. He tried to yell out but found that he did not even have the strength to speak.

He waved desperately but quickly realized that it was a government plane, one of the Russian Antonovs, circling, looking for something in particular. A few moments later he heard the bombs, loud, piercing crashes and booms that seemed to kill any hope that he had woken with that morning.

He tried to figure out what they would be bombing in such a desolate location and then pulled the map from his backpack. It did not come to him right away but eventually he figured out they were bombing any and all of the bridges. The government did not want the people evacuating to Ethiopia. They wanted them dead.

With no bridges to cross and no food to eat, Jack looked at the children and had very little hope that any of them would make it. That day they walked only a short distance. It was too hot and they had very little energy. Jack held Cindy Lou and Emmanuel most of the day.

They slept in the reeds by the river even though the mosquitos were relentless and vicious. Jack would routinely slap the back of his neck and kill dozens of feasting mosquitos, his hand red with his own blood.

That night Jack heard other people on the river bank and watched in silence from a distance as a man in a small rowboat made several trips ferrying people to the other side. It was less than a half-mile from where they were sleeping in the reeds. They were clearly not government soldiers and the people crossing looked as weary and hungry as they were.

He shook Raphael gently to wake him and told him what he had seen.

"It has to be you," Jack said to the boy, who relished the responsibility despite his emaciated state. "Seeing someone like me would spook them too much, and they would probably stop what they were doing and run. But you? You could find out what it would take for us to get on the boat and cross the river. You could tell them about me in advance so they don't all go running when they see a white man coming out of the bushes."

Raphael wanted to laugh but had no strength. He nodded and started walking through the high reeds hoping simply that he could make it to the boatman before a Nile River crocodile ate him. The full moon shone on the river, giving him enough light to see where he was going.

Jack waited, not able to sleep while the boy was walking in the darkness. He walked in small circles around the sleeping children and stood on his toes to see if Raphael had made contact yet. He was angry at himself for sending such a young boy to do something like this but he knew that his options were limited. There was really nothing else he could do but wait for the boy to come back.

It took hours.

The boy waited in the cover of the reeds until the ferryman came across and there was no one left for him to take across. The sun was rising and large white birds glided gracefully along the top of the water, letting the tips of their wings skim the very top layer of water. The frogs had stopped singing a while earlier.

Raphael spoke to the ferryman at length and told him everything that had happened to them so far, even the story about the lion, which he did not believe and laughed to himself about it. The man did not seem to be paying attention as he had heard the same story thousands of times already. He tied the boat up and got out. He started walking away from Raphael and turned around when he was only a few steps away.

He eyed the boy up and down and Raphael did not know whether the look was one of disgust or one of pity. At this point it didn't matter much as long as the man could get them across the river.

"Tell the white man and the others to be here at nightfall," he said in a curt, rude voice. "Tell no one else."

TWENTY FOUR

THAT DAY JACK made it his mission to let the children rest in the shade—where it was still sweltering—while he went out and looked for food. He was extremely weak and now his stomach felt sick from drinking water from the river. He stopped many times that day to throw up in addition to the terrible diarrhea that he had. After a few times, when the sickness came, there was nothing left for his body to give back and so he wretched and tried to go to the bathroom but nothing happened except dry heaves and terrible cramping.

It was very hot that afternoon, piercingly hot, and Jack wanted nothing more than to go back to the river and drink more of the wretched, disgusting water. The river water did not move at all, it was more like a gigantic puddle, an incubator for mosquitos and Jack was sure that was the source of his malady.

He was sweating terribly and his forehead was throbbing. He wished for a lot of things but right now Jack wished he could just lie down somewhere cool and shady.

But he kept walking, keeping his bearings about him, looking for fruit, cassava, or better yet an open bodega where he could get a Snickers bar and ice cold Pepsi. Maybe he could also pick up the late edition of the *New York Post* and see what the Mets were doing lately. Maybe they had finally decided to call up that kid Strawberry.

Late in the afternoon he felt things go dark.

It started with a murky cloudiness around the outer edges of his vision and he knew something was wrong. He leaned against a dead acacia tree and tried rubbing his eyes right again but things only got worse. Everything around him was turning dark.

It got to where he could only see a tiny bit through the very center of his eyes and even that was very blurry.

There was a sweet smell in the air, similar to the fragrance of gardenias, strong and pleasant. And it was right at that moment that Jack realized he was going to die.

Funny, I've faced a lion, men with guns, a genocide, snakes, bombs, and truly evil people. Yet the thing that makes me sure I'm going to die is the sweetest breeze I've breathed in since being in the Sudan. Get yourself together, Jack. It's just a flower blooming somewhere. Still, I'm so tired and just want to sit against this tree for a while and rest. It's OK, you've worked hard and you've come a long way. You deserve a little nap under this tree with this wonderful odor in the air.

He dreamt of home and the kids on the basketball court and Papo selling coquito ices. Someone had opened the fire hydrant and the kids had stopped playing ball and instead took turns running through the water.

It was one of those perfect summer days in the Bronx when everyone was in a good mood and just happy to enjoy a cold drink or some shade. Some of the older Puerto Rican men were playing dominoes and Jack could hear them arguing about whether the Dominican style of play was better than the aggressive Haitian style of play. Someone mentioned that Haitians force the losing players to put twigs and debris in their hair as a mark of shame. They all agreed, however, that no one played dominoes as well as the Puerto Ricans.

They were sipping rum and talking very loudly.

Jack looked up at one of the buildings in the neighborhood, one he did not recognize, and he could see Jenelle dropping rose petals from the window. She sprinkled the entire street below with pink and red flower petals and the scent wafted up like perfume. It mixed with the water from the hydrant and everyone was happy. Jack waved desperately at Jenelle but she just looked right through him and that's when he knew he was dreaming. He tried calling her name over and over, screaming it at times, but his voice made no sound at all.

Jack thought he saw Cindy Lou picking petals up from the grimy street and placing them in a little basket. He couldn't quite make out her face but was confident it was her.

He dreamt of Old Man Dukes and Felicia, Mike Morgan and the Sullivan twins all drinking cold beer at the pub. He could see them all clearly doing the things that he always remembered doing, like throwing darts and telling improbable stories, but they couldn't see him. He was there but it was more like he was watching a film of it in the dream. He tried talking to them but they could not hear him.

They left the bar and walked in single file toward the basketball court like fathers picking their kids up from school. The kids left with them, as if they were really their sons, holding hands and talking enthusiastically about their day. They spotted the open fire hydrant and they all ran through. Jack tried running through as well, to cool off, but he just couldn't seem to reach the water.

Finally, though, one of the kids, little Stevie Casanova, seemed to recognize Jack and cupped his hands on the hydrant's spout, sending some water high up into the air. Jack followed the stream of cold, clear water in slow motion with his eyes and opened his mouth as it came sprinkling down on him. He had never felt so perfectly wonderful as in that moment. The water smothered the fire inside his body. He could almost feel smoke leave his skin with each drop that fell.

Jack held out his tongue and drank in as much of the water as he could.

The boy waved and Jack could see it was Emmanuel. But it didn't seem strange to see him there in the old neighborhood with all the other kids. The dream ended and Jack opened his eyes.

It was dark but a different kind of dark and Jack smiled in his mind to feel the rain falling from the black thunderclouds above. He opened his mouth, as in the dream, and let the precious water come straight down from heaven into his mouth. Jack forced himself to stand, getting closer to the source, and spread his arms wide so that every inch of his skin could feel the life-saving quarter-sized droplets coming down. They burned his flesh in a beautiful way and all Jack could say over and over was "Thank you, God. Thank you, God."

He started back toward the river and the children, and though his eyes were not back to normal, his vision was much better than it had been before his nap. And now he felt confident that he would live long enough at least to get the children across the river and closer to the border, closer to safety. It was hard to tell what time it was with his blurred vision and the darkened storm-filled sky. He hoped it would was almost time to meet the ferryman.

The rain continued to fall lightly and made the ground soft enough for Jack to dig up some leafy plants that he hoped were edible. The worst of the stomach cramping from earlier had passed but Jack still not had regained his appetite. He knew he was starving to death, as were the kids, and there was not much time left. He knew that Raphael could tell him if the plants were safe to eat. Jack ran his hands over his ribs and was shocked at how soft and loose his skin had become and how clearly he could make out each individual bone. He was thankful not to have a mirror handy.

The starvation diet, he laughed. That Scarsdale doctor has got nothing on this weight loss plan. Wonder if this will be the newest fad? Forget going to the gym or investing on expensive home exercise equipment. Just come to the Sudan, find yourself in the middle of a genocide, travel through bug-infested jungles, wade through snake-infested swamps, have chance encounters with lions, and you'll be sure to drop 30 or 40 pounds in no time. This diet comes with a money back guarantee.

He smiled at his own silliness and held the plants out to let the rain fall on them and clear away any dirt.

He made it back to the river but was several miles from the children and he worked his way down the river walking slowly and carefully not to step on any snakes or crocodiles. He also kept his eyes open for any bird nests, hoping to find some eggs but there were none. The critters had already taken care of that.

The rain stopped finally and Jack was thankful once more that the sky remained cloudy and for at least the rest of the day the sun would no longer be able to punish them.

"Thank you, God. Thank you. I will be forever grateful if you keep that wretched sun hidden for just a little while longer. Please, God."

The scent of flowers was long gone and the humid smell of rain on the red clay rose slow and thick from the earth. It was earthy and strange but Jack preferred it to the flowers and the sense of dread that came with it. The odor changed to smoke then something cooking.

Hallucinations are a terrible thing. I can almost make out a barbecue. That is way too cruel of a smell to be just a figment of my imagination.

Then he remembered a cartoon he had watched with his mother about two friends that had gotten shipwrecked on an island. They were Mexicans or Cubans or something. One was tall and skinny and the other was fat and short. They started seeing each other as a hot dog on a bun and a hamburger with all the fixings. His mother would tease him and say she was going to pour barbecue sauce all over him and eat him up.

He smiled at the memory.

Jack reached the camp and was greeted by hugs from Cindy Lou and Emmanuel who looked remarkably better than they had in a while. Nearby was a small fire that Raphael managed to keep going by using Jack's backpack to keep the rain from falling on it. It smelled of some sort of soup or stew and Jack walked over.

"There was a catfish on the shore," Raphael said proudly. "It was still breathing so I knew it would be fresh and safe for us. The birds had not reached it yet. I cut out all the bad parts and cooked it in some water and a few of these plants."

"Raphael," Jack said, kneeling down as the stomach cramps started up again, "you never cease to amaze me."

"Does that mean something good?"

"Yes, it means something good." Jack laughed and reached to hug the boy. Raphael held him tightly for a long time.

"Are you alright, Mr. Jack?"

"I think so. I can't really see too well right now. Do I look that bad?"

"You look a little sick." The boy's face turned serious. "You should sip a little of the broth."

Jack knew he was right. But the thought of swallowing anything made his stomach churn. Yet he needed something to give him energy and sustain him. And the truth was it actually smelled pretty good.

"Raphael, I don't know where we would be without you."

"I think we, or you, would still be here, right here on this spot. But we wouldn't have this fish to eat."

Jack laughed out loud and Raphael smiled and giggled as well.

"Have the children eaten?"

"Yes, of course, they ate first."

It made Jack proud and sad to see how quickly Raphael had been forced to grow up. But there was no other choice. Grow up or die. He was a handsome boy who was eager to smile and Jack liked him very much.

If I ever had a son I would want him to be just like Raphael, without all the suffering of course. He really has been a lifesaver and he never, ever complains. This child has a great mind and great sense of spirit and life. I will do all I can to make sure he doesn't languish in some awful Kenyan orphanage. Oh Jack, there is nothing you can do, really.

He turned his attention to the younger kids and was amazed to see how just one cup of fish broth and a small piece of catfish could bring Cindy Lou and Emmanuel back to life so quickly. They were playing a hand game, similar to "Patty-Cake" and were laughing out loud. The mood had changed considerably with the food and knowledge that they would soon be on a ferry.

That gave him hope.

Perhaps salvation lies on the other side of this river with water that doesn't move. Maybe we will find the border and we can get to safety. Maybe the people will have food and water for us and treat us kindly.

Jack took a sip of the warm fish broth and instantly felt better. It was soothingly hot and tasty. He drank plenty from it and was even able to rip off a piece of fish and eat it without incident.

"Raphael, I don't know if I am saving your life or if you are saving mine."

"Maybe we are saving each other's."

TWENTY FIVE

THE BAND OF travelers, fortified with catfish broth and the hope of making it across the river, set off just before nightfall. They had made it nearly there when they were startled by a man who jumped out of the tall reeds.

"You are to wait here," he said while not moving his gaze from Jack's white skin. "I will come for you when it is your turn. Do not speak or make a sound."

He continued looking at Jack's arm.

"You can touch it if you'd like," Jack said but the man did not understand. He reached and pulled the man's hand onto his arm and smiled. The man nodded and smiled back. All of his front teeth were missing. He put his finger up to his mouth and waved goodbye.

"Maybe he thought you were a ghost," Raphael said and everyone laughed quietly.

"A ghost? Gee whiz, I was thinking maybe I was a just a vanilla flavored African!"

The ground beneath them was murky and they could hear the river, now roaring from the rains earlier in the day. Jack stood on his toes to look out over the reeds at the rushing water. There were four or five hippopotamuses floating around near the middle of the river. Their mouths were wide open and they were flashing their sharp teeth. A small white bird kept diving down on them, likely picking ticks off their backs.

The mosquitos came out in full vengeance once the sun was down completely. The four slapped and swatted at their necks and arms tirelessly and as quietly as they could. No matter how many blood-engorged insects they killed with their slaps, there remained thousands more ready to take their place at the feast.

Cindy Lou started crying and Jack tried shielding her as best he could from the bugs.

"At this rate, I will be run out of blood before we get on the boat," Raphael said bitterly but tried to smile when Jack laughed.

"You're right, little man. Hopefully they will come my way, since I have way more flesh, fat, and blood than you little ones combined."

Then summoning all the strength he had, Jack stood and spun in place with his arms spread wide like a helicopter blade, trying to keep the mosquitos away.

He made a sound like an engine whirring and the children laughed. He was happy they were in good spirits despite the situation. When he finally stopped he was very dizzy and weak.

The night went by slowly and Jack tired of slapping mosquitos. He would wait until he could feel more than one at a time and then would give the back of his neck a strong whack. The most he counted at once were six dead mosquitos on his hand after a slap. The cramps came back and his eyes remained blurry. He did not know the symptoms of malaria but was sure by now that he had it.

When the moon was high above them and the Southern Cross clear in the far sky, the man returned.

"Come now," he whispered to them.

Cindy Lou and Emmanuel had fallen asleep hours earlier on Jack's lap and he struggled to stand and carry them at the same time. The man reached over scooped Emmanuel from his arms.

"Come. We must go now. Soldiers coming."

Jack's heart quickened at the words and a wave of despair washed over him.

Soldiers? Even this far south? Are they planning on chasing us right up to the border? If they hate these people so much then why not just let them leave?

The man led them in a single file walk with Raphael following and Jack in the rear still clutching Cindy Lou.

The ground was increasingly muddy and swampy and Jack lost both of his shoes to the mud on different steps. If he had more strength or if he wasn't holding a sleeping child then he might have fought to dig the shoes from the deep mud but he just couldn't.

He tried to say something to the man leading them to the boat but he was already too far ahead. The last thing he wanted to do was yell and draw attention to themselves, especially from soldiers.

He was resigned to let them go.

Twice more he sank knee deep into the mud and each time wanted to cry. Cindy Lou slept through the entire ordeal. Jack shook his head and smiled at her.

"Sleep, pretty angel, sleep and dream only of good things. We won't tell anyone what happened to my shoes."

They finally arrived down at the small wooden boat but only after a long deep incline down very slippery rocks. Jack knew there was no way he could walk down the embankment with Cindy Lou in his arms and so he sat on his rear and slipped down the entire way slowly on his backside.

He was exhausted by the time he made it to the bottom.

When he saw how small and rickety the boat was and how fast the river was moving, he started to have second thoughts. But they were loaded into the boat before he could utter a word of protest. The man who led them to the boat sat in the back and held a wooden oar.

Jack took the watch from his wrist, though it had not worked in days, and gave it to the man in the back as payment. But the boat owner, the older man with the perpetual scowl, yelled something at his partner and he reluctantly gave it back. Before Jack could protest and offer something else, the men had started rowing.

"Hold on, Raphael. Please, hold on tight."

Once on the open water the air became very cold and Jack's teeth began chattering loudly. He held Emmanuel and Cindy Lou in his arms but could tell the cold was making them uncomfortable. He used his knee to brace himself under the inside of the boat and leaned his weight way over toward the other side so that he seemed to be directly in the center. There was no other way to hold the children and keep his balance without eventually falling out of the boat. The wood of the boat dug into his knee and he could feel blood dripping down onto his bare feet.

The trip across took more than an hour but was much smoother than Jack had anticipated. Only once was there a splash of cold water into the boat from heading into the current too directly. A few other times there were sprays of water and only the cold air made it uncomfortable. By the time they were three-quarters of the way across, Jack had shivered himself warm.

Several crocodiles scampered into the water from the banks as the boat approached. The slowing boat caused the children to finally wake from their slumber. Jack tried thanking the two men that had ferried them across but they were anxious to get back and did not acknowledge him. Finally he grabbed the arm of the older man with the scowl and shook his hand. The man let go coldly and pointed down the path alongside the river.

Jack nodded and thanked him again. They stayed on the shore and watched as the men got back in their boat and headed back across.

"That was an incredible favor those two men just did for us," Jack said aloud but to no one in particular. "There is no way we would have made it across the river without them. Thank you, Mr. grumpy boat man."

They were all very hungry but the rising sun warmed them and they set out down that road again. When it was barely light out, Jack felt Raphael tap him on the shoulder.

"Mr. Jack, can I ask you something?"

"Of course. What is it?"

"Why aren't you wearing any shoes?"

Jack looked down at his toes and wiggled them.

"Well, I'll be," he exclaimed. "I'll bet those darned mosquitos must have taken them off while I wasn't looking."

Raphael looked and nodded and then realized the joke. He looked down at the whitest toes he had ever seen and smiled.

"I lost them in the mud back there across the river," Jack conceded.

Raphael plopped himself down on the ground and started undoing the straps to the sandals that Ahmed had made for Jack.

"What are you doing?"

"You don't have any shoes so I am giving you back yours."

A tear welled up in Jack's right eye.

"No no, please, tie those shoes back on. I am just fine. My feet need to tan a little anyhow. Come on, let's keep going."

"But—"

"I don't want to hear any more about it. Come on, Ethiopia and Kenya have got to be just around the corner. We've been at this for weeks already. And I don't know about you guys, but I am ready for a hot bath and a warm meal and a cold beer."

He regretted saying the words as they were leaving his lips as he instantly felt pangs of hunger not just in his belly but over his entire body. If it was possible for eyelids and wrists to get hungry then Jack's would have been.

He knew the kids were starving as well. The stamina received from the fish broth was long gone.

Jack truly did believe they were nearly at the border but they walked for the next three days and did not see a single person or any sign of hope. They had not eaten since finding a dried out coconut they broke apart the morning after the boat ride and each took a piece to chew on. There was nothing really to eat from the coconut but the illusion of sucking on the dead fruit was better than nothing. If it wasn't food, it felt like it.

On the third day they walked along slowly, silently as if to their graves. By this time Jack was sure the children knew they were never going to make it. His vision had worsened and he kept a hand on Raphael's shoulder most of the time to make sure they were following the right path. His feet were bloody with scabies, blisters, and other parasites and his knee had become infected after injuring it on the boat.

His breathing was different now, more labored than before and he could feel his heart alternate between palpitations and very slow beating. Emmanuel was able to walk a lot of the journey on his own and Jack and Raphael took turns carrying Cindy Lou, who had not spoken in two days.

The walking had become too much. Emmanuel and even his older brother had stopped. Raphael tried to vomit but could not. They found a very small bit of shade beneath a palm and sat down.

No more. I'm not going to force them to keep going. This is madness. They are only children. Look at me for crying out loud. If I can't do it then how can I expect them? No, I want their last few moments on this earth to be something good and nice and not this wretched walk. I've had it with this walk. Enough is enough.

"Let's rest here a while," he said in a raspy whisper that surprised even himself. "Here, come close."

Emmanuel and Cindy Lou each sat on one of his knees while Raphael sat next to Jack leaning his head on his shoulder. His nose was bleeding.

"I want you to know how proud of you I am, all of you. This journey we have taken, well I know many grown men, strong men who could not do this, not for a second."

Jack closed his eyes and nodded for a moment.

"Whatever happens from this point out, I want you all to know something. I wish the three of you were my children. I wish we were in a safe place, back home where I live and I could look after you and send you to school and play basketball in the schoolyard. I love all three of you as if you were my children. Life is not always hard like this. Sometimes there are good things, good times, and good people."

The children said nothing. They began drifting off.

Jack closed his eyes again and could feel everything around him start to move. He wanted to dream but sleep did not come, only this sensation of movement and swirling air that was just the hallucination of a dying man.

He opened his eyes and his vision was lost, gone. There was no blurriness left, only unending darkness. He took a deep, long breath and started to sing.

"Close your eyes and I'll kiss you,
Tomorrow I'll miss you.
Remember how much I love you.
And then while I'm away, I'll write home every day,
And send all my lovin' to you."

TWENTY SIX

JACK COULD FEEL his body rising up off the ground. There were hands all over him and there was a lot of yelling. There was intense heat. He could feel the flames.

It was surreal and he felt completely discombobulated.

Oh God, this can't be what going to heaven feels like.

He opened his eyes but could see nothing. He could hear the children screaming and could feel his legs dragging on the ground behind him, hitting everything in their way. It took a moment to gather his wits even without his sight. Two men were holding him—one under each arm—and dragging him quickly through the brush. Branches and limbs were cracking against Jack's face and his feet were being bloodied against sharp rocks and jutting roots.

The worst part of it was listening to the children screaming and being powerless to help them.

The men must have been holding torches. He could feel the heat occasionally get too close. Somehow or other he was still able to hear the children's muffled cries.

Jack tried to yell something at them to stop hurting the children but couldn't.

He had no way of knowing how long they moved like that through the night but it was long enough to stop caring about his face and feet hurting anymore. The measure of pain had leveled off and got no better or worse as they traveled deeper into the woods.

Again he was speaking over and over but only sputterings of words came from his lips only to be quickly covered by a hand over his mouth and a harsh rebuke from one of his captors.

Let me speak! All I want to do is let the children know I love them. Oh God, let it be over quickly for the children. Please take them with you, God, please look after them. Remember them when they enter into your kingdom.

Jack could feel and taste the blood running down from his forehead. It was salty and not all together unpleasant. But mixed with sweat it rolled down and burned his eyes and so he just kept them closed.

Then, just as he thought he would be dragged into eternity, the men stopped and dropped him harshly to the ground. He could hear them discussing something but he couldn't understand. They started arguing and he lifted his arms as if to signal surrender but no one responded to his actions.

He could make out the sound of people running and finally they lifted him again. Only this time they raised him higher than before. It felt like more of them. They placed their heads in his back and moved him into the back of a truck where he fell lifeless onto the cold, refreshing metal. He reached and could feel the children. Cindy Lou put her hand in his and he kissed it with a mixture of his blood and tears.

Oh Cindy Lou, all you've known is suffering in your poor, little pathetic life.

The diesel engine roared to life and moved forward with a startling jolt. The ride was bumpy and Jack tried his best to keep from falling asleep. The stink of the fumes kept pouring into the back of the truck, which was open. It was choking and thick.

More than once Jack thought of gathering the kids in his arms and jumping off the moving vehicle to safety. Of course he was barely strong enough to keep breathing, let alone carry out some daring rescue.

The night air became warm, then hot, and Jack knew it was the following day. The blood had dried on his face and was no longer sticky, only itchy. No one spoke in the back of the truck and Jack did not know if they were alone or if one or more of their captors was guarding and watching them as well.

He hoped all three children were still alive.

After a long while on roads that felt like dried river beds, the truck moved to smoother ground and picked up speed. The breeze coming into the back of the truck felt good and the various fragrances wafting in along the way were nice. Jack imagined a river, with dozens of gardenias or cherry blossoms lining the banks. He pictured children fishing and women in colorful dresses washing clothes together and singing songs. He laughed to himself, recognizing it was the first nice thing he'd allowed himself to imagine in days, maybe longer. He realized how much he missed smiling and laughing, doing it himself and seeing and listening to it.

He imagined the people were speaking English and started to smell food. He couldn't make it out exactly but was sure there were plates of tacos and refried beans somewhere near.

Yeah, right.

Then he heard it.

It was unmistakable.

Wow, this is some hallucination. The last time I heard that was, well, I guess it was at Jenelle's school.

Jack had not realized that the truck had come to a full and complete stop. He was still lost in the fantasy, trying to make out the voices speaking English, the wonderful aroma of food and some fool picking on a banjo.

Banjo?

That's the things about banjos. You can never mistake it for any other sound, not really. It's the instrument that sounds out of tune and in perfect tune all at the same time. Jack started coming out of it.

It was a banjo playing somewhere. He felt delirious. This crazy nightmare didn't seem to have an ending. What was going on? Jack was not altogether sure he hadn't passed away and was just experiencing some out of body phenomenon. He always imagined it would be a little more peaceful, maybe some angels and harps—definitely never with a banjo.

Then the yelling and cheering started, causing Jack to brace for blows or gunshots that never came. He instinctively placed his hands up over his face.

"Oh my God, thank God, thank God." Jack could never mistake George White's booming voice. "Somebody get Dr. Haridopolos. Jack, Jack can you hear me? Jack, thank God. Holy smokes!"

He climbed into the truck and held Jack in his arms. George shook with emotion.

"I had stopped hoping Jack, stopped hoping but never gave up. I had stopped allowing myself to believe I'd ever see you again. Holy smokes. Don't die on me now. We've been searching for way too long."

"Searching?" Jack managed is a raspy voice. His throat was killing him and he motioned for water.

George pointed at one of the aid workers.

"Get some water over quickly, please," he barked.

"Searching?" Jack repeated, his voice was barely audible.

"I've circulated Xerox copies of your ugly mug to just about every tribe, every village on both the border with Kenya and with Ethiopia." There was laughter and sadness in George's voice. "The villagers and natives called you the ghost when they saw your picture. It was because they had never seen anyone so white. They thought something was wrong with the picture. I didn't like it but after a while I begged with them to help me find the ghost. I promised some sort of reward for anyone that found you and delivered you here."

"Here?"

"You made it to a UNICEF relief station just over the border. Welcome to Ethiopia, Jack."

"Have you been here all this time?"

"Here and flying my little bird up and down the border hoping to spot you somehow. We've been looking for nine weeks. God, I can't believe you're actually here. I can't believe you're alive, really."

"Did you say nine weeks?" Jack coughed and it felt as if something inside him cracked open and started oozing warm fluid throughout his body. "George, we've only been on the road for a few days."

George looked around and shook his head. He wiped something from his eye.

"It's been nine weeks since I let you walk away from my plane and not a minute's gone by that I don't wish I could change that moment and just fly you and kids out of there. Can you ever forgive me?"

"Nine weeks?"

George said nothing.

The words were too heavy, too exhausting and Jack began to weep as the enormity of the journey started to become real once more. All of it, every second of it, flashed in a moment before his eyes starting and ending with finding Jenelle at the school.

He tried to stop crying but could not. His body shook uncontrollably.

"Where is Dr. Haridopolos?" George yelled once more.

George pulled Jack carefully from the truck and hugged him dearly.

"Jack, you're safe now, my friend. No one is going to try and hurt you again. It's going to be alright. I know it doesn't seem like it now. But it will."

"I can't see. Are the children alright? Little Emmanuel, Cindy Lou, and Raphael, are they OK?"

"Well, somehow, all three are managing to smile. That can't be a bad sign. Your eyes? We've been seeing a lot of that, something to do with the water. Doc will fix you up in no time. She'll get you on some strong antibiotics if I can ever get her over here."

Jack felt a tiny precious hand enter his and squeeze his tight. For a fraction of a second it felt like Jenelle's.

"You saved us, Mr. Jack," Cindy Lou said softly. "I love you."

Jack reached for the little girl. He knelt down, and using whatever strength he had left, he picked her up in his arms. He surprised himself that he still could. She rested her head on his chest and he kissed the top of her head over and over. Her breathing was very heavy and he knew she had fallen asleep.

"Make sure the doctor sees the children first," Jack whispered to George. "They have been through so much and need food and medicine."

He stopped himself from beginning to weep once more.

"Of course, Jack, whatever you say," George said, placing his hand on Jack's shoulder. "Is there anything I can get you while we wait for the doctor?"

"Yes."

"Anything. What would you like?"

"Well," he managed a wry smile, "I'll take a dozen White Castle hamburgers, onion rings, and a large Coke with unlimited refills."

"How about water and a can of Spam?"

"That'll do just fine."

TWENTY SEVEN
Ten months later

"IT ALL STARTED with the *fiat*, with the simple 'yes.' It was the yes that changed the world. It was the yes that saved the world. But think about it. How many times do we hesitate when a simple yes is all that's needed. We avoid getting involved or making a promise, afraid of the commitment, of what it might take to make good on the promise or the yes.

"But look here at this beautiful manger the Knights of Columbus have generously spent so much time putting together. Look at the result of a 'yes,' look at the little child of love, the savior of the world. Look at those around him who said yes, we will go and witness the birth of God. Look at the wise men who had so much faith that they said 'yes' to following a star. Can you imagine doing that today?

"Look at Joseph who said yes, I will still marry Mary and raise a child, even as he fought through his initial doubts.

"They could have all said no and where would we be today?

"How easy it would have been for Mary to say no. Can you imagine what was going through that poor girl's mind when the question was asked of her? Put yourself in her shoes for a moment and ask yourselves what your answer would have been.

"Tonight, or should I say this morning, as you leave Midnight Mass, and head home to your warm beds or for that glass of eggnog, as you admire the splendor of your Christmas trees, as you open gifts presented to you by those who love you more than anything else in the world, I want you to think about offering your services to those in need. If someone asks you for help this Christmas season and beyond, don't think about it. Just say yes. Now that would be the perfect Christmas gift to give God this year. Don't you think?

"Now let us stand for the profession of faith."

Many parishioners stared at Jack throughout the ceremony, recognizing him from news reports and television broadcasts or from the time he threw out the first pitch at the Mets game at Shea Stadium.

He didn't mind. He wanted them to know about what he experienced and what was happening to the children in a faraway part of the world. He also thought that seeing him in church might help them with their own faith. He heard the murmurings. Some questioned how he could continue to believe in God after what he went through. But they had it all wrong. He never blamed God for allowing what happened to happen, he gave God all the credit for allowing him and the children to survive.

He smiled politely at them during the service and many made an extra effort to shake his hand during the "sign of peace."

He could feel their sincerity when they looked him in the eyes and said slowly "May God's peace be with you."

Even Father Tony honored Jack by asking him weeks earlier if there was a specific hymn he'd like to hear during Midnight Mass. "Bring a Torch Jeanette Isabella," was his reply.

And sure enough Jack wept when he heard it.

"Ah, ah, beautiful is the mother,

Ah, ah beautiful is her son."

The same was true after mass. It seemed as if just about everybody wanted to come and shake Jack's hand or wish him a Merry Christmas. Old Man Dukes was there and so were the Sullivan twins and their families. Jack nodded over at them and they waved.

"Will Felicia and I see you tomorrow, Jack?" Dukes called out over the crowd.

"You bet. Merry Christmas."

"Merry Christmas to you, Jack."

Wisps of bitter cold Bronx air swept into the church every time someone opened the door to head home. Jack bundled his coat up and put on his Mets ball cap. The thick eye glasses he'd worn since returning from Africa stuck to his face in the cold.

He felt a mittened hand enter his and smiled at Cindy Lou, who was wearing a green Christmas dress with a lovely red bow. Emmanuel held his other hand and pulled him out of the church with Raphael following closely behind. It was the first time he had left home without his cane since returning.

"Hey now, what's the hurry?" Jack laughed, knowing full well what it was.

"We just want to get home, daddy," Cindy Lou giggled.

They stepped out and it was freezing out and the sky looked a funny shade of black with a little orange mixed in.

"I can't believe it," Jack smiled.

"What is it?" Raphael asked with just a twinge of nervousness.

"Look up."

The three children looked and the slow brilliant white flakes circled down toward them from a seemingly never-ending sky.

"It's snowing! It's snowing!" Emmanuel exclaimed and held Cindy Lou's hands as they danced among the falling flakes that were now coming down quickly and sticking to the sidewalk and street.

"Yay!" she answered and let go of Jack's hand to play.

"There is nothing like a White Christmas," Jack said. "It couldn't be more perfect."

But of course it could, he thought for a moment. He stared up at the sky and the falling snow.

Merry Christmas, my love.

"Are you OK, dad?" Raphael asked. It sounded as if his voice was starting to change a little bit.

"Yes, of course, big guy. I just get emotional around Christmas time. It's such a magical time and to be here with you three right here and right now makes this the very best Christmas I have ever had in my life."

"So tell me again, dad. Is this the same place that you used to live in before? Is everything the same?"

"Yep. Same neighborhood, same friends, same building, and the very same apartment, not much has changed really. The only difference now is that no one can ever throw me or us out of it."

"Why is that?"

"Because I own the building now, along with a few partners."

"Are we rich?"

Jack laughed.

"Well, I had saved all of my paychecks from the airport, so let's just say we're doing alright. And when we need money there is nothing more I'd like than to get a little hot dog stand and listen the Mets on the radio while you guys play in the school yard."

"That doesn't sound very exciting," Raphael laughed.

"Son, I have definitely had my share of excitement to last many lifetimes. Now I'm ready for some peace in my life. I don't need much to make me happy, just you guys. The only thing I want is to watch you all grow up in peace and love. I want to live to be a very old man who can look back at his life and smile."

"Dad, can I ask you something?"

"Anything."

"Well, is there a certain age that a boy gets when he is too old to kiss his father?"

"You will never be old to kiss your father."

"Good."

They walked a few steps in silence before Raphael stopped and smiled.

"Merry Christmas, dad." He reached up and kissed Jack on the cheek.

"Merry Christmas, son."

They continued on their way home singing Christmas carols—the children loved "Rudolph the Red Nosed Reindeer" the most—and vying to see who could catch the most snowflakes in their mouths. There were no cars driving by and the crowd from church had dispersed. No one else was around.

Jack's eyeglasses caught more flakes than his tongue and the children kept laughing every time he took them off to clean them.

"Maybe I should get wiper blades for my specs?"

There was at least an inch of snow on the ground by the time they reached the old brownstone. Jack's eyeglasses were nearly frozen over.

Maybe in the morning I can teach them to make snow angels.

"Do we have to go straight to bed?" Cindy Lou asked.

"Well, I can make us some hot cocoa and we can look and see if 'A Christmas Carol' is on the television."

"I thought you told us that was a ghost story. I don't want to have nightmares."

Jack chuckled.

"It is a sort of ghost story. But it's a happy one, not at first. At first things are hard and a little scary but then it all gets better. You are going to love it. That movie will only leave you with sweet dreams," he promised.

They entered the building and starting climbing the stairs.

"Can we open just one present tonight?"

"Absolutely not, Cindy Lou. I told you what our tradition is going to be. We never open gifts until Christmas morning."

"Oh please, daddy, please."

Jack smiled and sighed deeply, knowing he would never be able to deny her anything.

"Oh, alright, maybe one."

www.ingramcontent.com/pod-product-compliance
Lightning Source LLC
Chambersburg PA
CBHW061615100726
47898CB00002B/674